THE
FIRE DANCE

THE
FIRE DANCE

HELENE TURSTEN

Translation by Laura A. Wideburg

Copyright © 2005 by Helene Tursten
Published in agreement with H. Samuelsson-Tursten AB, Sunne, and
Leonhardt & Høier Literary Agency, Copenhagen

English translation copyright © 2014 by Laura A. Wideburg

First published in English in 2014 by Soho Press
853 Broadway
New York, NY 10003

Library of Congress Cataloging-in-Publication Data
Tursten, Helene, 1954–
[Eldsdansen. Engish]
The fire dance / Helene Tursten.
p. cm.
Originally published in Swedish as Eldsdansen.
ISBN 978-1-61695-010-1
eISBN 978-1-61695-011-8
1. Women private investigators—Fiction. I. Title.
PT9876.3.U55E5413 2014
839.73'8—dc23
2013025799

Printed in the United States of America

10 9 8 7 6 5 4 3 2 1

*To my nieces
Karin, Sara and Lisa.*

THE
FIRE DANCE

Prologue

THE NOISE AND heat from the crowd rose toward the ceiling and mixed with cigarette smoke in a thick smog around the chandeliers. People crowded at the enormous bar and tried to catch the bartender's attention. The atmosphere was frenzied and excited, as it usually was in the Park Aveny Hotel bar during the annual meeting of the Göteborg Book Fair. Some guests were already showing signs of incipient intoxication. Famous cultural personalities, as well as some not-so-famous ones, were hanging around the bar, though a few of them had wandered to the pub's armchairs and were starting to doze.

People kept coming and going through the revolving door, mingling as they headed toward the bar or to join the groups sitting at tables. Many still kept one eye on the entrance— a high-level celebrity could walk in at any moment since most of the important authors were booked at the hotel. Unfortunately, most of the people who appeared were publishers and their employees, a goodly number of librarians and one or two poets, drunk from the attention given to their readings.

So many eyes were on the door that people remembered the moment she stepped into the lobby and paused just inside the revolving door. Even if their other memories were diffuse—or totally absent, in some cases—many people reacted to her entrance, and not just because of her extraordinary appearance. Many witnesses recalled a certain "vibe" or "aura" about her.

She was tall and thin. She wore a black miniskirt that ended just below her rump, shiny bright pink tights and black knit leg warmers that were pushed down around her ankles above her ballet flats. Even without high heels, her legs appeared to be sensationally long. She wore a short black leather jacket over her thin pink T-shirt, which revealed more of her small, perky breasts than it covered. Metal studs decorated her jacket. But despite her conspicuous outfit, her pale face drew most of the attention. It was heart-shaped with high cheekbones, and her full lips seemed made for kissing. The way she pursed them, however, made it clear that any attempt to kiss her would be met with failure. Her eyes only magnified that message. They were slightly almond-shaped and had thick, long lashes, which she accentuated with heavy black eyeliner. But her brown eyes themselves showed no emotion. As a hungover poet would say later during questioning, "Her eyes were bottomless wells that led to the permafrost of her soul."

She turned her head to search the crowd. When she found the face she was looking for, she began to walk straight toward a table in the middle of the pub. All her movements were graceful and smooth.

One man, his back to the entrance, had not seen her when she came in. As she passed him, he lost his grip on his frosted beer glass. He blew on his hands and shook his fingers as if they'd been frozen with cold.

A children's book author, who was already hammered, began to pull on his suit jacket clumsily, complaining about the draft from the door.

The truth was that the woman could move through the compact crowd with ease, and yet every person drew away from her, either intentionally or unconsciously.

She reached the table she wanted and quietly regarded the boisterous people gathered there. One by one, the young people, uniformly dressed in black, fell quiet and looked at her with astonishment. There was only one man who didn't seem to have noticed her. He kept singing:"*Poeira, poeira, poeira, Levantou poeira.*"

His voice was deep and pleasant, and his entire appearance differed from his companions in their black uniformity. A skintight red T-shirt emphasized his buff upper body, and his jeans clung to his narrow hips. Around his neck, a wide gold chain glittered against his café au lait skin, and a few tiny gold rings in his earlobe shone with an intensity to match his gleaming white teeth.

When he finished singing, he calmly turned to face the silent young woman. His entire face broke into a smile.

"*Hola!*" he exclaimed with great happiness.

He gestured for her to join them at the table.

A slightly worse-for-wear blonde, her eyelids soot-colored and her lips painted black, gave the newcomer a disgruntled look. She left her seat beside the man and headed to the restroom on unsteady feet.

The silent woman sat on the chair and stared at the man without blinking. Totally unaware of the icy chill she was spreading all around her, he draped his arm over her shoulders. Begrudgingly, she allowed him to draw her close. The tension in her face and body began to soften somewhat. One of the young men began to recite a poem at a volume more suited for a poetry slam. The brown-eyed woman kept watching him. Though it appeared that she didn't understand the poem, she applauded politely when he was finished. She even smiled a little at a joke the black-clad poet made.

A BOUNCER IN a dark suit walked between the tables to warn the pub's customers that it was closing time. A few older people had come to join the group at the table. At the center was a tall man with scraggly white hair who was twice as old as most of the others, but he was a famous author and seemed to know one of the young people in the group. The sulky blonde had returned after an extremely long visit to the restroom.

"Let's go up to my room and keep the party going," the white-haired author offered, his words slurring. "I have a suite on the top floor."

They all got up and headed toward the elevators. As the doors opened, everyone jostled inside, pushing and shoving a bit, but laughing all the while. Everyone except the woman in the miniskirt and pink tights.

"I'm leaving," she said.

These were the only words she said all evening. The others called to her and tried to convince her to join them in the packed elevator. She didn't turn back, but walked steadily past the security guard toward the wide stairs. The last they saw of her, before the elevator doors shut, was the reflection of the chandeliers shining down on her pageboy haircut.

PART ONE

1989 – 1990

SHE HAD TO pee but tried not to think about it. She had to bike as fast as she could in order to get to the convenience store. Tessan's mother would not wait for her. She was that kind of mother. If you weren't where you were supposed to be on time, there'd be no ride for you. She had to get that ride or her dance class would be over before she even got there since the bus took twice as long. Her bicycle was almost new, and she pedaled as hard as she could. The narrow gravel road spread out before her. There were no streetlights, and it was getting dark. She didn't mind that, as she knew the way by heart, but she felt uneasy thinking about what could be hiding behind the shrubbery along the side of the road. What if there was a flasher behind one of the bushes?

Stupid flashers, stupid flashers, stupid flashers, stupid flashers. The words tumbled in her brain while her feet mechanically drove the pedals.

She began to feel relief as she caught a glimpse of the streetlights on the main road. Once she got to the turnoff, she had to wait to let some cars pass. She got off her bike and glanced at the convenience store on the other side of the street. Her heart skipped a beat as she saw Tessan's mother's red car parked in front of the building. She leaped back onto her bike and darted across the street, almost getting hit by a truck but missing it by a hair. The truck braked with a loud squeal, and the driver laid on the horn. She skidded in beside the Audi, and, breathless, jumped off the bike and threw it into the bushes beside the store. She grabbed the back door handle and scooted into the backseat. Tessan was sitting in the front seat, as usual, beside her mother.

"Really, Sophie! You were almost run over! That could have been a terrible accident. And you didn't lock your bike."

Her pulse was pounding so hard in her ears that she didn't hear what Tessan's mother was saying. She panted, trying to get her breathing under control.

"Didn't you hear me? You have to lock your bike," Tessan's mother repeated. She was very strict. She often sounded irritated, though she routinely tried to hide it with pleasant words.

Sophie got out, dragged her bike out of the bushes and led it to the bike stand. She locked it and hurried back to the car.

Drive now, drive now, drive now, drive now . . . the words ricocheted through her head with the same rhythm as before.

Finally the car was moving and leaving the parking lot. Sophie leaned back in her seat and relaxed with a great sigh.

Made it, made it, made it, made it . . .

An ice-cold wind was blowing in from the sea. The chill bit Sophie's ears and fingers as she biked back home a few hours later. In her hurry, she'd forgotten her mittens and knit cap, of course.

In the distance, she saw swirling blue lights pulsing through the darkness. Farther away she could just make out people moving in front of a red glow.

Her legs did not want to keep moving. She couldn't make it the last few hundred yards. She didn't want to make it . . . *don't want to . . . don't want to . . . don't want to . . .*

• • •

"WE FOUND THE girl at the side of the road over there. It looked like she'd fallen over, and the bike was in the ditch below her. We were leaving the fire scene because we'd finished there, and our headlights caught her just sitting there. We thought it was strange, because the ambulance should have spotted her when it passed by just a few minutes earlier."

"Did she say anything?"

"No, she just looked at us."

"Was she in shock?"

"Absolutely. We drove her to Östra Hospital. Her little brother and her mother had already gone."

"Did you talk to her in the car?"

"No. I wrapped her in a blanket and sat with her in the backseat. I tried to say something comforting, but she didn't say a single word. It was odd."

"What was odd about it?"

"Hard to put my finger on it . . . just the fact that she didn't say anything. She wasn't calling for her mother or brother. She didn't even ask about them. She wasn't crying, either."

"She just sat and stared?"

"That's right."

Superintendent Sven Andersson looked at his newest inspector thoughtfully. She'd joined the department just a month earlier. He had a hard time hiding his irritation that he'd gotten a female inspector, and one with two small kids to boot. He didn't like it one bit. The superintendent sighed and got a questioning look from his fresh-baked detective inspector.

Irene Huss had a great deal of respect for her new boss. He had a good reputation as a policeman, even if he had some rough personality quirks and was known to have a short fuse. She'd been nervous her first few days on the job, but she was beginning to get used to him. As long as she did her job, he would come to change his mind about her. And besides, women officers were no longer so unusual on the force.

"It's been three months since the day you and your partner found the girl on the side of the road. Let me tell you, she still just sits and stares, saying nothing at all!"

The superintendent's voice rose; his anger was apparent. Or perhaps he was just frustrated, not angry. Irene knew that the superintendent had no children of his own.

Irene raised her eyebrows but remained quiet. She didn't really know what she should be saying. She was not part of the Björlanda District house fire investigation. She and her colleague, Håkan Lund, had been the first patrol car on the scene, but that was all. The only thing she knew about the investigation was what she'd read in the newspapers.

"Both Hasse and I tried to get her to talk, but it was impossible! She just sat and glared at us with those big brown eyes of hers."

"Is she able to speak? I mean, are you sure she's not mute?"

"No, she can talk. She's apparently the silent type, even before the fire, I mean. Do you know how old she is?"

Andersson gave her a look before he replied, "Read it for yourself. It's all in the paperwork. You and Sophie Malmborg are going to take over the questioning."

"But why should I . . . ? I mean, if she won't talk to you or Hans . . . "

"You've just answered your own question. She does not want to talk to us. Why? Maybe because we're men. So the shrinks say. We're going to test that by putting you in. You're a woman. You have kids yourself."

Irene was floored. This was a big case to be just dumped in her lap. A man had died in the fire, and there still were lots of unanswered questions. There were even indications that Sophie might know something important, or maybe more than that . . .

"Or do you think you can't handle it?" Andersson challenged.

There was a threat beneath his sarcasm. *If you can't figure this out, you won't stay long in this department.*

Irene felt her stomach turn into a lump of ice. Then a warm wave swept through her body and she forced herself to look her boss in the eye and steady her voice before she replied.

"I'll talk to her."

"Good. She'll be here tomorrow."

IRENE SAT AT her desk in the office she shared with Tommy Persson. He'd started working as a detective inspector the previous year, and he was also the one who'd convinced her to apply for the job in the department. They'd met at the police academy in Stockholm, and they'd become good friends—perhaps, in the beginning, because they were the only ones from Göteborg at the academy. Irene's then-boyfriend, Krister, had been wary of Tommy at first, but now they were all close, and Tommy had even been Krister's best man in their wedding five years ago. Irene was seven months pregnant with the twins when she married, and she thought she looked like the *Potemkin* in her wedding pictures.

She was twenty-four at the time. Her own parents had been older when she'd been born. Her mother, Gerd, was thirty-six and her father, Börje, forty-five. Irene found it funny that her parents had the same age difference she and Krister had.

"So here you are—daydreaming!"

Tommy's happy greeting jerked Irene out of her thoughts.

She hadn't heard him open the door. He was grinning from ear to ear as he headed for his desk.

"Martin can say 'Pappa!' Well, he says 'pa—pa—pa—pa.' It's almost his first birthday. He's obviously advanced for his age, just like his old man."

Tommy was filled with pride. Martin was his first son with his wife, Agneta. Irene was the boy's godmother.

She couldn't help but smile. "Great! Or should I say congratulations? Just be happy that pa—pa—pa is all he can say. Once he's started talking, you'll wish you were back in the good old days. I was almost late this morning because Jenny threw a fit the minute we walked in the door at preschool."

"Did she want to go?"

"Oh, yes, she loves preschool. But she wanted me to promise to buy her a pet tiger before I left."

"The tiger she wants to keep in the yard?"

"That's the one. She's not letting go of the idea."

Krister and Irene had brought the twins to Borås Zoo one fine Sunday afternoon in August. Jenny and Katarina had run around from animal to animal and jumped with joy whenever they caught sight of a new one. Katarina liked the monkeys the best, but Jenny had fallen head over heels for the tigers. She wanted one for herself. She said they could put a high fence around the backyard they shared with the other people in their townhouse row. Jenny was not dissuaded by the argument that tigers were dangerous and might like to make a meal of the residents. She insisted it would be the nicest tiger in the world. She'd raise the tiger from a cub and teach it not to eat meat, so the neighbors would be safe. She started to save all her allowance toward the tiger, putting her money into her red plastic piggy bank. Jenny called it her tiger bank. Every bit of money that came her way would go toward the tiger.

Last weekend, Jenny demanded that Irene open the piggy
bank so she could count the money. Irene struggled with the
lid on the piggy's stomach, but finally got it open. She
counted to thirty-two Swedish kronor and 50 öre. Jenny
looked at Irene with her big eyes and asked breathlessly, "Is
that enough?"

"No, a tiger is pretty expensive. Keep saving and maybe
you'll have enough money in . . . oh . . . two or three years.
Or maybe you could buy something else that you'd like."

"A Barbie house!" Katarina suggested.

"No, I want a tiger!" Jenny said with determination.

Katarina loved to play with her Barbie doll. She could
occupy herself for hours combing the doll's long hair and
changing her clothes.

Jenny, on the other hand, was completely uninterested in
Barbies. She would rather stand in front of the mirror and
sing, imitating her idol, Carola.

"She's old enough now that she's beginning to understand
she will hardly be able to come up with enough money for a
tiger, so this morning she decided to see if throwing a fit
would work. It was awful. All the preschool teachers came
running. They probably thought I was abusing that child,"
Irene said with a sigh.

"If I know Jenny, I believe she'll settle with this tiger issue
one way or another." Tommy was laughing.

"I'm sure she will. Speaking of children, I just got the word
from Andersson that I'm supposed to take over the questioning of that girl, Sophie Malmborg."

The smile disappeared from Tommy's face and his voice
had no more laughter in it as he said, "That's a tough case.
Why'd you get it?"

"Well . . . for one, she refuses to talk to Andersson or Borg.
And two, I've met her once before, right after it happened. An
additional reason seems to be that I have children."

"But the twins are only four! Sophie is eleven," Tommy objected.

"Right. But kids are kids, according to the boss."

"Of course. Kids are *not* his thing," Tommy said, his smile returning.

IRENE SPENT THE rest of the workday going through the thick folder from Superintendent Andersson and stayed a few hours after her shift had ended. She had no reason to hurry home, as her mother had picked up the twins from preschool already. They'd enjoy themselves with their grandmother until Krister came home at five. He had just gotten a part-time job as a cook at a new gourmet restaurant on Avenyn. He was thrilled to death that he'd gotten the job, despite the fact that he could only work thirty hours a week. The owner had been surprised and had tried to convince him to go full-time, but Krister told him that his wife was a policewoman in the criminal unit. "There are no part-time jobs there, so I'm the one who has to take part-time work for the sake of my girls."

When the owner realized that Krister was not about to change his position, he reconsidered and hired his first-ever part-time cook.

On Monday afternoon on the sixth of November, 1989, Sophie Malmborg had taken the school bus home as usual. She was in a rush, as she had a ballet lesson at 5:15 P.M., and a classmate's mother was going to drive them to the House of Dance. The friend's name was Terese Olsén, and the mother's name was Maria Olsén.

The school bus had stopped by the convenience store at around 3:35 P.M. The bus driver had seen Sophie go to the bike rack and unlock her bike. She had to ride about one kilometer down a narrow gravel road to get

home, which would have taken, at most, ten minutes.
Probably less. According to her mother, Angelika
Malmborg-Eriksson, Sophie would gobble down a few
sandwiches and a glass of milk and grab her ballet bag,
which would have already been packed the night before.
She'd then bike back to the convenience store, where
Maria Olsén would pick her up. She had been driving
her every Monday for the past year.

According to Maria Olsén, Sophie Malmborg had
come biking up at top speed a little after the predeter-
mined time, which was unusual, as she was always
prompt and often early.

If the time given by the bus driver was accurate,
Sophie would have arrived home at 3:45 P.M. at the
latest. In order to make it back to the convenience store,
she would have had to have left her home at about 4:20,
or 4:25 at the latest, especially since she'd been running
late. What had happened while Sophie was at home? No
one knew except Sophie herself.

After ballet class ended at 8:00 P.M., Sophie's
mother, Angelika Malmborg-Eriksson, had taken her
turn to drive the two girls. They shared the same clas-
sical ballet class. First they dropped off Terese Olsén,
then they drove toward their own home but stopped by
the convenience store so Sophie could get her bike. It
was too large to fit in the Golf. Angelika Malmborg-
Eriksson had been alone when she drove up to the
house—or what was left of it.

Irene took a break from reading and leaned back in
her chair. She remembered how the beat-up Golf had
slammed to a halt right next to the patrol car and Angelika Malmborg-Eriksson had leapt out almost before the
car stopped.

"Frej! Where's Frej?" she'd screamed, her voice filled with fear.

An old Saab Combi had driven up just then, and a young boy got out, holding the hand of the large woman who had driven the Saab. It seemed as if he were unsteady on his feet and needed the woman's support. It was likely that he'd been scared by the commotion and the devastation of the fire and wanted to be anywhere but there. The heavy, pungent smell was suffocating enough to make anyone want to get away.

The boy and the woman had walked toward Angelika, who had become quite hysterical. When Angelika caught sight of the boy, she ran to him, laughing and crying in turns, holding the boy to her tightly as tears streamed down her cheeks. The woman who had come with the boy went to the fire chief and asked him a question. The chief shook his head and, judging by his gestures, delivered some bad news. With a grim expression on her face, the woman walked back to the mother and son. Irene Huss and Håkan Lund were standing close by.

The woman said, "They weren't able to enter the house. It was completely engulfed when the fire trucks arrived. So they don't know if he . . ."

She stopped and cast a glance at the boy.

Håkan took her by the arm and gently but firmly pulled her away from the other two.

"Can someone have been in the house?" he'd asked.

She'd bitten her lower lip hard before she replied, "My brother, Magnus Eriksson. Frej's father."

Irene had heard the woman's statement and turned back to the glowing inferno. If a person had been in that building, there would not be much left of him.

Two days later, the fire investigators found some remains of a skeleton, including the lower jaw, which the forensic dentist had used to determine that the remains had indeed belonged to Magnus Eriksson.

ANGELIKA MALMBORG-ERIKSSON WAS a dance instructor at the House of Dance who also taught at the College of Dance in Högsbo. The school, built in the fifties and later abandoned, had been renovated for the college. The trip between the House of Dance and the Malmborg-Eriksson home in Björkil was more than ten miles. Since public transportation in Göteborg left something to be desired, Sophie and her friend Tessan had to be driven to their ballet class. This was also part of the paperwork from the initial investigation.

Sophie had danced her whole life. According to her mother, she'd been dancing before she could walk.

Angelika had provided all the information about her daughter for the paperwork. Sophie hadn't been helpful to the officials. Angelika insisted that Sophie had said nothing to her about the fire, either. The girl had kept to herself, though her deep, dark eyes took in everything she saw. It also appeared that she'd talked to her father, Ernst Malmborg, the composer. Angelika Malmborg-Eriksson was still upset when she told Superintendent Andersson (who had given up on hearing a word out of the girl) that Sophie had refused to move back in with Frej and herself after her latest visit with her father. Apparently, Social Services had located an apartment for Angelika and her two children since there was nothing left of their house to return to. Everything they owned had been lost in the fire, except a few pieces of outdoor furniture that would be useless in a fourth-floor apartment in the Biskopsgården District. Angelika had protested her daughter's decision mightily, but finally had to give in, at least "until the worst was over."

Irene checked the date for that statement and found it was given the day before Christmas Eve.

Is the worst over now? Why couldn't Angelika and her children live with Magnus Eriksson's sister after the fire? It appeared that she had a good relationship with the little boy.

Irene flipped through the various papers left in the folder. She didn't find any interviews with the sister. Irene vaguely remembered that the woman had introduced herself, but she couldn't remember her name. She'd check on that tomorrow, after she had her meeting with Sophie at ten.

At the back of the folder, there were three short reports as appendices. The first one touched on a fire in a haystack during April of 1985. The owner of a riding field had mucked out bad hay into an area behind the stable. The plan was to burn it at a later date. At nine the same evening, a neighbor had called to say that the hay was on fire. The neighbor's house looked out over the owner's field, so he'd spotted it, and by the time the fire trucks arrived, the fire was already under control and could be put out quickly.

The fire investigators determined that it had been arson. The technicians had found two bottles of igniter fluid nearby. They were so close to the fire, unfortunately, that they'd actually started to melt, so no fingerprints could be lifted from them.

There was a report from a witness who said that someone on a bicycle had been seen in the vicinity shortly before the fire broke out. The witness was the same neighbor who'd called the owner. He was an elderly man and his eyesight was no longer the best, but he was absolutely sure that there was a person outside the stall. He wasn't sure whether it had been a man or a woman; he could only say that the bicyclist had black pants and a dark, long-sleeve shirt or coat.

The second report concerned a more serious fire that had broken out at a summer cottage early in September

1989. The cottage was somewhat isolated and it took a while before the fire was discovered by a couple walking their dog. The cottage had burned to the ground. The technicians were able to determine fairly quickly that it had been arson. Someone had piled rugs, bedcovers and other textiles in the center of the floor and set them on fire. Chemical analysis determined that the suspect had used igniter fluid as well.

The newspapers had picked up on this one. PYROMANIAC IN BJÖRLANDA. People began to fear another arson would be committed by the alleged pyromaniac. Still, all remained quiet on the arson front until the beginning of November, when Magnus Eriksson had died in the Björkil cottage fire.

The last report concerned a case of smoking in bed. It dated back to Christmas 1988, at 7:47 P.M. The fire department had been called to the Malmborg-Eriksson cottage. According to the report, there was a hysterical woman screaming into the phone: "It's on fire! He's on fire!"

By the time the ambulance and the fire trucks arrived, the fire had already been put out. Magnus Eriksson had an ugly burn on his right hand and lower arm, but was otherwise not injured. According to the report, he'd been heavily intoxicated, and his wife wasn't sober, either. Their seven-year-old son had also been in the house.

Magnus Eriksson had been taken to the hospital for treatment of his arm. His wife said that her husband had felt tired and decided to go upstairs to rest. When she'd gone upstairs an hour later to tell him that the movie he wanted to see on television was about to start, she saw that the room was on fire. She yelled and was able to wake up her husband, then showed great presence of mind and rushed to get a plastic bucket in the bathroom, where a pair of dirty shoes had been soaking. She threw the water on the fire. The bed itself had not started to burn, just the shag rug beneath it. The investigation determined that Magnus Eriksson had fallen asleep after he'd lit a cigarette. His arm had been dangling from the bed and the cigarette had fallen down onto the rug.

Irene noted that Sophie Malmborg was not mentioned in the report—probably because she had been spending Christmas with her father, Ernst Malmborg.

THE FIRST TWO fires had been arson and had been set within a one-kilometer radius of the Malmborg-Eriksson home in Björkil.

It could be a coincidence, however statistically improbable it might seem. Or, as Superintendent Andersson had written in his barely legible handwriting: *One fire—perhaps. Two fires—hardly. Three—absolutely not.*

Irene had to agree with her boss. Three fires within half a year and within such a small area was hardly a coincidence.

"I CAN HONESTLY say I'm nervous. We hardly ever question children, and when we do, it's usually in cases where we suspect that the child is the victim of a crime. This case is different."

Irene and Tommy were drinking coffee together in their shared office.

"Do they seriously think that she set the fire?" asked Tommy.

"The home started to burn shortly after she left on her bike. Perhaps it really is a coincidence. Magnus Eriksson could have fallen asleep with a burning cigarette and set fire to the rug or the bed. It happened before, less than a year ago. But that it would happen twice . . ."

Irene sighed and shook her head.

"It doesn't appear all that believable," Tommy agreed. "Have the technicians found the cause of the fire yet?"

"No, and they were not able to determine where the fire started. The house burned to the ground. There are two reports concerning arson in the vicinity of the house during the past six months. In those cases, plastic bottles containing igniter fluid were found. That would not have been needed here. The technicians found a huge number of bottles with high-proof alcohol. They were all over the place. All the arsonist would have had to do was pour some alcohol onto the floor and throw a match in it."

"Was he a drunk?"

"Don't know. In the report concerning the bed fire, they stated that he was heavily intoxicated. Still, it was Christmas and it's not unusual for people to overindulge—add some more vodka to the glögg and the like."

"Maybe he was celebrating Gustav Adolf's Day on the sixth of November and bought a cake and a bottle in honor of the king who founded our city of Göteborg," Tommy joked as he imitated drinking straight out of the bottle.

Irene grimaced to show what she thought of the combination of cake and strong spirits. "A terrible way to celebrate. But still, we don't know for sure that he was an alcoholic. There's nothing else about it in the material, but that could be something to check up on."

"Maybe so. I'll go ahead and take this on—dig up something on that Eriksson guy. Something tells me you're going to have a tough time with Sophie and her mother."

"You're right about that."

"Are you going to use the large interrogation room?"

"I think so. We can use the video camera then. I can always start by talking to the mother . . . Angelika."

"Is someone going to be in the adjoining room?"

"Yes. Probably someone from Child Protection or Social Services. They've been observing all the interrogations so far. So has her mother. Sophie has been determined to have psychological damage of some kind. After all, she's only eleven—twelve next month."

Tommy looked at Irene thoughtfully. Finally, he sighed and said, "It's not like we've been trained to question children."

"No, and it's not like we have experience with it, either. Social Services usually handles it whenever the suspect is underage."

"The suspect . . . so you think she's a suspect?"

"I have no idea. I should meet her first. It would be best if I didn't jump to conclusions beforehand."

"What are you going to do if she refuses to speak?"

Irene raised her palms. "No idea!"

She got up to head to the bathroom before she had her meeting with Sophie and her mother. As she walked, she realized that she should have worn a different set of clothes. She had on jeans and a hoodie. It made her look a little childish. It didn't help that her hoodie had the emblem of the Swedish Police Sport League on it. Should she put her hair up to make her appear older and more proper? She studied her appearance in the mirror over the sink and decided just to use barrettes to pin her hair back behind her ears. She tried smiling at her mirror image. Perhaps the girl would prefer to talk to a young woman instead of two middle-aged men, she told herself encouragingly. She certainly hoped so.

SOPHIE LOOKED ESPECIALLY pale and thin in her all-black outfit. Her large boots, her tights and her cotton sweatshirt, emblazoned with a college logo, were all washed-out shades of black. She was unusually tall for her age. In fact, she was just as tall as her mother. They both wore the same dark eye shadow and had dark hair, but that was where the similarities ended. Angelika Malmborg-Eriksson was tiny and thin-boned. She rattled on quickly and nervously, gesturing a great deal.

According to the reports, Angelika was thirty-one years old, but she appeared much younger. Her bright red angora turtleneck sweater was burled, and its wide shoulder pads revealed it had been around for a few years. Still, the color suited her. She'd managed to find glossy lipstick to match. Beneath her sweater, she wore tights that disappeared into her black high-heeled boots.

Sophie sat and watched them. Her stillness so penetrated the air around her, that it felt like the molecules had stopped swirling and started to vibrate in place. Irene became intensely aware of the temperature shift around the girl. It was hard to tell if it was warmer or colder, but something was there that Irene would later describe as an "energy field." The phenomenon was so unusual that Irene started to wonder if it was due to her own nervousness about the interrogation.

Irene introduced herself and offered her hand. Angelika's small, thin hand felt hot and tense but otherwise lifeless. Sophie gave no indication that she wanted to greet Irene. Irene picked up the girl's right hand gently. It was fragile and cold, like a thin pane of glass, and it lay in Irene's hand passively. Irene shuddered. She felt uncomfortable in the girl's presence. Sophie's unusual gaze revealed neither fear nor nervousness, neither sorrow nor joy. In fact, it showed nothing at all.

How could a mere girl be so disengaged? She did not appear to be totally withdrawn, as from time to time she would look at the person speaking. But for the most part, she looked straight ahead or at her hands, loosely clasped on her lap. Irene noticed that her nails were bitten all the way to the quick, but there was no other sign of nervousness. Was this disengagement Sophie's way of channeling her inner tension? Perhaps, but Irene had never seen it before, nor heard anyone mention experiencing anything like this.

Angelika perched herself graciously on the edge of the chair, and began chattering before Irene could even formulate her first question.

"Sophie and I have been talking. The truth is that Sophie did not know whether Magnus was home or not that day. He must have gone to sleep before she came home from school, because the whole house was dark. Nothing was on fire when

Sophie left the house. She didn't smell any burning odor. There must have been an electrical issue."

"Is this true, Sophie?" asked Irene. She peered directly at the girl.

Instead of meeting Irene's gaze, Sophie turned her head slightly to look at the point in the room where the video camera had been set up, offering Irene only a view of her face in profile. *If there was a change in her facial expression, perhaps the video tape will show it*, thought Irene. When Sophie turned her head back, her face was as expressionless as a porcelain mask.

Irene decided to concentrate on what Angelika was saying. At least Angelika was talking. Perhaps Sophie would relax and react to Angelika's words.

"I understand that your husband was a journalist. Which newspaper did he work for?"

"Different ones. He was a freelancer."

"Where did he write?"

"At home for the most part."

"So it's not impossible that he was home when Sophie returned from school," Irene stated.

"Well . . . there were times when he wasn't home."

Angelika gave Irene a quick glance. Her beautiful eyes betrayed something, but what? Before Irene could analyze it, the look was gone.

"Where would he be if he wasn't at home?"

"Out. Working. Journalists have to investigate places and figure things out. Meet people. That kind of thing."

They'd deviated from the line of questioning Irene had intended to follow before the meeting and she was now improvising. The whole idea had been to get Sophie to talk. Still, Irene felt that there were many other questions in this investigation that still needed answers. With each response, a whole new bevy sprang up. Perhaps Irene would still get a few pieces of the puzzle from the mother.

"What kind of journalist was Magnus?" asked Irene.

"What kind?" Angelika repeated, confused.

"Well, did he write about sports or movies or food or news?" Irene clarified.

"He . . . he wrote about anything . . . anything going on. And then he'd sell the article to a paper or a magazine."

"Which ones?"

"Different ones. *GT* and *GP*. Other magazines. *Norra Hisingens Nyheter*. And *Björkils Bulletin*."

"Those two are locals, right?"

"Yeah, though the *Bulletin* is more like an advertising supplement."

Irene was beginning to realize that Magnus Eriksson had not exactly been a shining star in the lofty skies of journalism. Perhaps she was mistaken, but Angelika's nervous shifting position on her chair seemed to indicate that Irene was on the right track.

"How long had you been living in the Björkil cottage?"

"Three . . . almost four years."

"Where did you live previously?"

"On Linnégatan."

"That's a nice, central location. Was it in one of the newer buildings?"

"No, an older one. It was a really comfortable apartment. High ceilings and large rooms. The kitchen was old, but it was really beautiful. And it had a gas stove and stuff."

"Why did you decide to move?"

Angelika looked away and then back at Irene.

"They scheduled it for renovation. They were showing us other apartments in the area, but they were too expensive."

"So you bought the cottage."

"No, we rented it from Magnus's sister. It's on her property. We were only going to live there for one year."

"But you've been there for almost four years," Irene observed.

"That's how it turned out. Rents closer to town were just too high."

Tears appeared in Angelika's eyes and Irene could hear the desperation in her voice.

"Don't freelance journalists earn good money?" asked Irene.

Angelika unconsciously curled her lips before she replied. "It depends. Sometimes things go well for a time and then it can take a while before another article is sold."

"But you work as a dance instructor. Don't you have a good salary?"

"Dancers are not paid well. We have terrible employment contracts. I also work as a freelancer and dance in various events and shows. In order to have a more steady income, I've started teaching at the House of Dance, and I have a few hours at the College of Dance, too. They're in the same building complex."

"Do you teach every day?"

"No. Mondays, Tuesdays and Sundays in the afternoons and evenings."

"So that's why Sophie had to get a ride from her friend's mother and you drove the girls home."

"That's right. I have a long day on Mondays. I work from one in the afternoon until eight in the evening. Sophie and Tessan dance in the last session I teach. Classical ballet, level three. Level four is the highest level. Girls and boys have to be at least thirteen. Most of those kids then go on to study at the Dance Academy high school program. It's extremely competitive there and tough to get a place."

"And if you complete the Dance Academy program, you go on to the College of Dance, right?"

"Correct. I only teach there at specific times—when they're doing a series of classical ballet and show dance. Those are my specialties."

"Are those your specialties as well?" Irene asked, turning to Sophie.

She was hoping that the direct question would surprise the girl and elicit an answer before she had time to think. Irene's trick didn't work. Sophie lifted her gaze from her hands directly to Irene. Her face was completely blank.

Irene was beginning to feel resigned to failure. She wasn't able to handle the girl's silence, and it was looking like she wouldn't find out the truth about the fire in Björkil. On the other hand, Superintendent Andersson and Hans Borg, who were old, experienced investigators, also had to throw in the towel when it came to Sophie Malmborg. Strengthened by the thought, Irene decided to continue to talk to Angelika.

Irene had an idea. She got up and looked at Sophie.

"Sophie, you can stay here by yourself for a minute. I would like to chat with your mother alone. I promise that we won't be gone long," Irene said calmly. Before Angelika could react and start to protest, Irene turned to her and said, "Come with me."

She placed her hand on Angelika's shoulder and smiled at her encouragingly. Angelika unwillingly stood up and went with her into the hallway. Irene stuck her head into the adjoining room and asked the psychologist from the Child and Youth Social Services Department to keep an eye on Sophie for a moment, then led Angelika to her office.

"Please come in," she said.

As she'd hoped, Tommy was in. He was reading a stack of papers. When Irene opened the door, he looked up and smiled in his happy way at Angelika. Angelika smiled back at Tommy. The change was instantaneous. The elegant woman seemed to stretch and then glide across the floor. Her thin fingers fluttered over her shiny hair as she coquettishly tucked a strand behind her ear. With a bit of sway in her hips, she walked over to Tommy. Tommy had gotten to his feet and was holding out his hand. Angelika graciously put her tiny hand in his, and her voice dropped an octave as she introduced herself.

"Hello. My name is Angelika Malmborg-Eriksson."

"Tommy Persson."

The sultry look she gave him could have aroused a eunuch. Irene had seldom seen a more open sexual invitation. Of course, Tommy was good-looking, but women usually didn't fall head over heels over him the first moment they saw him. At least, not that Irene was aware of. Tommy was looking with obvious delight at the beautiful woman who had unexpectedly entered his office and disturbed his routine. Irene decided to start speaking to disrupt the rise of so many pheromones.

"Tommy, I've asked Angelika to come to our office for a moment. There are some questions I'd like to ask which are not suitable for Sophie's ears. Personal questions . . . some about Sophie herself and others . . . well, you know, the ones we were discussing earlier when we were looking over the reports." Irene turned to Angelika and asked, while trying to smile in a natural way, "Would you like a cup of coffee?"

"Yes, please," Angelika replied. She did not take her eyes off Tommy.

"I'll go and get one," Irene said.

Neither Tommy nor Angelika seemed to notice that Irene left the room. Irene felt a slight unease. Perhaps it wasn't a good idea to leave Angelika alone with Tommy. He usually had a good effect on women, but Angelika's reaction was a bit extreme. Would he be able to handle that fox? What if—she stopped and then said to herself, out loud, "Get a grip! This is your old buddy! If anyone can handle Angelika in the right way, it has to be Tommy!"

She intentionally stayed away for a while to give Tommy time for his questions. Irene had no idea what they would be, but she was hoping that he'd intuit what she intended: ask about Magnus's alcoholism and anything he could about Sophie. She'd acted impulsively asking Tommy to take over, but Irene was hoping her trick would work. She felt drained of energy and initiative. Sophie was like the smooth surface of glass: hard, cold, flat. Still, you could see how brittle the glass really was. She would have to proceed carefully so that the girl wouldn't break. Or was Sophie unbreakable? It was hard to tell, but Irene did not want to be the one to shatter that protective shell because then they might never find out the truth about that Monday afternoon in November.

When Irene returned to her office with the steaming mugs of coffee, she heard Angelika talking.

"The problem was that Magnus had no insurance. He wasn't in the union. And he didn't have any kind of private insurance, either. We have no home insurance at all. We're not going to get a single öre. We lost everything we had in the fire."

"I'm sure you'll get some compensation from the state . . . child support and the like."

"Sure, but it won't be enough. I don't want to live in a housing project for the rest of my life! I want to move back to the city!"

Irene interrupted them by placing the mugs of coffee on the table. "Perhaps Sophie will get worried if we're away for too long. We can take our cups with us. I'll just quickly ask you the questions I have. By the way, do you think Sophie would like some coffee? Or a cup of tea?"

"No. A cup of water is fine for her."

Angelika looked unhappy at Irene's return, probably because Angelika's cozy chat with Tommy had been interrupted.

"How is Sophie doing in school?" Irene asked abruptly.

Angelika looked surprised. "Well, she's not the brightest

bulb in the package. Her teachers complain that she never says anything in class and that she's slow. But she manages to pass her tests."

Irene noticed the lack of concern in Angelika's voice. Apparently, Angelika didn't care one way or another how Sophie did in school.

"Does she have many friends? Or a best friend?"

"She doesn't have a lot of free time. She dances on Mondays, Tuesdays and Sundays."

Now Irene heard the obvious irritation in Angelika's voice.

"She doesn't hang out with any friends during the little free time she has?" Irene continued stubbornly.

"No, she doesn't. Well . . . Tessan Olsén, of course. They're in the same class at school and take the same ballet class."

"Do they get together when they're not dancing?"

"Not really." Angelika took some time to reply. Irene scanned Angelika's attractive face, which now looked cross and sulky. She did not want to talk about her daughter. Why?

"Do you have any idea why Sophie doesn't have any friends?"

"How should I know? She's so damn strange! She's always been an oddball."

Angelika's outburst was unexpectedly heated—even to Angelika herself. She stopped mid-rant and looked helplessly at Tommy. He hadn't changed his friendly expression.

"I mean . . . she's always been hard to understand. All this not talking business, that's nothing new. She's just like her crazy father. She can keep quiet for days on end. Days! And if something doesn't suit her fancy, she gets just as stubborn as he does. She'll never end up being a dancer if she keeps going like this."

She glanced at Irene as if to say, *And then she might end up looking like you.* Though she was in pretty good shape, Irene suddenly felt clumsy and huge. She knew her feelings were irrelevant, but she couldn't shake them.

"Is she still living with him now?" asked Tommy.

"Yes, and it's just as well. Frej is not doing so well after the death of his father. And, quite frankly, neither am I."

"Do you know if she's talked to her father about the fire?"

Angelika shook her head. "No idea. Ernst and I never talk to each other unless absolutely necessary."

"Do you share custody?" Irene asked.

"Yes, but she can't live with him during the week. It's too far from school. Now she wants to change schools, so she can live with him all the time."

"Where does he live?"

"The Änggården District." Angelika pouted. Her glossy red lips revealed that she didn't like this conversation one bit. Irene realized that they were running out of time. She tried to think of a follow-up question, but nothing came, so she just said, "Let's get back to Sophie."

They walked back along the hallway in silence, Irene hyperaware of every inch she measured in stocking feet. She was annoyed with herself for letting Angelika's chatter get to her.

It appeared as if Sophie had not moved at all. The woman from Social Services was sitting in a chair next to her, but got up when Irene and Angelika entered the room. When she walked past Irene, she whispered, "Can we talk for a second afterward?"

"Sure," Irene replied.

The next few minutes were just as unproductive as before. Sophie would not speak. Irene concluded it was useless to keep trying, so she decided to end the interview. Angelika appeared relieved. Sophie didn't change her expression as she got up and followed in her mother's wake out of the room.

With an audible sigh, Irene let her forehead fall into her hands once the door shut behind them. The woman from Social Services opened the door again almost immediately. She was about thirty years old and wore an enormous knitted purple poncho over a wide, black wool maxi skirt. She'd wrapped her frizzy blonde hair at the top of her head with a leather strap and stuck a chopstick through it. She sat down on the chair across from Irene and observed her through her thick, round glasses. She got right to the point.

"There's no use questioning her. Sophie needs peace and quiet. You police have no idea how to deal with children in this situation."

"No, perhaps not, but we do need to find out the truth about a suspected crime."

"What basis do you have for suspicion? That Eriksson fellow had previously set fire to his room by smoking in bed. You're torturing Sophie. She can sense your suspicion. Silence is her only defense against you and your questions."

"Why can't she at least just give us a 'yes' or a 'no'?" Irene exclaimed helplessly.

"I believe she really *can't* answer you. She doesn't remember. She received a great shock when the house she lived in burned down and the man who had been her father figure for the past nine years died in it. Children often react to trauma with silence. They repress the event."

Irene studied the psychologist. She seemed like a leftover from the seventies. Still, Irene knew she was right.

Nevertheless, if Sophie could not remember what happened, it was now the responsibility of the police.

THE PSYCHOLOGIST HAD barely left when the door was jerked open again by Superintendent Andersson.

"So things went straight to hell in a handbasket for you, too," he stated dryly.

He sat down heavily in the chair the psychologist had just vacated. He was not yet fifty, but Irene thought it was high time for him to start a diet. She could see his stomach hanging over his belt. She looked back up at his face and replied, "Yes, unfortunately, it did. But I believe that—"

"We will stop all interrogation on this matter. It's a waste of time. We have tons of other cases on our plates. Keep in touch with that scarecrow of a woman from Social Services. If the girl ever opens her mouth, maybe we can try again."

Irene knew he was right, but she still did not want to give up. She took a deep breath and said, "I think we should talk with all the adults close to her. Maybe they can give us some hints we can use if we need to question Sophie again."

Andersson's forehead wrinkled. "Where are you going with this?"

"If we do a thorough investigation," she began eagerly, "perhaps we can reconstruct a course of events and . . ." She stopped when she saw the darkening expression on her boss's face.

"So you believe that a thorough investigation has not been done?"

Since Hans Borg and the superintendent himself were the ones responsible for the initial investigation, there was only one way to answer that question.

"Of course it was thorough. But I mean that—"

"Well, then. We're not going to use up any more time on this. We'll wait for Social Services to contact us. For now, go help out Tommy with those rape cases from Guldheden."

Without waiting for Irene to reply, the superintendent got up and walked out the door, slamming it behind him.

IRENE HAD A scheduled training session every Saturday afternoon. Two years before she'd had the twins, she had won the European competition for women's jiujitsu. Back then, she'd trained practically every day, but once the girls were born, she'd been forced to cut back to only a few hours every week. She still belonged to the highest level in Sweden: black belt, third dan. Since there still were so few women at the elite level of the sport, her classmates were usually men. The Göteborg police force had its own jiujitsu group, so Irene could train during work hours. Still, her Saturday hours were the most important because she worked out with the highest-level people from her former club. The dojo was in the district of Majorna, but since the building was scheduled to be torn down, it was soon going to move. Irene felt melancholy about the move. She'd worked out in the old building for almost thirteen years; it was like her second home.

Krister was supposed to work all of Saturday, and Irene's parents were going to take care of the twins. Jenny and Katarina had been ecstatic when Grandpa Rune promised to take them sledding for the day. Irene worried that he might be overdoing things. He'd recovered from the operation he'd had that summer, but Irene worried that he had seemed more tired lately. Of course, he was seventy-two years old, but he'd always been healthy and energetic prior to his illness the year before. The diagnosis of prostate cancer had been a shock to them all, not the least for Irene's mother, Gerd. Gerd still had a few years to go before her retirement from the post office. She'd said many times that she dreamed of traveling the world with Rune once she was done working. She hadn't considered the possibility of a serious illness.

Hope they've had fun in this great weather, Irene thought as she climbed into her freezing car. Twilight had come, but a light pink shimmer still dallied on the roofs of the houses. Here in the center of town, yesterday's snow had turned into slush. Irene hoped that the slope in their townhouse neighborhood still had enough snow for sledding. The temperature had hovered around freezing the entire day, so perhaps snow still covered the tiny hill in the playground. It was the first winter the Huss family had spent in the townhouse neighborhood, and the twins had gotten used to their new surroundings quickly. They'd found lots of new friends, but that had created some friction between the Huss family and their childless neighbors, who did not appreciate the children running through their flowerbeds during their wild games. Mr. Bernhög had come over to Irene and Krister to complain many times. Their relationship with the neighbors remained strained, but it was something they had to deal with now that they were living in a townhouse.

INSTEAD OF TAKING her usual route over the Västerleden highway after her workout, Irene drove over the Älvsborg Bridge. Sinéad O'Connor's new hit, "Nothing Compares 2 U," was on the radio. Irene sang along with the refrain and let her thoughts run freely.

Even if Superintendent Andersson had decided to put aside the Björkil fire case, he couldn't stop her from going out and taking a look at the area on her own time. Even though they were swamped with other cases, Irene couldn't let this one go. Perhaps it was a nagging feeling that she'd failed somehow. Perhaps it was the riddle that was Sophie. During the past few nights, the girl and her dark eyes had been haunting Irene's dreams . . . and there was that unusual electric aura surrounding her. There were too many unanswered questions in this investigation. For her own peace of mind, Irene decided to keep digging. She was now convinced that they would never get the truth from Sophie.

Lost in thought, Irene missed the turnoff and had to drive a few hundred meters past it before she could turn back. The road was not plowed, but there wasn't much snow left, so Irene had no trouble driving on it. The shadows had deepened between the trees, but the thin snow cover reflected the last glimmer of the fading sun.

Irene sat in the car for a while and looked at the blackened remains of the house. A bit of the northside wall and the foundation were still there and looked like rotting teeth standing upright in the twilight. The rest of the remains were piles shoved into various corners of the burned area, covered by the thin snow.

What had happened that late afternoon in November?

There were a number of scenarios.

The first one was the one Angelika insisted was the truth as Sophie had told her: the girl had come home, had a snack and then rushed off on her bicycle to make it to class. She did not notice that Magnus Eriksson was sleeping in the upstairs bedroom, and she also had not smelled any indication of a fire.

In that case, there were also four possible ways the fire could have started.

The first was most probable: Eriksson had been smoking in bed and had fallen asleep while his cigarette was still lit. It had happened before.

The second was that the unknown Björlanda arsonist had struck again. Perhaps the arsonist had thought no one was home when he lit the fire.

Naturally there was a third possibility: there could have been a short in the electrical system of the old cottage. However, the technicians had not found any indications that this was the case. In fact, they'd stated just the opposite. The electrical system had been replaced and was completely new.

Then there was the question of candles. Angelika had been asked whether there were any candles in the house, which could have been lit and not snuffed out. Angelika had replied that she had no candles in the house at all since she'd not yet put out any for Advent. She was certain that her husband would not have lit any candles and then forgotten about them. "He wasn't the kind to have any candles around," she'd said firmly.

So that left the theory that kept bothering Irene. Sophie had come home from school and found her stepfather asleep, or passed out drunk, more likely, and therefore unable to wake up. The girl, in cold blood, could have set a fire and then ridden away on her bicycle for her ballet class.

Premeditated murder.

Would an eleven-year-old girl be capable of such a crime? If Irene had been asked that question a few weeks ago, she would have said a definite no. Now that she'd met Sophie, she was no longer so sure.

But why would Sophie have wanted to kill Magnus Eriksson? According to Angelika, they'd gotten along just fine, even though "Sophie is the way she is." They probably didn't have a close relationship, but it appeared that Sophie didn't have a close relationship with anyone, with the possible exception of her father. Ernst Malmborg was second on Irene's list of people to contact.

Irene opened the car door and got out. She took her flashlight, as nightfall was approaching. The snow crunched beneath her snow boots. She felt the temperature falling. She turned on her hefty stick flashlight and let the beam dance over the snow-covered remains of the house. She hadn't expected to see much, and there really wasn't anything to see. There were tracks left from birds and small animals in the snow.

Not far from the main house, there was an outbuilding that was so rickety it seemed that the only reason it hadn't yet fallen over was that it hadn't decided which way to go. Irene walked up to it and unlatched the hook that kept the broken door closed. The hinges creaked as she opened it. The interior was almost entirely empty. There were a few broken gardening tools in a corner, and an empty cement bag fluttered in the draft from the open door. There was a rustling sound in the trash along the side of the wall, and Irene realized that the old shed still had some tiny inhabitants. She let the beam sweep over the junk on the floor.

The voice behind her almost gave her a heart attack.

"What are you doing here?"

Irene swung around and the flashlight beam fell across a heavyset woman with a German Shepherd. From the dog's chest came a low growl. The woman held the leash in a tight grip as she stood in a wide stance.

"Get that flashlight out of my face! Get out of here before I call the police!"

THE WOMAN'S KITCHEN was redolent of freshly baked cinnamon buns and good coffee. All the kitchen fixtures were avocado, which, together with the fir cabinet doors, revealed a renovation completed in the early seventies.

Irene sat at the kitchen table and enjoyed a cinnamon bun while the German Shepherd snored at her feet. The hefty woman stood at the stove filling a small pressed-glass bowl with sugar cubes. She had on black corduroy pants and a black turtleneck covered by a beautiful knitted poncho in various shades of blue. The metal clasps on her clothing caught the light from the kitchen lamp.

"You must forgive me. There have been so many strange people running around. Curious people or people looking to steal something. Just the thrill of gawking at a place where someone died . . ."

The woman stopped speaking and her gaze fell on the flaps of the box holding the sugar cubes. Irene understood that this was a sensitive conversation. The woman had turned out to be Ingrid Hagberg, born Eriksson, the sister of the deceased. She had taken the death of her brother very hard.

Once Ingrid had realized that Irene was a policewoman, she'd immediately invited her in for coffee. Irene, who knew she could use a cup, had agreed. In their conversation, Ingrid Hagberg revealed that she'd been widowed a few years previously and had no children.

"So you see, when Magnus died, it was a big shock for me. He was the only relative I had left . . . well, and Frej, of course . . ."

By now, Ingrid was at the table, and she stopped mid-sentence to look down at her hands resting on the tabletop. They were unusually large for a woman's. Her fingers were red and swollen, and the fingertips were covered with deep cracks.

"So Magnus was your only sibling?" Irene asked. She took another bite of the bun, breathing in the scent of cinnamon.

"There were three of us all together. I was the oldest. Magnus was the youngest. Between us was Einar. He died in a moped accident. He'd gotten a moped for his fifteenth birthday and crashed it into a car the next day. Mamma grieved her way into an early grave—she had a heart attack a year later. She was only fifty-six years old. That's the age I'm going to be this coming year, though not until October."

Ingrid took another bun. The woman was heavily overweight, and Irene thought she would be better off shedding a few pounds given her family's health history, but there was also a sense of warmth under Ingrid's rough exterior. Irene decided to change the direction of the conversation.

"You mentioned Frej. How did you happen to arrive at the house with him in tow? You arrived at the same time as Angelika."

"Yes. Well, I was keeping an eye out for Angelika's car. My farm is just across from the convenience store, so I can see the bus stop from my kitchen window. I can also see whenever a car turns onto the road to the other farm. It's the only house on that road, so there aren't a lot of cars turning off there. I can recognize Angelika's Golf—it has a dim headlight. So when I saw her car, I took Frej and drove after her. Of course, I couldn't leave him here by himself. Though I still don't know whether or not I did the right thing. Now he's seen the house . . . the remains . . . but he wanted his mother and how could I have known?"

Ingrid's eyes were almost pleading. Irene nodded as if she understood. Of course the situation was difficult to deal with. Ingrid apparently felt very responsible for her nephew and, not only that, she'd never had children of her own, so she wasn't used to them. Irene took the natural follow-up question.

"Why was Frej with you that Monday?"

Ingrid looked away, and Irene could tell that her confidence evaporated.

"Magnus had asked me to pick him up from the school bus," Ingrid replied shortly.

"Did you often pick him up?"

"Sometimes. Angelika teaches on some days and doesn't come home until late in the evening. She has her daughter with her, of course. The girl also does ballet."

"But Magnus was home writing, wasn't he? Why couldn't he pick up his son himself?"

Ingrid's lips formed into a thin line, and she looked like she didn't want to reply. She ran her chapped fingers through her grey-streaked hair. For a brief moment, she appeared truly angry, but then she sighed heavily and sank down into her chair. When their eyes met again, Ingrid's were filled with tears.

"Magnus had some problems. He and Angelika . . . that woman drove him to drink!" she whispered.

"How so?"

"That little bitch! She was always cheating on him. I

warned him when he met her. I could tell at first glance what she was all about. A real whore! She was after his money, of course."

Ingrid's broad face flushed bright red from her outburst. Shaking with anger, she grabbed another cinnamon bun and ate it in three quick bites. Irene's ears had pricked up at Ingrid's last sentence.

"Magnus had money?" she asked.

"Yes, he did. He'd won some, and then he'd sold his half of our parents' house to me and my husband. The same house that just burned. Magnus and I had grown up there. It was only five acres, so my husband and I bought it. Magnus wasn't interested in keeping it. We redid the cottage so we could rent it out and maybe even sell it eventually. Then Magnus and Angelika lost their apartment . . . it was supposed to be renovated. So I let him rent the cottage."

"So the house had been your childhood home," Irene stated with surprise.

"That's right."

"Was it insured?"

"Yes."

Irene hurriedly thought of how to put the next question delicately. "You mentioned that Magnus was having problems and had started to drink. Was he drunk that afternoon when the cottage caught fire?"

Ingrid nodded. "I would go past when I walked Rex every afternoon . . . to check on the situation, you might say. I was worried. Sometimes I noticed that Magnus had . . . had a bit too much, and I offered to pick up Frej at the bus stop. Then I'd keep Frej at my place until Angelika came home."

"When did you pass by that particular Monday?"

"Right after two in the afternoon. The usual time I go past there with my dog."

As if he understood he was being talked about, the German Shepherd got up and put his head onto Ingrid's lap. Ingrid scratched him tenderly behind the ears. Irene could see that Ingrid's thoughts were far away from her pleasant kitchen.

"So at two P.M., you found Magnus under the influence?"

"Yes. It wasn't that bad, but I still told him I would go ahead and pick up Frej."

"Did you talk to your brother later that afternoon?"

"No."

"I read in the report that you were the one who called in the fire alarm. How did you find out? And when?"

"It was right before five. I just happened to look out the window and I could see flames over the tops of the trees. There's just a bit of forest between our properties. I realized at once that it must be the house burning, since there aren't any others on that road. So I called the fire department."

"You didn't go over there yourself?"

"No, Frej was asleep and I didn't want to wake him up. I also didn't want to leave him alone."

"Weren't you worried about your brother?"

Ingrid looked at Irene for a long time before she answered. "No, not then. When I was at his place around two, he told me he was planning to go to Göteborg to turn in an article."

"So you assumed he wasn't home when the house caught fire."

Ingrid nodded and looked down. A tear fell on the back of one chapped hand. She rubbed it dry on her pants. Then she took a deep breath and looked directly into Irene's eyes. "He borrowed some money from me. For the bus. He said he had to get some new clothes, too. It was that article he was going to turn in . . . he said it was important that he look presentable. He hoped that the newspaper would give him a job."

"Which newspaper was it?"

"I think he said it was *GT*."

Irene made a note inside her head to contact *Göteborgs-Tidningen* and see if Magnus Eriksson had an appointment to turn in an article on the same day he died.

"When did you start to worry that he might have been in the house after all?"

Ingrid gazed again at her work-worn hands for a long time before she answered. "The fire trucks and police cars came and went. An ambulance, too. Magnus didn't show up. As I said, I can see when the buses stop outside the convenience store. Every time a bus stopped, I expected him to storm into my kitchen and demand to know what was going on. Still, as the evening wore on and he didn't show up, I realized he wasn't coming. I was still hoping up until the last . . . but . . ."

Ingrid couldn't keep talking. Her despair appeared genuine. Irene got the feeling that Magnus Eriksson's sister was the only person who was actually grieving the fact that he had passed away. One could only guess what Sophie was thinking. Angelika seemed mostly angry that he hadn't been insured. She needed money. On the other hand, Angelika did seem to think that Frej missed his father.

"Why didn't you call the House of Dance and try to reach Angelika?" asked Irene.

Ingrid Hagberg stiffened. "We never talk. I didn't even think of calling her."

Ingrid got up and went over to the sink and tore off a huge wad of paper towels. She blew her nose. Her back was to Irene as she suddenly said, "Do you think she did it?"

"Excuse me, who do you mean?" Irene asked, confused.

"That she did it. The girl. Do you think she set fire to the house?" Ingrid said with emotion.

She turned and looked at Irene. Her eyes were now red

from crying. Still, Irene could see something glowing inside them that resembled hate.

"There is nothing to indicate that Sophie caused the fire. Neither on purpose nor by accident," Irene said as calmly and definitively as she could.

She got up from the table and thanked Ingrid for her time and for the coffee.

As she drove away from Ingrid's house, she glanced in her rearview mirror. The woman and her German Shepherd stood like unmoving silhouettes in front of the open door and watched her go.

IRENE AND TOMMY sat with the investigative material from the Guldheden rape cases in front of them, but somehow they'd gotten onto the topic of the Björkil fire. Irene told Tommy about her meeting with Ingrid Hagberg and how she had been unable to get through to Sophie. She was feeling more and more frustrated.

"If only I could figure out what she's hiding behind that mask of hers! What do you think?" she asked her colleague.

Tommy shrugged slightly.

"No idea. My son screams and the tears flow like a waterfall when there's something going on he doesn't like. When he's happy, he bubbles with laughter. He can't even try to hide what he thinks. Perhaps when kids get a little bit older, though . . . maybe if they're ashamed or if they don't want to talk about something . . . or want to protect someone."

"That's right. Kids are loyal and they don't tell. Who do you think Sophie is protecting? Or do you think she's just trying to protect herself?"

"I believe we should just leave Sophie to Child Protection Services. She's a hard nut to crack. Maybe she'll open up to them. Maybe then we'll have another chance to question her. It was interesting that you got the sister to admit that Eriksson had an alcohol problem. It corroborates what I've found out," Tommy said.

He pulled out his notebook from the top drawer of his desk and began to read out loud.

"Magnus Eriksson was forty-two years old when he died. He'd worked the last ten years as a freelancer because no newspaper would give him a full-time job. For one, he didn't write well. Two, he wasn't dependable. Never met his deadlines, according to my source at GT."

"Your source at GT?" Irene interrupted. "Who's that?"

"A guy who went to the same high school as me. Kurt Höök. Nice guy. We've never been that close, though we have some friends in common. So that bit he told his sister about GT offering him a job was an outright lie. According to Kurt, they hadn't bought anything Magnus Eriksson wrote in over five years."

"So he never went to town to turn in an article that Monday."

"Nope. He probably headed to the state liquor store and straight back home."

"So it's likely he was soused already when the fire broke out and didn't even notice when things started to burn."

They were actually getting somewhere with setting the last moments of Magnus Eriksson's life into place. The only missing piece was how the fire broke out and whether or not Sophie had a part in it. Did the fire start after she left the house? Or did she use a bit of blind courage to set the fire herself?

"By the way, what do you know about Ernst Malmborg?" Tommy broke Irene's revery with his question.

"Ernst who? Oh yes, Sophie's father. No, I don't know a thing about him."

Tommy smiled at her in a teasing way. "You're probably the only woman I know who isn't interested in celebrity gossip. As a matter of fact, I remember fairly well what was in the papers twelve years ago. Kurt Höök helped me fill in the blanks. Even though I was only seventeen at the time, I remember how Angelika looked back then. I thought she was a real fox. I couldn't see how she could settle down with an old man like that."

Irene raised her eyebrow in surprise. "Who? What old man?"

"Ernst Malmborg. He was over fifty and she was barely twenty! He was disgusting. And she didn't even know that I existed!"

He smiled again and gave Irene a swift glance. Irene remembered quite well how electrified the meeting between Tommy and Angelika had been just a few days earlier. Now Angelika certainly knew that Tommy existed.

Irene quickly tried to turn back the conversation to Ernst Malmborg. "So it was a big scandal that a fifty-year-old and a twenty-year-old got together? These things happen. Rich men buy themselves young women who want a father surrogate with money . . . not that unusual."

"Well, it was a bit more trashy than that. Ernst was married when he met Angelika. His wife was a famous actress who'd starred in a number of movies. She was more famous than he was. She was older, too. They had no children, but they'd been married a long time. When Ernst met Angelika, she got pregnant right away. His wife fell apart. There were whole columns about it in the papers. On the same day Sophie was born, Ernst's ex-wife committed suicide."

As Tommy recited the story, Irene began to remember fragments of it. Wasn't Ernst's wife named Anna-Britta or Anna-Lisa or something like that? Irene had a vague memory that the woman had overdosed and had been found dead in her apartment, but since she couldn't remember for sure, she asked Tommy.

"How did she die?"

"The usual, with some embellishments. She'd taken a huge amount of pills, not so unusual for suicides. The reason most people don't succeed is that they start to feel nauseous and throw up. So to be sure that she'd really die, she'd tied a plastic bag around her head, and she suffocated."

Irene shivered. There'd been a great deal written up about her films after her death. Her work with Ingmar Bergman had been highly praised. Irene had never seen any of his films, but she knew that working with Bergman was one of the highest honors a Swedish actor could receive.

Tommy turned a page in his notebook and continued. "According to Kurt, there was some speculation at the time of her death. Obviously she'd been depressed and bitter, but her doctor had thought she was starting to recover."

"Isn't that when the risk is greatest, though? When the depression starts to lift and the patient has enough energy to go through with it? A suicide, I mean."

"Exactly. And that's how people reasoned back then. It was headlined as a suicide. The body was found at nine in the morning by her housecleaner. The autopsy revealed that she'd died between nine and eleven the previous evening. At that time, Ernst and Angelika were at the maternity ward."

"What was her name?"

"Anna-Greta Lidman."

"So Ernst left Anna-Greta for Angelika?" Irene was honestly curious now.

"Yep, and Ernst Malmborg inherited everything from his ex-wife. They'd not yet filed for divorce. He married Angelika in the spring at the same time they had Sophie baptized. Within a few months, rumors were spreading that the marriage was already headed for the rocks. Angelika supposedly had an affair with a Frenchman: the instructor for the dance group she was in. It was all over the tabloids. Later she met Magnus Eriksson."

"Was Magnus Eriksson also a dancer?" exclaimed Irene, dumbfounded.

"Of course not. They didn't meet in the dance world, but

through the tabloids. He'd gotten the assignment to interview her about her first wonderful year with Ernst Malmborg.
It all ended when she left Ernst for Magnus."

Even if Angelika had left her first husband for another
man twenty years younger, Magnus was still ten years older
than she was. Perhaps Angelika just preferred older men. But
didn't Magnus's sister just say that Angelika was only out for
Magnus's money?

"Ingrid Hagberg said Magnus Eriksson had a lot of money
when he met Angelika. What happened to it? Did he drink
it all up?"

"According to Kurt, alcohol had not been Magnus's
greatest problem at first, even if it took over in the end. He
was a gambler. He frittered away every cent he had."

"Didn't Angelika get any money after the divorce?"

"Nothing. He'd made her sign a prenup."

"That explains—"

Irene stopped when their office door opened and Superintendent Andersson stuck his balding head inside.

"How's the questioning going?"

Both Irene and Tommy knew he meant the questioning
of the rape victims in the Guldheden case. There were three
women, all between eighteen and twenty-five.

Tommy shook his head and said, "We'll have to question
them again. All we know is the perpetrator was young,
strong and muscular. Blond. Swedish. But the last victim has
a different description. Says he was dark-haired and not all
that tall. Just normal sized."

"Do you think we're dealing with two different guys?"

"It's possible."

"All right. You two keep going on this case. We'll take it
up tomorrow at morning prayer."

Andersson closed the door behind him. Irene and Tommy
returned to the pile of paperwork on their desks.

• • •

THE NEXT DAY, a brutal murder took place in Kortedala, and the case fell to Irene and Tommy. From the beginning, it was suspected that the killing involved the drug cartels. But both the murder case and the rapes at Guldheden proved to be much more difficult than they had first appeared.

Time went by. The fire at Björkil fell further down the scale of important cases. Irene called child services once in the spring and talked to the psychologist who had been with Sophie at the police station. According to the exhausted psychologist, Sophie had never spoken about the fateful day. In fact, she never talked at all. The psychologist's last words were not at all hope-inspiring.

"You over there in the police department have to understand that Sophie has a handicap. She is different from other people. We have evaluated her and we're trying to help her, but it can take a long time before she even wants to talk to us. Perhaps she never will. At least about the fire. We'll just have to wait and see."

Irene sighed and hung up the phone.

Child services never contacted them again, and Irene never called back. The fire at Björkil was eventually registered as accidental due to smoking in bed.

PART TWO

2004

"I ASSUME THAT we might have been the last people who saw her. It seems that no one else saw her later that night . . . or rather, maybe it was already morning . . ."

"When did you arrive at Park Aveny?"

"Well . . . around midnight. Or quarter past. I really don't remember. It was a while back. We were at a publishing house party, and it was really pleasant. Lots of food and drink. Honestly, there was a great deal to drink and that's probably why I don't remember the time so well. I usually don't drink to get drunk, but the Göteborg Book Fair is a special occasion. You can say that it's the party of the year for the book world. A writer's life is pretty lonely. No co-workers. No one to have coffee with or to bounce ideas back and forth with. And then it's like this . . . this huge party and everybody comes. All kinds of people, other colleagues, publishing houses, media . . . and as a writer, you're the center of attention. It's a huge contrast to sitting in front of the computer all day. Of course, you're pulled into the flow! It's only once a year. And we usually go to Park on Thursday evening after the publishing house party. That is, all of us who have our books published at Borgstens. It's like an after-party where you meet all the people you know. Most of them, anyway. Also a lot of people who . . ."

"Was Sophie already there when you arrived?"

"No, I'm fairly sure she came later on. It looked like she

knew that dark-haired guy . . . quite good-looking . . . Marcelo, that's his name! If I remember correctly, she was just standing next to him all of a sudden. I was at the table next to theirs—we hadn't moved to their table yet—but I saw her from where I sat."

"Who is Marcelo?"

"Marcelo? Oh, he's another dancer, I believe. He's a friend of Pontus Backman, you know, the new star in the heavens of poetry. Max and I both know Pontus because we have the same publisher. Although I don't write poetry, not in the least. I'd never be able to put a stanza together. I just plod away at my detective stories. When you're as old as I am, you have to keep doing what you know. By the way, I have two published books about growing roses. That was before I started writing crime novels. I was a journalist at *Gardening* magazine and—"

"Did she come alone?"

"Yes, indeed. I'm absolutely sure about that. At any rate, she was alone when she turned up next to Marcelo."

"So you didn't see her when she came into the bar?"

"No, it was impossible. There were so many people in the foyer. People were constantly coming and going through those swinging doors . . . do you call them swinging doors? What do you call doors that go around and around without stopping? Revolving doors?"

"Right. What time was it when she appeared at your table?"

"Between twelve thirty and one, I think . . . somewhere around then."

"When did you decide to break up the party at the table?"

"One thirty. They close the bar then. We thought it was much too early for us to quit. So a group of us decided to head up to Max Franke's suite. He always brings a whole case of really good wine to the Book Fair. Max is one of our most famous authors. We've been good friends since we were kids.

These days we have the same publisher and his first wife, Barbara, and I were close friends during our days at the School of Journalism. It was—"

"Was Sophie going to go with you to that suite?"

"Yes. Max and her father were related . . . I think they're cousins . . . you know that Ernst Malmborg is her father?"

"Yes, I do."

"Yes, well, I guess most everyone knows that. It was a huge scandal when—"

"So Sophie was supposed to go up to the suite. What happened then?"

"The suite was on the top floor. We all packed ourselves into the elevator. Sophie didn't want to get in with us. Said she'd rather take the stairs."

"She said nothing more than she'd take the stairs?"

"Not that I heard. Just that she wanted to take the stairs. And she must have. The last I saw of her was her back. She was heading toward the stairwell. And from what I hear, that's the last anyone saw of her."

Detective Inspector Irene Huss nodded slightly, as if she agreed. The author had just given her a witness report, which, for the most part, agreed with what they'd already figured out. Which was not much.

The woman on the other side of the table, Alice Mattson, seemed to be nearing retirement age. Irene had never heard of her before. She didn't have the time or interest to read all that much. Still, she'd bought one of Max Franke's paperbacks at the Landvetter Airport bookstore and read it on her vacation to Cretet. It was a detective novel set in Stockholm. According to the back cover, Max Franke had sold an incredible number of books, and he'd become one of Sweden's most well-known authors. Now he was a part of the investigation that she was conducting.

As soon as she'd read the first chapter in the book, Irene

had found herself irritated at all the mistakes the investigators were making. There were also a surprising number of wine enthusiasts and opera lovers in the literary police department. She'd been a policewoman for seventeen years, and she only knew one single colleague who listened to opera. Strangely enough, that was her boss, Sven Andersson. He also kept a great number of CDs with music from the fifties and sixties. His favorites were Glenn Miller and Louis Armstrong. On the other hand, Andersson drank strong beer and schnapps. He thought that wine was for women.

Irene thanked Alice Mattson for taking the time to come down to the police station and file a report. The tiny, plump author chirped that it hadn't been any trouble at all. She was going to put down the cost of the car ride from Sävedalen as "research" on her taxes.

"Do you know that I've never been inside a real police station before? And I've written thirteen mystery books! My heroine has a flower shop and just has the habit of wandering into criminal investigations," she confided to Irene before she disappeared through the reception room.

Irene tried to hide her irritation and made a mental note to never buy a single book by Alice Mattson.

IRENE SAT DOWN in her office to think. It felt odd to stir up ghosts from the past. There had been times when the girl had turned up in her dreams: her large, slightly almond-shaped eyes and the emotionless expression. But had she truly been emotionless? Had she just lowered a protective curtain to avoid revealing anything? Irene had thought about Sophie Malmborg's gaze as the years went by. She never figured out what it meant or what Sophie was hiding.

And now Sophie was dead.

Fifteen years after the house fire out in Björkil.

Irene turned on her computer but couldn't focus on the screen. She stared out of the one window in her office. The rain had created patterns in the thick dirt. Twilight was falling. She ought to turn on the ceiling light but just kept sitting in her chair as the darkness gathered. Her thoughts went back in time again to try to piece together what had been gathered in the investigation.

She could hear the clattering of china in the hallway. The scent of coffee and cinnamon buns seeped beneath the gap in her office door. Or perhaps it was just her imagination, since she already knew that she'd need something sweet with her coffee.

ACCORDING TO NUMEROUS witnesses, Sophie Malmborg had arrived late, perhaps around twelve thirty, at the bar. She had come to join a group of friends who had arrived at least an hour beforehand. The group consisted of three men and a woman. Everyone knew one another. Around 1 A.M., Max Franke, Alice Mattson and the publisher, Viktor Borgsten, had joined the young people. The older group was just as drunk as the younger one. According to poet Pontus Backman, Max Franke went up to Sophie's table and bellowed: "Well, if it isn't my itty-bitty cousin!" or something to that effect. Then Max had hugged Sophie, who was as stiff as a statue. "A really strange girl, that one," Pontus concluded at the end of his testimony. The poet had no clear memories about the rest of the evening. The only thing he *did* remember was waking up at the apartment of the sulky blonde. Her name was Kia, and he never caught her last name. He didn't ever find out what it was, as he hadn't seen her since September. Kia lived in the Majorna district and was an art student. Pontus stroked his thin goatee tiredly and sighed. "Her apartment reeked of paint and turpentine. If I didn't already have a headache, I would have gotten one from the smell. And I'm getting another one now."

He gave this last sentence as half an apology. Irene would be able to swear on a stack of Bibles that Pontus Backman was even now severely hungover. His stinking breath hovered in the air between them—cigarette smoke, garlic and red wine.

He had no recollection of the elevator ride to Max Franke's suite. Therefore he also had no memory of anything Sophie might have said about taking the stairs instead.

Irene's conversation with Christina "Kia" Strömborg brought nothing new. As Irene caught a glimpse of her in the reception lounge area, she strongly suspected that Kia was high. Kia wore black clothes and a black blanket with a white pattern that she'd cut a hole in and was wearing like a poncho. She'd tied a grey scarf around her waist to keep it in place. All her movements were jerky and nervous. She was walking close to the wall like a caged animal and appeared unable to make her body pause long enough to sit down.

Kia had hardly known Sophie, it turned out. She only knew her by reputation. "Sophie was all hyped up—clothes and all—and just glommed onto Marcelo. But what could he do? He was addicted to her." Kia's narrow fingers kept plucking at the lint on her blanket.

As Irene could tell from Kia's national identification number, Kia was just twenty-six years old, but she looked much older. Her skin was pocked with acne scars and her heavily bleached hair hung in clumps. Apparently she was trying to grow dreadlocks but with limited success. The coal-black makeup she wore on her eyelids had run.

"What do you mean Marcelo was 'addicted' to Sophie?" Irene asked.

Kia gave Irene a look that Irene could not read. She answered shortly, "They lived together."

"How long had they been living together?"

Kia gave a dry laugh, which crunched like leaves in the autumn sun. "Don't know. She had a house of some kind."

Irene had checked out the house and found it was true. Ernst Malmborg had died of cancer at seventy-three in the summer of 2002. His only child, Sophie, had inherited everything he owned, which was a substantial fortune: 400,000 Swedish kronor in the bank, a summer cottage on the ocean by Ljungskile and a large house in Änggården. For the most part, the wealth of the estate had come from Ernst's inheritance from his first wife. He hadn't been careless with his fortune, and had husbanded it. As soon as probate concluded, Sophie sold the summer cottage for a million Swedish kronor. She had been a wealthy young woman when she died.

Was that why she was killed? Her next of kin was her mother. Certainly Angelika Malmborg-Eriksson could use the money, but how often would a mother kill her own child for the sake of money? The reverse was more likely.

There were other indications that the motive was something completely different.

Sophie had disappeared that night from the Park Aveny Bar. The people in the elevator had seen her walk toward the stairwell. According to Angelika, Sophie had a phobia of elevators. She never took them, or even escalators for that matter. The security guard who had been posted at the stairwell actually saw her go up the stairs. The same guard had seen her on the second floor right outside the elevator doors when he did a check of the stairwell a few minutes later. She was holding her cell phone, and it looked like she was sending a text message. She seemed to be concentrating, so he continued up the stairs on his rounds without saying anything to her. He'd walked all the way to the top floor. On the way back down, he hadn't seen Sophie. None of the other employees had seen her leave the building. They were totally occupied in putting the bar back in order after the rowdy night.

Thomas Magnusson, the security guard, was the last person to see Sophie alive. He was in his third year at Chalmers University, and he had the job on the side to earn some extra cash. Irene and Tommy had run his name through an electronic search, but they hadn't found anything remarkable. Magnusson didn't even have a parking ticket. His record was so clean that it was suspicious. He was blond and well built, and his honest blue eyes and clear, steady voice gave her no reason to be suspicious of his testimony.

Sophie Malmborg disappeared from the bar of the Park Aveny Hotel at approximately 1:40 A.M. on Friday, September 24th, 2004.

She had received a text message on her cell phone at 1:38 and sent a reply two minutes later. The sender had been in the vicinity of the hotel, but could not be identified, as a prepaid phone card had been used. That text message was the last sign of life from Sophie.

She had disappeared without a trace for three weeks.

On Saturday, October 16th, a storage shed in the industrial area of Högsbo had burned to the ground, and a charred corpse was found in the rubble. Another few days passed before the body was positively identified as Sophie Malmborg.

Irene had not yet gone to the site of the fire. She'd only seen the pictures. There was not much left of the building.

Irene got up from her desk to look at the map hanging on the wall. The location of the fire was in the oldest area of the industrial park at the end of a narrow cul-de-sac, not far from the rifle range. A thicket of hawthorn and birch trees had grown up around the abandoned building. No other industrial buildings were nearby. The shed had belonged to a tire company, which had closed years ago. Recently, the entire area had been bought by a pharmaceutical company that planned to demolish the shed and the buildings nearby and start construction on a lavish new office complex.

All the buildings in the area had been searched thoroughly. Although there were signs of unauthorized inhabitation, there were no traces of Sophie. The police quickly were able to determine that Sophie had not been kept hostage in any of the other buildings. It was also highly unlikely that Sophie had been held in the burned building since, prior to the fire, most of the roof had caved in. The weather had been cold and rainy the three weeks that Sophie had been missing. The chill dampness would have killed her in just a few days. And the area was not so deserted that someone could come and go for weeks on end unseen. Someone would wonder. Even if the suspect only appeared at night.

So the questions remained. Where had Sophie been kept the three weeks she had been missing? And who had been her captor?

"So, where do we go from here?" Superintendent Andersson began.

He helped himself to a slice of mocha cake, which he rapidly stuffed into his mouth, washing it down with large gulps of coffee.

The other people around the table contemplated his question, ignoring the cake, which Birgitta Moberg Rauhala had brought in for her birthday. They all felt they needed to stay focused. The discovery of Sophie Malmborg's body had made the papers with large, boldface headlines. Journalists were blocking the entrances to the main police station and the telephone lines were constantly busy. Irene could empathize with the journalists a bit. The case was sensational.

"We'll have the autopsy report tomorrow or Wednesday. Then we can see what they've found out about Sophie," Tommy said.

"Poor girl," said Birgitta, shivering.

Birgitta's husband and colleague, Hannu, who had recently returned to work after his paternity leave, nodded in agreement. Little Timo was now going to nursery school. Irene thought it was good to have Hannu back in the department again. His substitute, Kajsa Birgersdotter, had returned to her position in general investigation, but after the New Year she was scheduled to start a new position in the narcotics division.

Kajsa was the person who had received the missing person report. Angelika Malmborg-Eriksson had been expecting Sophia for a dance recital on September twenty-fifth. When she was unable to reach her the following day, she reported her daughter missing. When the charred body at the Högsbo industrial park was identified as Sophie, Kajsa had handed over the investigation to her former colleagues in the Violent Crimes unit.

Irene sneaked a glance at Tommy. Kajsa had been a source of comfort for him right after his divorce. Tommy's divorce had been a complete surprise for Irene—and also a hard blow. Tommy and his ex-wife, Agneta, had been best friends with her and her husband, Krister. Nothing would be the same again. No more shared vacations or midsummer celebrations . . . no more New Year's Eves together . . .

Suddenly Irene was aware that everyone at the table was looking at her. She said, confused, "What? I was just sitting here and . . ."

"We know. Taking a cat nap," said Jonny Blom.

"Thinking," Irene countered. She stared at Jonny angrily. It didn't help a bit. Jonny was grinning, as he'd been able to get in his little dig.

"Yes? And what was the result of all your thought?" asked Andersson.

Irene mentally pulled up her earlier speculations about the case. "We can all agree that it is a remarkable coincidence that Sophie burned to death in that shed. Especially the burning, I mean. Fifteen years have gone by since we questioned Sophie about what really happened at Björkil, but we could never get her to talk. I think we must start again there: the fire at Björkil when Magnus Eriksson died."

Fredrik Stridh swallowed the last bit of his slice of cake. He indicated that he wanted to ask a question. "Tommy told me that you'd gone to the scene of the fire fifteen years ago. Why? You were working at the central station."

Since both Fredrik and Birgitta had still been in training when the Björkil fire had taken place and Hannu was just starting at the Police Academy, Irene and Tommy had gone through the case with the entire group last Friday. Obviously Fredrik had been wondering how Irene and her colleague, Håkan Lund, who both worked in the central district at the time, had come to be in the northwest corner of Hisingen.

"Håkan and I were chasing a car thief. We lost him near Torslanda. When the alarm had come in at around five, we were the closest patrol car to the scene. All the cars in the seventh district were at the station for the shift change. We had been planning to head back to the station ourselves for the same reason, but as it turned out, we took the call on the fire in Björkil. We weren't able to leave until about nine that evening, which is when we found Sophie next to her bicycle by the side of the road."

"Did she say anything to you?"

"Not a word. I interpreted it as shock, but I'm not so sure."

The superintendent gave her a gloomy look. "So you really think we should drag up that old investigation again?"

"I believe we *do* need to look at it."

"Well, yes, I am aware that you were unhappy about how the investigation had gone before you took it over. Still, it didn't last long. It was written off as a case of smoking in bed." He didn't even try to hide the sarcasm in his voice. When he was in that mood, no good came from arguing with him. Irene knew her boss much too well after all the years they'd spent working together. Perhaps he was aware of the holes in the case and also thought that the investigation of the Björkil fire had gone wrong. Andersson stared at her, but when Irene said nothing, he decided to keep talking.

"We must question everyone who was at the Park Aveny Bar the last night that Sophie was seen alive. There are no traces of her in the hotel, so she must have left. Why didn't anyone see her go? There can't have been that many young women walking around town in bright pink tights, am I right?"

The superintendent had a point there. He fell silent and began to drum his fingertips on the table.

How had Sophie left the hotel unnoticed? Her trail after that was still a puzzle. They'd grilled the security guard, Thomas Magnusson, to within an inch of his life, but no results. It had been a fine night with clear skies. There'd been crowds of people—most of them young and in various states of inebriation—walking up and down Göteborg's main boulevard, Avenyn. Perhaps no one noticed Sophie because they were all too intoxicated.

"She went out the rear door. She did not want to be seen," Hannu said calmly.

This was a theory they were all considering: the suspect had gotten Sophie to sneak out the back door of the hotel.

"Still, someone must have seen her. Someone must have driven her somewhere. We will have to have an all-out search. Question everyone. Taxi drivers, hot dog sellers, doormen and the usual gang. Fredrik, Jonny, Birgitta, you're on it," Andersson said.

He wrinkled his brow in thought for a moment. Then he hit the table with the palm of his hand.

"Tommy and Irene. You're the most familiar with what happened fifteen years ago. Go dig up that old crap again. And you, Hannu, since you're a . . . well, you can go talk to that foreign kid who lived with the girl."

It was obvious that Andersson meant that Hannu should question Marcelo because he thought Hannu was also of foreign extraction, but he was completely off the mark.

Hannu was Swedish. He came from the Finnish-speaking area of Sweden called Tornedalen, so he did have a Finnish tinge to his Swedish when he spoke. That is, if he spoke at all. He was a man of few words. Why he would be the best person to talk to a Brazilian was anyone's guess. Irene knew that Andersson didn't make these kinds of gaffes on purpose, but she was starting to wonder. With a pang in her heart, she remembered that Andersson had mentioned retiring at the beginning of the year. In spite of everything, she was fond of her boss.

IRENE SPENT ALL of Tuesday going through the material about the fire in 1989. Now that she had fifteen more years of experience, Irene could see all the holes in the earlier investigation clearly.

Not a single detective had interviewed Sophie's father, Ernst Malmborg. Now it was too late.

There'd been a short interview with Magnus Eriksson's sister, Ingrid Hagberg, on the day after the fire, as she'd been the one to raise the alarm. Since her boss had told her to set aside the investigation, Irene had not dared to write a report about her informal conversation with the sister, and now she could remember only fragments of their talk.

There were no conversations recorded between Frej Eriksson and investigators. He'd been only eight years old when his father died, and he'd been at his aunt's place when the fire broke out. According to Ingrid Hagberg, he'd fallen asleep after having a snack. *The boy must have had a long nap*, Irene thought. Ingrid had said that she couldn't go to the scene of the fire while the boy was sleeping at her place. She had not wanted to awaken him. The fire alarm had come in at 4:56 P.M. Irene had seen Ingrid and Frej arrive at the scene at around 8:45. This meant that the boy had been napping for over three and a half hours. It wasn't completely impossible, but it was strange for an eight-year-old to have an afternoon nap last so long into the evening. *Don't people wake kids up if they nap too long? Just to make sure the kids sleep at night?* Well, Ingrid did not have children of her own, so perhaps she didn't think about it.

Not a single one of Sophie's teachers had been interviewed.

She would have to contact child services. They must have records on Sophie's personality and mental states.

Perhaps it would even be possible to track down Tessan, the girl in Sophie's ballet class? Her mother, Maria Olsén, had driven the girls to their ballet class. Hans Borg had talked to her, but the questioning session had been brief. Why had Sophie been out of breath when she'd biked to the store? Usually she was already standing there waiting in good time.

This was the detail that had made the police suspicious about Sophie in the first place. Did she set fire to the cottage, whether or not she knew Magnus Eriksson was sleeping there? Was this why she was burned to death fifteen years later? Or was this pure coincidence that both the girl and her stepfather died in the same manner?

Irene had no idea.

The only thing she could do was to go back to the beginning. But fifteen years had passed. Irene didn't feel very optimistic that a renewed criminal investigation would yield results.

AN IDEA CAME to Irene about how she could find more information about Ernst and Sophie Malmborg. Perhaps it was a long shot, but she'd try.

When she arrived home, she spent a few minutes with her overeager dog, Sammie, who was always overjoyed when a family member returned home.

Jenny was in the kitchen, stirring a pot. Katarina was out practicing jiujitsu and wouldn't be home until after eight. Krister would turn up at any minute. It was a rare day when the entire family sat at the table for dinner.

"Hi, sweetie, what are you making? It smells wonderful!" Irene called to her daughter in the kitchen.

"Lentil soup. I've made baked bananas for dessert," Jenny informed her. "You can go ahead and pour yourself a glass of wine."

Jenny had been a vegan for a few years now. Lately, she'd developed an interest in cooking. Since Krister was a professional chef, he found inspiration in her vegan creations. He'd lost about twenty pounds, a very good thing, but Irene found that she couldn't reconcile herself to vegan food. She begged them to limit the vegan meals to three times a week. On the other nights, Jenny had to fend for herself and often got by on leftovers from the previous night.

Irene could hear the jangle of Jenny's many thin silver bracelets as she stirred the soup.

Recently, Jenny had been dyeing her hair raven black and wearing a lot of red and lime green. Many years had passed since Irene had argued with her daughter about her choice of clothes. Jenny was grown now and could wear whatever she wanted. Her old-fogey mamma had been forced to realize that her daughter's role as a singer in a rock band with a punk edge demanded a certain look.

"Pappa called. He's running late. Someone got sick," Jenny said from the kitchen. Irene sighed as she thought about her poor husband, who often had to stand in when one of the other cooks got sick. He'd been complaining of being too tired lately, which was certainly to be expected. Gladys's was one of Göteborg's most popular restaurants and even had a one-star rating in an international guidebook, so expectations from both the boss and the patrons were high.

As soon as Sammie had enjoyed his fill of petting and tickling, Irene went into the living room to search through the bookshelves. She found the paperback by Max Franke. His name was in bigger letters than the title. As she pulled the book from the shelf, a few grains of sand fell to the floor—a greeting from the sunny beaches of Crete. On the back cover was the name of the publisher and there she found what she was looking for: Borgstens Förlag AB. She wrote down the name on a slip of paper and put it in her wallet.

ALL THE GATHERED detectives sat as straight as candles in a candleholder as morning prayer was about to start. Even Superintendent Andersson sat quietly in his chair, waiting, because, as they found out that morning, Yvonne Stridner intended to grace them with her esteemed presence. Professor Stridner was practically a legend as the Head of Forensic Medicine in Göteborg and was known as one of the best pathologists in Europe. She herself would have insisted she was one of the best in the world.

A few minutes after the clock showed it was time to start, they could hear the energetic click of Stridner's high heels on the hallway floor. Professor Stridner appeared in the doorway and surveyed the auditorium before making her entrance. She walked to the podium, leaving a waft of expensive perfume in her wake. She shrugged off her fur coat and fluffed her bright red hair. As always, her clothes were modern and tailored. This autumn morning, she wore dark brown linen trousers and an emerald green angora sweater with an eye-catching brooch fastened to the collar. The brooch was a leopard whose glittering red eyes caught the light. Irene assumed that the red stones were real rubies.

Yvonne Stridner spoke without further ado.

"Since I was coming to meet with the chief of police

anyway, I thought I would inform you of the results of Sophie Malmborg's autopsy to save us all time."

Stridner stared down the auditorium, and Superintendent Andersson shrank as her sharp blue-green eyes bored into his. Most people would have had the same reaction.

Satisfied with the attention of her audience, Stridner continued.

"Sophie was still alive when the fire began. Her nostrils and lungs are filled with soot. The soot particles reach as deep as the alveoli. In the lower lobes of the lung, the concentration of soot is fairly slight, which means that she was breathing shallowly. The cause of death was carbon monoxide asphyxiation. The fire was intense, but the lower body was not totally incinerated since it was covered by a thick rug. Therefore, we were able to run a number of tests. Prior to her death, she'd had a small meal, which consisted of tomatoes, cheese, bread, peppers and olives—probably a slice of pizza."

"A capriccioso?" smirked Jonny, who couldn't hold back a grin.

The glare Jonny received from the professor would have stopped a tiger in its tracks. They could hear the ice in her voice. "You must order an analysis from the lab if you need to know the kind of pizza in question. That is not my job." She took her glare from Jonny and redirected it at the superintendent.

"I would like to continue without foolish interruptions."

All Andersson could do was nod and send a warning glare at Jonny, who, for once, looked down at the floor and kept completely still.

"The toxicology report showed high levels of various sedatives and other narcotics in the contents of the intestine and in the tissues. Mostly diazepam and ketobemidone hydrochloride, as well as traces of dextropropoxyphene. The body also suffered from malnutrition. And . . ."

Yvonne Stridner stopped for a fraction of a second and a wave of emotion quickly flashed in her eyes. When she started to speak again, there was little indication that she had been troubled, but Irene noticed a trace of tension in her lips that hinted the professor was trying to keep her cool.

"Sophie Malmborg had an ugly fracture in her radius—that is, a crack in the bone of her lower arm that dated back to a few weeks before she died. She must have suffered a great deal of pain. So she may have been both abused and drugged. But considering the amount of drugs in her system, she was probably unconscious before she died."

Yvonne Stridner paused for a moment. Irene dared to raise her hand and Stridner nodded at her.

"Was it possible to find out what she was wearing?"

"Although the body was severely burned and the soft parts of the upper body were basically carbonized, we did find some textile fibers beneath the body. The technicians have them. However, she was lying on a mattress which had melted from the heat, so the analysis was more complicated."

"You're saying textile fibers. Could there have been some remnants of a leather jacket?"

"No, these were most definitely textile fragments. But please direct those questions to your technicians. They have also examined the remains of the rug."

Superintendent Andersson cleared his throat and carefully put his question to Yvonne.

"Have there been any other signs of abuse? I mean . . . torture or . . ."

"No, though what we have seen so far can be considered torture as far as I am concerned. She may have had that fracture since the day she disappeared. Three weeks is a long time to be in severe pain."

Forcing someone to endure that kind of pain and then killing her in such a brutal way! So awful, so inhumane! Mixed emotions of sorrow and wrath began to rise in Irene, and she was surprised by how strongly she felt.

Andersson found the courage to ask another question. "I meant, are there any signs of sexual . . ."

"Not that we can tell, but given the state of the remains, it is difficult to say for sure. I have sent some uterine samples to the lab, but we don't have the results yet. On the other hand, ketobemidone hydrochloride was found in the rectum from ketogan suppositories."

"What is that?" Irene hazarded.

"Ketogan is a preparation often given for extreme pain, for example, cancer or a heart attack. Of course, as an opiate, it is addictive. Since this was found in high concentration throughout the body, I believe she also received ketobemidone hydrochloride in the form of either pills or injections."

"And the other medications? What were they for?" Irene asked.

"Diazepam is found in Stesolid, for example. It's for anxiety management and cramp reduction. Dextropropoxyphene is found in various analgesic combination preparations. Analgesic means pain reduction."

"Is it hard to get these medications?" Irene asked.

"They are classified as narcotics, except for dextropopoxyphene, though even the latter needs a prescription. The person who kept her captive probably had to steal these medicines. I advise you to check the reports of recent pharmacy thefts."

Stridner wheeled around to lift her fur coat from the chair where she'd draped it. As she put it on, she asked, "Any more questions? None? Then I will let you know later if any other results turn up."

Her last words were spoken from the hallway as she disappeared through the door.

The auditorium remained silent for a long time after the departure of Professor Stridner.

Finally, Andersson said, with feeling, "*Goddammit.* Let's catch this devil bastard!"

Irene agreed with him wholeheartedly.

He stood up and continued, "Everyone stick to your assigned task. Dismissed."

IRENE PHONED BORGSTENS Förlag AB in Stockholm and was able to talk to the publisher, Viktor Borgsten, himself. He had a pleasant voice and seemed to be a personable man.

"I'm sorry I don't have more information about what happened that night at the Book Fair. We'd had a big party because Hollywood had bought the rights to Max's last three books, and we'd just signed the paperwork. It's going to be a big production. One of the best-known American directors is going to take it on, so we really had something to celebrate."

"I understand. I'm actually calling to reach Max Franke. He was related to Sophie and we're tracking down more information on the family."

In all honesty, Irene didn't know what she was really trying to find out from Max Franke, so she was intentionally vague. She was just following her instincts.

The publisher gave her an email address and a few telephone numbers and actual house addresses. Max had two houses in Sweden: one in Stockholm and one on the island of Gotland. He also had a house in Provence.

Irene decided to call the Stockholm number first and was in luck. Max picked up the phone after just a few rings. Irene introduced herself and began to question Max with some hesitation.

"We know that you were questioned earlier in connection

with Sophie's disappearance. We have also talked to others who were at the Park bar. According to one of them, you called Sophie *fröken flicka*"—little miss—"or something similar. What exactly did you say?"

There was complete silence on the other end of the line. Irene began to fear that he'd hung up, but after a while he said, "I was going to say that you asked the dumbest question I'd ever heard . . . but . . . well, I believe I *did* say something like *fröken franka*. I've called Sophie that before."

"What does *franka* mean?"

"It's an old Swedish word meaning 'female relative.' She's . . . she was my cousin's child. Ernst and I were first cousins. Our mothers were sisters. They were twins, in fact."

Irene was thinking fast. How could she get as much information as possible about Ernst and Sophie? She didn't have time to travel to Stockholm and meet Franke in person. The department didn't have the money to cover the cost, either, if Sven Andersson had any say in it. What could she ask? Then she had an idea.

"As you know, Sophie died in a fire. This has made us take another look at what happened when Magnus Eriksson perished in a fire years earlier. It could be just a coincidence that Sophie's murderer decided to burn her to death, but we cannot exclude the possibility of a connection. Therefore, we have to look at what happened fifteen years ago, or even further back. In other words, we need information from people who knew the individuals involved back then."

"What do you need to know?"

"Anything and everything."

"Everything?"

"Yes. The minutest detail, one that doesn't even seem important, could turn out to be the key to the entire investigation."

"Yes, yes, I know. I've written crime novels for twenty years."

There was another long pause, but Irene could tell that he was thinking hard.

"I'll tell you what I'll do," he said at last. "I'll write down everything I know about Ernst and Sophie's lives—just a synopsis, so don't expect literary quality. I'll email it to you when I'm done. This is just between you and me, though. Don't release it to anyone. I don't want to see any of this show up in the evening tabloids."

Irene promised to hold his information in strictest confidence and then gave him her email address. She felt pleased with herself when she hung up the phone, but her sense of contentment evaporated approximately five minutes later, when Tommy entered their shared office, shaking his head.

"You had a good idea, but it led nowhere."

"According to the address records, she should still be living at her farm."

"Well, she still owns it, but she's moved to assisted living in Torslanda and her property is for sale. Would you like to buy a horse farm?"

"Not really. I can barely manage a townhouse. Too bad things didn't work out. It was a good theory."

"Yep. A farm is another place to keep a prisoner without anyone noticing. But Ingrid Hagberg was hit by a car about three months ago. She was crossing the road to buy something at the little convenience store across the street. Ever since then, she's been hospitalized with a brain injury and can't take care of herself. They moved her to assisted living last week."

"Maybe we can still speak with her," Irene said.

"Maybe. If she *can* speak."

Irene tried to plot their next step. They'd found Ingrid Hagberg to be a dead end and the email report from Max

Franke would take a few days. Suddenly Irene knew her next step.

"There's one person on the scene fifteen years ago who's never been questioned."

FREJ ERIKSSON HAD testified that he was a student at the College of Photography in Göteborg, and Irene was able to reach the school's main office and left a message that the police would like to speak with him.

Frej called Irene's cell phone after lunch, and they agreed to meet at 5 P.M. at the police station to give him time to finish up his projects for the day. Irene asked him where he lived, and to Irene's surprise, he gave Sophie's address. That meant she had two tenants: her half brother and Marcelo Alves.

Frej had to cut the conversation short to rush off to class, but his willingness to talk gave Irene a sense of relief. She'd been afraid he'd be as closed-mouthed as his sister.

Irene had found a photograph of Magnus Eriksson among the old investigation material on the Björkil fire. It was a passport picture taken three years before his death.

He had an average-looking appearance, thin, blond hair and regular features, but he had a weak chin that was too small for the rest of his face. According to his passport information, he was 180 centimeters tall and weighed 86 kilos. He had blue eyes and wore glasses.

Why would Angelika fall for a man with such a humdrum appearance? No one during the investigation fifteen years ago had said that he was a pleasant, happy guy. No one said anything positive about him at all. He was an alcoholic and a gambler. Maybe he was a womanizer as well? Irene would have to ask Angelika what she had seen in him.

Money? He'd had a great deal of it when he met her. According to Ingrid Hagberg, Angelika had run through

Magnus's money fairly quickly, but since he was a gambler, he'd probably lost a lot himself. After a few years, all the money was gone. The Eriksson family had to move from their centrally located apartment in Linnéstaden and rent the cottage in Björkil. They'd stayed there for four years, up until the day the place burned down. What had happened to the family during those four years?

Frej had been fairly young, so the move probably didn't mean as much change for him. But Sophie had had to change schools and friends, and it was a much longer commute to the dance studio.

So during the four years at the cottage, the family's finances had further deteriorated. Magnus Eriksson had started to drink more and work less. Perhaps he even gambled away whatever money he earned as soon as it came in. His death at age forty-two might have come as a relief for Sophie and Angelika. Who had the most to win?

Angelika. She got no money from his death, but she did get her freedom. However, wouldn't she have asked for a divorce rather than kill her husband? She also had a watertight alibi for the time of the fire. She had first taught a ballet class between four and five in the evening and then led Sophie's double-length classical ballet class until seven thirty that night.

But why would Sophie kill her stepfather? There was no obvious motive. Perhaps his drinking disgusted her? Maybe he threatened her or frightened her? Maybe there was some kind of abuse? It was high time to contact child services.

It took a long time for Irene to find the right person within the clinic for child and teen psychiatry. Finally, she was connected to a secretary who located Sophie's file as well as the name of the child psychologist who had been caring for her.

"Majvor Granath is out on a work-related errand at the moment, but she should return soon. I'll ask her to contact you," the friendly secretary said.

While Irene waited for the return call, she flipped through the old reports from the investigation. It struck her as odd that so much time had passed from the moment Ingrid Hagberg had called in the alarm to when she had appeared with the boy at the site of the fire. It was also strange that she did not try to phone Angelika. Irene decided on a visit to Ingrid Hagberg, hoping there would be a way to communicate despite the brain injury.

Majvor Granath called at around four in the afternoon. She seemed harassed and her tone was brusque. Irene patiently described what had happened to Sophie and how it might be connected to the fire fifteen years earlier. The psychologist was quiet for a long time before she spoke, and her voice shook. "Poor little Sophie."

She seemed truly upset.

"Yes. It's a horrible murder," Irene agreed.

"I don't mean just her murder. I mean Sophie's entire life. She tried, she really did. But the odds were against her from the start."

"What do you mean by that?"

"Well, I really shouldn't say anything . . . patient confidentiality, you know . . . but perhaps what I know can help you solve this murder. So I do want to talk to you. Of course, I can't tell you everything, but some things . . ."

"I would be very grateful for whatever you could tell us. Sophie was a mystery to us."

"And to us as well. She just didn't let people into her life. Still, I did get to know her a little bit. We counseled her for just about four years. Then her case was handed to the clinic for child neuropsychiatry for further examination. We received the results of that examination, but I never saw her again."

"How was Sophie as a child?"

"You could say that she was an odd child even when she was very little. Her mother said that she had trouble getting close to Sophie even during her first few years. Sophie didn't start to talk until she was four. She usually played by herself. When she came to us, she already had problems with anorexia. She was healthier when she became a vegetarian, but she was still extremely picky with her food. Even though she was anemic, she refused to take iron pills. She often ate the same thing day after day."

"Do you know if she remained a vegetarian?" Irene asked.

"I wouldn't know. I haven't seen her in . . . eleven years."

The psychologist stopped talking for a moment and seemed to reflect on what she was about to say.

"Sophie always had personal quirks, and they intensified after the house fire. She fulfilled the criteria for Asperger's syndrome, but there was still much that did not fit that diagnosis. She also had her special gift, that is, dance. Sometimes she would dance for me. It was something else to watch her! In dance, she changed. With music, she seemed to be illuminated from within. I can't really describe it any other way. Usually people with Asperger's have some motor development challenges, but Sophie absolutely did not. Perhaps because she started so young. Most of her problems were not physical, but social. I'd say that although she displayed some characteristics, she did not fit an actual Asperger's diagnosis. At the clinic for pediatric neuropsychiatry, they found she had schizoid personality disorder."

"Was she seriously mentally ill?"

"No. You must not confuse the diagnosis of schizoid personality disorder with schizophrenia. Schizophrenia is a serious psychological illness where the patient loses all contact with reality and often must be hospitalized and medicated. A person who has schizoid personality disorder can live his or her entire life without needing to have any psychiatric care whatsoever. Nevertheless, Sophie's disorder created real problems in human relationships. It appears that her father carried similar traits. This condition is often genetic. Sophie was well aware that she was different from most people."

"Did you ever talk about her experience with this?"

"Yes, but not much. She rarely spoke at all. If she did, it was only in response to a direct question. She never started to speak spontaneously. I believe that Sophie communicated best through dance, but she was still the only one who ever truly understood what she was trying to say. It was not by chance that she became a choreographer."

"Did she ever say anything about what happened the afternoon of the fire?"

"No, she never talked about it at all."

"Did she ever mention her relationship to Magnus Eriksson?"

"She never talked about anyone in her family after the first year. Then she talked a great deal about her brother. She worried about him very much. I believe he was her only friend."

"Did she ever tell you why she wanted to move back in with her biological father?"

"No. She just said she would rather live with him forever. She told me that during her very first session. In fact, that was the only thing she said that first time. And she continued to live with him the entire time we were treating her."

"Did you ever have any indication that Sophie was abused by Magnus Eriksson?"

"That suspicion is always in the back of our minds, so we tried to see if there was any indication of abuse. But we never found any proof. Still, she certainly had a secret, which she kept to herself."

"What happened after she stopped treatment?"

The psychologist took her time before answering. "I heard that she'd done well at the School of Dance and that she wanted to continue her studies as a choreographer. Her mother said that she was a talented dancer, but that she had gotten too tall and too heavy for a professional career. I kept telling her mother not to say those kinds of things to Sophie, since the girl suffered from a severe eating disorder. But . . . just between you and me . . . I don't think her mother ever understood the seriousness of the situation. It seemed to me that they never related well to each other."

"In other words, Angelika Malmborg-Eriksson never understood her daughter."

"Exactly. I felt sorry for Sophie. She was talented and kind, but her personality pushed people away. The only person who seemed to understand her was her father. Otherwise she was very much alone. She struggled to find a place in society, and I believe—no, I'm absolutely sure—she found it in dance."

Irene had just thanked Majvor Granath for her time and hung up the phone when her office door flew open and a young man exploded through the doorway.

"You're Huss?" he demanded.

"You're Frej?" Irene retorted.

Irene knew it had to be Frej from the remarkable resemblance to his father. He had stringy blond hair hanging from beneath a black hat, and though he had developed a slight beard, it was too thin to hide the weak chin he'd inherited from Magnus Eriksson. As he walked into Irene's office, he shot off a charming smile, and Irene could tell he'd inherited a few things from his mother as well. He politely took her hand and introduced himself before sitting down in the visitor's chair. He had a solid handshake, and he looked at Irene steadily. It did not appear that Frej was suffering from any

social disorders. He wore jeans and a thick down jacket with
a fur-lined hood. Beneath the open jacket, Irene could see a
light-blue flat-knit sweater.

Frej stood up again abruptly and shed both the jacket and
the sweater. Before Irene could say anything, he said, "Don't
mind me. It's just too hot in here for me to keep them on.
We've been taking photos outside all day."

Beneath the blue sweater, he was wearing a black T-shirt
with the slogan U2 4-EVER. Irene was surprised to see that he
had well-defined muscles and nothing of his father's doughy
figure.

"My aunt, my father's sister, knitted this sweater for me.
It's a nice one, but it's too warm to wear anywhere but outside during cold weather."

He smiled pleasantly, and Irene smiled back. "Do you
often visit your aunt?"

"I see her, like, once a week or so."

"She was hurt in a car accident . . ." Irene left her sentence incomplete to see what he would say.

Frej nodded. "Yeah, she was hit by a car. Drunk driver.
They caught him. He hit Aunt Ingrid when she was crossing
the street to the store. He bounced off her and hit a light
pole. He had, like, a two-point-oh and couldn't even stand,
that drunken bastard. The police had to drag him out of the
car."

"How badly was she hurt?"

"She broke an arm and . . . what's it called . . . the tail-
bone . . . but she was, like, unconscious for a week. Broke
her skull when she landed on the pavement. She went
flying, the witnesses said."

"Can she speak?"

"Yeah, but the elevator doesn't go to the top floor, if you
know what I mean. She forgets stuff. She gets sad and starts
crying. She wasn't like that before."

"One of my colleagues told me that she was planning to sell the farm."

"Yeah, she can't handle living there any more. She can walk for short stretches indoors with that rolling thing . . . you know, the one all those old people have."

"A walker?"

"Yeah, but outside they put her in a wheelchair."

"Does she still keep animals?"

"Nah."

"Did she rent out the stalls?"

"Yeah, for a while, until the riding club built their own stable. Aunt Ingrid was okay with that 'cause she didn't really like people tramping all over the place. So she never rented it after that."

Irene was positively surprised about Frej. There was nothing in this questioning that was anything like her attempt to talk to Sophie all those years ago. Frej seemed open and talkative—a police officer's dream.

"So who is watching the farm now that she can't do it herself?"

"Me."

"Isn't that hard? You live in Änggården and have to get all the way out to Björkil. And you have your classes."

"No problem. I got a car. Aunt Ingrid's."

"That makes it easier, of course. How long have you been living at Sophie's place?"

"Since last spring. I'm renting the upstairs attic loft."

"I see. So Sophie and Marcelo lived together in the rest of the house . . ." Irene stopped when she saw Frej's expression.

He'd raised his eyebrow and his smile dimmed.

"Wasn't Sophie living with Marcelo?" asked Ingrid.

"Living together? Sophie? Nah. Where'd you hear that?"

"Someone said—"

"That someone was wrong. Sometimes Sophie rented a room to other dance instructors. Like, the ones who come and teach for a couple weeks or a month or so and don't live here in Göteborg. Marcelo's been there since the end of August."

"Is he still there?"

"Yeah."

"What about Sophie? Where did she live?"

"On the ground floor, of course."

"It must be a big house."

"Yeah. Like, four hundred square meters or something like that."

Given Frej's openness, Irene decided to get more personal.

"We have to go over everything again," Irene said. "Initially, we were dealing with a missing person, but now we're investigating a murder."

His face paled, but he said nothing. He just nodded to indicate he understood.

"I therefore have to ask you what you were doing around midnight between the twenty-third and twenty-fourth of September."

"I've already said I was in the darkroom the whole evening and into the night."

"What did you do later on?"

"I went to bed."

"What time?"

"After two, I'm pretty sure. Maybe three. I don't look at the clock when I'm in my darkroom."

"So you had no contact with your sister on the night in question?"

"No, we just saw each other briefly when I was getting home from class around, you know, four or five in the afternoon."

"Did she tell you what her plans were for that evening?"

"No."

His response was the same as he'd given earlier. Irene thought hard about how to come to a different approach.

"Do you know when she left the house?"

"No idea."

A thought crossed Irene's mind. "Where is your darkroom?"

"In the loft apartment. That's why I moved into Sophie's house in the first place. The space was empty. The darkroom's across from my apartment in the loft."

"Any ideas at all where Sophie went after she left the bar at Park Aveny that night?"

"No."

"Any guesses?"

"No."

Irene decided to change her line of inquiry. In a neutral tone, she asked, "Who were Sophie's best friends?"

"She didn't have any friends."

His answer came at once without any pause to think things through. It was just a dry statement.

"Were there any people at all she liked to hang out with?"

"Yeah, of course. People in the dance world. But she, like, never invited them home or anything."

"Did Sophie have any enemies?"

"Not that I know of."

"Do you know anyone who hated Sophie enough to want to kill her?"

He took a short time to think, and he replied in a low, quiet voice. "No."

"Do you believe there might be a reason why Sophie was burned to death?"

"What do you mean by 'believe'?" He looked at her.

"Why do you think that she was locked in that shed, and why do you think the killer set it on fire?"

Frej shook his head slowly. In his eyes, there appeared only deep sorrow. "Not the faintest idea," he said seriously.

"What do you remember from that afternoon and evening when the cottage out in Björkil burned down?"

He appeared to ponder this for a while before looking back at Irene. "Not much more than Aunt Ingrid driving over there with me in the car. I can remember police cars . . . lots of people . . . then I really don't remember much. It's kind of strange, really . . ."

"Do you remember anything from before you arrived at the scene?"

"Nah. I was asleep. I really don't remember much from that day at all. I remember *nada*. I must have been in shock or something like that."

It really seemed he was trying to remember as much as he could. His apologetic look at Irene spoke clearly.

Irene decided to drop the subject. Instead, she said, "I must also ask you what you were doing the night of the sixteenth of October between two and four A.M."

He looked at her for a while before answering.

"That must have been . . . when that shed . . . with Sophie caught on fire. I was exercising until seven thirty on Friday night. Then I went over to Aunt Ingrid's place to make sure it was okay. The real estate agent was supposed to come by, like, Saturday or something."

He fell silent again.

"When did you leave Björkil?" Irene continued her line of questioning.

"Around ten, I guess. I bought a kebab from the pizzeria on Björlandsvägen and ate it when I got home. Then I worked in my darkroom for a while. But I was tired as hell so I, like, went to bed, around midnight, twelve thirty, thereabouts."

"Where is this pizzeria located?"

"Almost all the way to Brunnsbo. It's called Pizzeria Napoli."

It appeared there was nothing else to ask. Nevertheless, Irene thought that Frej had been very helpful. She thanked him for his cooperation and promised to inform him if anything else came up in their investigation.

It was almost six in the evening, but Irene remained sitting in her office to mull over her conversation with Frej Eriksson. Some pieces had fallen into place, but others were still missing.

Frej did not have anyone who could back up his alibi. Even if, against all odds, the employees of the pizzeria remembered he was there that exact evening, there was no one to say what he was doing in the hours when the fire broke out.

Did those two siblings really not see or speak to each other the entire evening? Did they have a difficult relationship? They'd been living in the same house for six months. On the other hand, maybe their relationship was strained, especially after Frej's father died. Sophie had gone to stay with her father while Frej stayed with Angelika.

And what was Sophie's real relationship to Marcelo? According to Frej, Marcelo was one renter among many, but most people only stayed for weeks or months. An entire semester, on the other hand? Perhaps it was time to have a closer look at the stylish Brazilian.

HANNU HADN'T REACHED Marcelo Alves the previous day. There'd been a gang murder at the Central Train Station, so Andersson had shifted them to the new investigation. There were a great many people to interrogate, and not all of them were willing to cooperate with the police. They either lied or refused to answer any questions.

Before they went home for the day, Irene told Tommy that she was planning to reach Marcelo. "Good," Tommy replied. "I'll try for another chat session with Angelika. It's about time we meet again—it's been fifteen years."

He smiled an odd smile as he said this, and Irene was left with a nagging sense of worry.

THE NEXT MORNING, Irene headed straight for Högsbo and the House of Dance; it was not that far out of the way from her office. This "Mecca of a dance school," as the website proclaimed, was an old, red brick school building built in the late fifties not far from Axel Dahlström Square. Then, twenty years ago, a brand new school was built less than a kilometer away since there was no room for expanding the older building. Instead, the House of Dance moved in—and after some time, the School of Dance joined them. The schoolhouse building had been renovated bit by bit. Walls were ripped out, ceilings were raised. The remaining inside walls were covered with floor-to-ceiling mirrors. There were also spaces for theoretical instruction, changing rooms and administration. At present, the School of Dance was seen as one of the premier institutions for dance instruction.

It was exactly 8 A.M. when Irene walked through the entrance to the House of Dance. On one side, she saw a coatroom and on the other a large cafeteria. A few young people were hanging around a table with steaming mugs. They did not match Irene's image of serious dance students. These kids had dyed hair and the same kind of clothes as any other arts students. Irene was reminded of Jenny, who was finishing up her last year of high school as a fine arts major in music.

Irene noticed one pale girl who wore all black. She'd dyed her hair pink and was wearing it in two braids across the top of her head, Gretchen-style. Irene could see an inch of her blonde roots showing at the back of her neck. An ebony-skinned young man sat beside her. He was yawning so widely that Irene, in spite of the distance, could see into his throat. He was wearing an oversized knit hat, which appeared to have been created from the motley remnants of various balls of yarn.

Farther down the hallway was a white sign with the word ADMINISTRATION. Irene thought it wise to start her search there. When she went to push open the door, she found that it was locked. The glass doors that barred the entrance to the rest of the school were also locked. Obviously, outsiders were forbidden to go past the cafeteria.

The girl with the pink braids called out to her. "The bell is broken. Knock hard and someone will come."

Irene knocked on the glass panel to the door, and almost immediately a woman wearing a light-blue leotard and white knit leg warmers came down the stairs. She was exactly what Irene had imagined a stereotypical dance student looked like. She was most likely one of the teachers. Her black hair, streaked with grey, was pulled back into a tight bun, and the lines in her face revealed that she was middle-aged. The woman smiled and opened the door for Irene without asking who she was or what she was doing there.

Bad security here, thought Irene. She changed her mind during the time they walked up the stairs. She realized that she hardly appeared to be either a potential student or a crazy terrorist. Perhaps she gave off the "cop" smell from yards away.

The stairs ended in a reception area. Irene continued toward an older woman sitting behind a counter, introduced herself and told her why she was there.

"Marcelo Alves? I believe I recognize the name, but I'm not sure. Wait a moment while I go find Gisela."

The sprightly white-haired woman walked down the hallway and knocked on a door. She entered and, a moment or two later, returned with a tiny woman in tow who held out her hand to Irene.

"Hello, I'm Gisela Bagge. I'm in charge of instruction here at the House of Dance."

Gisela appeared almost transparent. Her light blonde hair was cut in a short style with wisps springing up around her head. Her round blue eyes and her smile made Irene think of an angel. Her white dress completed the picture. The turtle-neck collar was as wide as it could be without sliding off her shoulders and falling straight to her ankles. She wore a wide red ribbed belt, which perfectly matched her suede boots.

"Let's go into my office," Gisela Bagge said.

She spun gracefully on her high heels and led Irene down the hallway to her office, a surprisingly small room with large windows facing the old schoolyard. Gisela sat down behind her desk and gestured for Irene to sit in the opposite chair. Irene could see the autumn mist and the emptying branches of the chestnut tree outside.

Gisela got right to the point. "Lilly told me you were looking for Marcelo Alves."

"That's right. It's part of our ongoing investigation into the murder of Sophie Malmborg. I understand Marcelo rents an apartment from her."

"I know. I was the one who put him in touch with her. Sophie usually rents . . . rented rooms to our visiting instructors at low cost. She started the practice after her father died."

"Marcelo has no telephone we can reach, so I thought I would try to find him here," Irene said, smiling.

Gisela smiled in return, and in the harsh light from the ceiling lights, Irene could see thin lines spread from the corners of her eyes like rays from the sun. Irene suspected that Gisela was about forty years old, but could easily be mistaken for twenty-five.

"If you want Marcelo, you have to come by later in the day. He rarely arrives here before two in the afternoon. Often later."

"But he has to be here in time to teach class, right? He is an instructor here," Irene said, puzzled.

"Yes, indeed, but we've scheduled his classes as late in the day as possible. Often in the evenings, in fact. You see, he's from South America—Brazil."

Gisela's expression indicated that she thought that should explain everything, but Irene didn't get it.

"I know he's Brazilian, but why would that keep him from giving lessons during the day?"

"Because he's Brazilian," Gisela repeated. She rolled her eyes and, laughing slightly, continued, "Marcelo has no sense of time. It's like the clock has no meaning for him. He just wanders in whenever he feels like it."

"It must be really difficult to have an instructor like that on the staff," Irene exclaimed.

"In the beginning, we fussed about it, but no more. He's usually here by the time his classes are supposed to start, and even though they're in the afternoons and evenings, they're full. The students love him."

"What kind of dance does he teach?"

"South American. He teaches students from the school and the House of Dance, but he also has classes for the general public. Salsa, merengue and lambada are especially popular. Marcelo has also given a class in focho, which is a Brazilian variation of foxtrot. Though, to be honest, I don't see much resemblance to our European foxtrot. That course appeals to a group we usually don't see here: the retirees. The class is extraordinarily popular and the participants idolize Marcelo. He flirts with the ladies and jokes around with the men, and when they leave, they look twenty years younger! It's truly amazing, especially when you realize he hardly speaks Swedish."

She laughed heartily at the same time she opened the top drawer of her desk. She rummaged around and handed a brochure to Irene. It was in a language Irene did not understand. *Capoeira. Boa vontade. Mestre Canelão. Nata—Brasil.* Above the text was a photograph of two muscular men with bare chests and wide, white pants. One of them was upside down, balancing on one hand and aiming a kick at the other man while managing to keep the rest of his body in the air. The other man was dodging the kick by bending deeply at the knees so that his body was on a level plane with a hand on the floor behind him for balance. Irene knew, after many years of training in martial arts, that these men were strong and the kick would have been deadly if it had hit its mark.

"And if that's not enough, he wants to start a group in capoeira," Gisela said, with a nod to the brochure.

"But this doesn't look like dancing at all," Irene protested.

"Oh, it's a kind of dance. And then again, it isn't."

"How so?"

Gisela seemed to think for a moment and then said, "Let me show you."

Before Irene could say another word, Gisela stood up and led the way to the door. They walked down the stairs and into the hallway. Gisela opened the glass doors that closed off the rest of the building, and they passed through. The smell of sweat and the sound of rhythmic African drumbeats let Irene know they were heading toward the practice rooms. They stood in front of a closed door now, and from within the room, Irene could hear a wailing stringed instrument above the drums.

Gisela pressed down on the door handle, and they walked into a spacious training room. A group—two girls and four boys—was warming up in front of one of the mirrored walls. The dark-skinned young man Irene had seen in the cafeteria had shed his knit Jamaican cap and no longer appeared at all tired. Hundreds of small braids hung down his back. Whenever he moved his head, the wooden beads at the end of each braid clicked softly. Like the men pictured on the school brochure, he was bare-chested and wore wide, white pants. He was in great shape. As Irene later learned, the man was Felipe Medina.

The girl with the pink braids was warming up next to him. She wore white jazz pants and a lime green top. The girl was as thin as Irene had guessed when she'd seen her in the cafeteria, but now the girl's muscles were apparent beneath her pale skin.

The warm-up was different than what Irene was used to with her jiujitsu. The music was upbeat and the movements were swifter. Irene watched as the music segued to something smoother, and everyone in the group turned upside down to stand on their heads. Felipe, maintaining his headstand, let his legs fall into a split, while the girl in the pink braids kept hers straight in the air. The entire group remained upside down for quite a few minutes. The tempo increased, and they abandoned their positions and began to roll around on the floor, moving faster and faster as the music became more frenzied. The bare chests of the boys glistened with sweat.

Then, as if a secret sign were given, they formed a semi-circle and began to clap their hands in time with the music. Felipe Medina and one of the boys stepped out of the semi-circle to face each other and began to move in what appeared to Irene to be an advanced *kata*. They changed positions at a lightning pace. Irene recognized much of their basic technique, but at the same time she could see a great deal of difference between capoeira and jiujitsu. In capoeira, there was no bodily contact. Like karate, the blows were made into the air. Of course, Irene knew there were full-contact karate competitions, seldom held, because any physical damage would be serious. Powerful kicks were another similarity between karate and capoeira. Periodically, Felipe rose into the air and spun his legs like the blades of a helicopter. Irene could see that the power behind a kick like that could be deadly. Other movements were pure acrobatics, yet everything followed the beat of the music. It was dance, but then again, it wasn't, just as Gisela had said.

Gisele and Irene left the capoeira practitioners and returned to the hallway. The beat of the drums still echoed in Irene's ears.

"I understand what you meant when you said it was more than just dance," Irene said.

Gisela Bagge nodded and smiled.

"Capoeira is an old African dance style. Slaves sold to plantations in Brazil kept up the tradition, and so that the slave owners would not forbid it, they said that it was nothing more than a traditional African folk dance. The name capoeira derives from an indigenous language of Brazil.

It means 'bush.' When the slaves escaped, they hid in the bushes, and some local tribes told the masters that they were in the capoeira. The dance is alive and well in Brazil, and it's even become popular as a martial art. Now it's also starting to come to Europe. It's a good sport for dancers because there are so many dance movements in it."

"Can Marcelo do capoeira?"

"Yes. He offered an intensive course this past summer. That's why Felipe and those boys became so good so quickly. On the other hand, all of them had dance training from the get-go."

They entered the cafeteria, and they each picked up a paper mug of coffee. Irene withstood the temptation to throw a five-krona piece into the machine vending various pastries. She was overwhelmed by the same feeling she'd had fifteen years ago when she first met Angelika, as if she were size XXXL. On the other hand, anyone could feel hefty beside the ethereal Gisela.

They walked back to her office. Irene put her mug down on the desk and blew her fingertips.

"I still have quite a few questions. Do you have time to talk?"

"Sure. I have a meeting at ten o'clock, but I'm at your service until then. Lilly will take my phone calls so we won't be disturbed."

"Thanks. Tell me, how did Marcelo end up here at the House of Dance?"

"He came here just over a year ago. The students wanted a course devoted to salsa, which is still quite popular. An acquaintance of mine in Oslo knew Marcelo, who had made a name for himself as a dance instructor over there. I managed to lure him here and he felt at home with us. Last semester he commuted between here and Oslo, but he stayed here in Göteborg this semester. Sophie had a great deal to do with that. Marcelo felt at home in the space he rented from her."

Irene felt this was the best opening to ask an important question. "Do you know if she and Marcelo were a couple?"

Gisela gave Irene a long look before she replied, "Both Marcelo and Sophie are . . . shall we say . . . problematic. Let's start with Marcelo. His problem is that he has no trouble at all with women, though I have to say, he does not see this as a problem. He sleeps with anyone he wants, and he often wants different women. For some reason, they never get angry with him. They seem to be grateful that he gives them some of his attention and warmth, even for a moment. The devil knows how he gets away with it!"

She finished speaking with a short laugh, and Irene had to smile in agreement. But at the same time, she wondered at Gisela's odd choice of words until she noticed the glistening shine in Gisela's eyes. Clearly this was a dangerous man whose heat left many female hearts in disarray. She decided to tactfully leave the subject of Marcelo behind.

"Why was Sophie problematic?"

"I got to know Sophie when I came here as a teacher fifteen years ago. She is . . . she was a very unusual person. At the same time, she was tremendously gifted as a dancer. She saw dance in everything. Last year she studied choreography and received top grades. As a matter of fact, a group here at the college is preparing her work for a premiere next Wednesday. It's a real experience, and I urge you to come and see it."

Gisela got up and pulled a sheet of red paper from a stack in her bookshelf. Black letters proclaimed:

THE FIRE DANCE
A saga in dance
Students of the College of Dance with dancers from Theater

Souls on Fire
Choreography by Sophie Malmborg
Music by Ernst Malmborg

The picture above the text showed black silhouettes posed against the dark red background.

Irene studied the picture and its text for a long time. Something stirred in her subconscious. A memory, a flash of recognition . . . no, she didn't understand what it was.

Gisela was also looking down at the piece of paper. With real sorrow in her voice, she said, "Now Sophie will never see her work performed."

Gisela had to swallow a few times before she was able to speak again.

"Sophie was insecure when it came to dealing with other people—especially men. As far as I know, she'd never slept with any man. To tell you the truth, I believe men were frightened by her intensity. She never flirted or played the coquette. She'd just retreat inside her shell. I watched it happen many times. Sometimes I had the strong feeling that Sophie needed to be . . . protected somehow."

"Protected from what?"

"People. Life. I can't explain it any better than that. I know what she went through when that Eriksson man died in the fire. She was a suspect!"

Her blue angel eyes looked accusingly into Irene's.

"So you don't believe she was capable of such a thing?" Irene countered quickly.

"Of course not! She never attacked anyone, ever! She was always trying to defend herself from other people."

"Did she have a . . . best friend here at the college?"

Gisela looked at Irene with sorrow and Irene could hear the sadness in her voice as she replied, "I was probably the person closest to her. I was her mentor, you could say. She needed someone who cared about her and encouraged her. At times she could be so sad, even if she didn't show it to the outside world."

"You must know her mother, Angelika, then, I suppose?"

"Oh, yes, I know Angelika fairly well. She's worked here for over seventeen years, you see, which makes her the teacher who's been here the longest. We knew each other from before, as well, since we studied dance at about the same time."

"How was her relationship to Sophie?"

Gisela paused, as if hesitant to reveal her thoughts, but then she spoke with determination. "Angelika was never as supportive as she should have been. She saw Sophie as . . . somewhat unsuccessful. Angelika said repeatedly that Sophie was too tall and not good enough to be a true dancer. Yes, Sophie was tall, but she had a gift. Her mother refused to see this. Sophie yearned for her mother's appreciation."

"What kind of a person is Angelika?"

Irene realized that she was skirting the level of gossip, but at the same time, she knew she had to find out more about the Malmborg and Eriksson families.

"Angelika is actually an extremely good teacher, but as a mother . . . unfortunately, she put more effort into her relationships with various men than with her children. She always had another guy lined up. Her last one was a Volvo executive. One of my colleagues once said she chooses her men by the bottom line, not for love. There's something to that, I'm afraid. Once her husband died in the fire, she moved from lover to lover and from house to house with Frej in tow. Sophie was smart to choose to live with her father."

"Has Angelika ever remarried?"

"No."

"What kind of a person was Sophie's father?"

"I really didn't know him, although we met a few times. I

saw that he and Sophie were very close. She was devastated when he passed away. It was a good thing that she got into choreography and was able to concentrate on her work. I know that she'd already completed her first version of *The Fire Dance* before she got into the department."

Irene looked at the clock on the wall. It was almost ten. She'd have to wrap up her conversation with Gisela.

"How can I get in touch with Marcelo Alves?" she asked.

Gisela thought a moment and then said, "Well, you see, one problem with Marcelo is that he doesn't speak good Swedish. His English is just as bad. You'll need someone to interpret for you if you want to question him. I'd suggest you come back sometime this evening, preferably after six thirty. Marcelo and Felipe work with the capoeira group then. Felipe speaks Portuguese, so he'll be able to interpret for you."

Irene thought about this suggestion. Krister was scheduled to work and Jenny would be practicing with her band. Perhaps Katarina would like to go with her and watch some capoeira? She might like it.

"All right, I'll be back this evening. Could you be so kind as to let Marcelo and Felipe know about it?"

"Sure," Gisela said. She took Irene's right hand into her two thin ones. Her hands felt like the wings of birds. "Promise me that you'll catch Sophie's killer. Do everything you possibly can. She . . . she had a tough life. No one deserves a horrible death—certainly not Sophie of all people!"

Tears began to run down her cheeks. Gisela was the first person Irene had met during this investigation who mourned Sophie to the point of tears. Perhaps Gisela really was Sophie's only true friend.

IRENE TURNED OFF Dag Hammarskjöldsleden. She'd decided to take a look at Sophie's house in Änggården and perhaps get in touch with Marcelo Alves. If he were home, she might be able to take a look around the property.

Of course, Sophie's residence had been searched at the end of September when she'd been reported missing. The investigators had found nothing suspicious, but nothing to show she'd left voluntarily, either. She'd never had a passport and all of her bank accounts remained untouched since the day she disappeared. The day after her burned body had been identified, Fredrik Stridh and Jonny Blom had gone again to search her house. They'd found nothing that time either, though her dance stuff was there. Fredrik had said the place "was pretty damn filthy for a girl's house."

But neither her colleagues at General Investigations nor at the Violent Crime Unit had taken a look at Marcelo Alves's apartment or Frej's attic rooms.

Huge noise abatement walls protected Änggården from the heavily trafficked highway and its pollution. Behind these walls were beautiful old townhouses. A rose-colored house was next to a light blue one; a grey house neighbored a green one. It was a pretty scene, even if it was rather un-Swedish. They reminded Irene of the townhouses in London, when she'd been there a few years back.

Most of the houses in Änggården were built during the first half of the twentieth century. The row houses had mostly wooden façades, while the separate houses had stucco. The trees that shaded the peaceful streets were often rare species, since many employees of the nearby botanical garden had lived in this area over the years. Irene knew quite a bit about the neighborhood since her mother's best friend, Rut, had lived there for decades. Irene's parents had almost bought a house there thirty-five years ago, when the one next to Rut's went on the market. In the end, though, the expense held them back, and they stayed in their apartment. Irene's mother was still living there by herself.

Strangely enough, Irene hadn't been in this neighborhood in over twenty years. The police rarely had business here—just a routine burglary once in a while.

The neighborhood was an elegant step removed from the rest of the city. The houses were freshly painted, completely restored and clean. Everything gave a strong impression of neat and tidy wealth, despite the heavy fog that draped the buildings. Irene drove around on the narrow streets for a while until she found the proper address and a parking spot not far away. She slowly walked back toward the high, wrought-iron fence in the stone wall, carefully inspecting the house on the other side. She saw a large wooden structure masked by overgrown bushes and fruit trees.

Originally, the wrought-iron fence had been painted black, but now it was reddish brown from rust. Its heavy hinges resisted with a groan. The entire garden gave off the scent of damp earth and decay. No one had taken in the harvest of fruit from the old trees, which had fallen to rot on a lawn that didn't appear to have been mowed that summer. Like the garden, which bore evidence of abandonment and decay, the house was in rough shape. In many spots, the stucco had fallen from the façade, and the broken gutters jutted out at odd angles. The window and doorframes had revealed grey wood where paint was long gone. It was the ugly duckling of the neighborhood.

Irene walked up the stone stairway and rang the doorbell. A bronze nameplate with a green patina revealed the name *Malmborg* in an elegant script. Irene could hear the echo of the doorbell on the other side of the heavy oak door, but no other sounds of movement. She pressed the bell a second time with the same result.

As she started back along the slippery stone pathway, which was almost entirely overgrown, she felt as if the house itself were staring at her back. She couldn't resist the impulse to turn around when she closed the gate behind her. The crumbling, ancient home appeared to brood threateningly from its place in the middle of the melancholy garden. Its black, empty windows stared at her. Involuntarily, Irene shivered. Sometimes, her imagination was much too vivid for a police officer.

MAX FRANKE'S EMAIL was waiting when Irene returned to her computer after lunch. Irene printed it out and was surprised by the number of pages, then thought, *Well, what else would you expect from a writer?*

Filled with curiosity and expectation, Irene sat down in her desk chair and began to read:

> *Please remember that this is for your eyes only. This has been written in haste and with no forethought for literary quality. My hope is that my memories of Ernst and Sophie, as well as the other members of the Malmborg family, will be able to help you solve Sophie's murder.*
>
> *My cousin Ernst and I were very close, ever since we were children. One reason was that we were born on the same day, the second of August, although he was born ten years earlier. We were also the only boys in our generation of the family.*
>
> *Ernst had an older sister named Elsy. Even though she was only fourteen years older than I was, I always considered her to be a cold, haughty old lady. I usually called her "Snooty Elsy." Not ever to her face, of course. I knew she wouldn't see herself that way. To tell the truth, I believe she was born with a genetic lack of humor (the most difficult handicap a human being can have). Like her brother, she was quiet and kept to herself. She was also tall and gangly and definitely not*

attractive. She never made any attempt to improve her appearance, either. She never married, but studied to be a pharmacist. Rumor has it she knew the entire range of pharmaceutical medicines by heart and even knew exactly which compounds each one contained. As far as I know, she never left Stockholm—not even for vacation! She lived in the family mansion in the Östermalm District her whole life. She worked for forty years at the same apothecary and died six months after her retirement. I'd say she died of sorrow, but my sister Bettan says she had a heart condition from birth.

Elsy and I never had a good relationship, perhaps due to the difference in our ages. We would meet at family events through the years, but that's all. The reason I started off this email with Elsy is that she and Ernst shared a great number of personality quirks, which they inherited from their father, Hilding Malmborg. Hilding married my maternal aunt, Alice. He was her exact opposite. My mother and Aunt Alice were identical twins. They were so similar that even family members had trouble telling them apart. Both of them were happy people and enjoyed life. They made similar choices—except the choice of a partner. My mother married a journalist, Gustaf Franke, who was socially competent and extremely extroverted. Meanwhile, Hilding Malmborg was the exact opposite of my father.

Hilding was a professor of biology and studied the exciting field of snake nests. Quite honestly, he was more interested in the lives of creepy-crawlers than he was in those of his own family, never mind other members of the human race. As time went on, he turned into a really odd duffer, and at the end of his life, he was definitely showing signs of dementia. My Aunt Alice was fifty-nine when she died of colon cancer. After she died, cousin Elsy lived with her ever-more-senile father in the family mansion. I believe that he eventually had a fatal stroke either in 1973 or 1974, as far as I can recall. The last time I saw Elsy was at his funeral. After that, we only exchanged birthday and Christmas cards. She died in 1990, and I am absolutely convinced that she never bothered to read a single book I wrote.

I have three older sisters, but only Bettan made the effort to see Elsy on occasion, the main reason being that Bettan lived close by, also in the Östermalm District. But Bettan said that she went over to see her because she felt sorry for her. They didn't have much in common, besides being unmarried. Bettan is the oldest of all my siblings. She's a nurse, trained by Sophia Nursing School, and for all these years she's worked at Sophia Hospital. She is the sister who has the most caring nature. She'd often say, "Poor Elsy. She is so alone. I try to cheer her up and invite her over for dinner and conversation. She never invites me back. At times, I'd try to tempt her to come with me to the theater or to a nice restaurant, but she wouldn't want to go. She'd always say she was under the weather or that it would be too expensive. Quite honestly, she never was much fun."

In my most evil thoughts, I always suspected that Elsy was Bettan's equivalent to a medieval hair shirt.

Ernst was similar to his sister in appearance, but what was ugly and unfeminine in her was masculine and attractive in him. At least, that's what the women around him would say. Still, most of his difficulties with women would come later in life, after he was somewhat renowned, which increased his attractiveness level.

Ernst was my substitute big brother, and he probably saw me as the younger brother he never had. I admired *him a great deal and was unbelievably flattered that he wanted to celebrate his birthdays with me. There'd be a big group of us under the lilac arbor at our family's summer place in Roslagen. I could always invite all my neighborhood friends, as well as my sisters, and sometimes their friends would come, too. At times my maternal uncle, Kalle, and his large family from Gävle would attend, too. They'd stay at a bed and breakfast, and I'd be really jealous of them. That bed and breakfast was famous for its extravagant breakfast spread. Rumor had it that fresh waffles with whipped cream and marmalade were served every single morning.*

Ernst would come with his parents and sour-faced sister, but he never brought a friend; he never seemed to have any. They stayed at the guesthouse on the property, which was fairly large and had two bedrooms. Bettan and Ernst were the same age and they'd hang out, sometimes with Bettan's friends. Elsy would sit nearby as the rest of us played cards or Chinese checkers. As I think about it, she must have been in her twenties, but I have her in my memories as a real old boring biddy even then. The Malmborg family would stay with us for four or five days, swimming or sunbathing if the weather allowed. Then they'd head back home, probably because Uncle Hilding was afraid his snakes would starve in their nests.

Ernst had revealed mathematical genius already by age four. Elsy was also good at math, but not compared to her brother. Hilding probably rubbed his hands together in glee as he dreamed of his son's bright future career as a mathematician. However, the old biology professor was disappointed—Mozart and Bach dashed his dreams. When he was eight years old, Ernst found some old 78s in an attic. He would spend whole days

winding up Aunt Alice's gramophone so he could listen
to them. A few weeks later, he asked if he could have
piano lessons. The family owned a piano. His sister
had already banged on it for years, but she was hopeless. Her long-suffering piano teacher had already told
her parents that she was completely tone-deaf and had
no musical talent whatsoever. After that, there were no
more piano lessons for Elsy.

Ernst, on the other hand, was a musical prodigy. He
attended the music academy in Stockholm and graduated with highest honors. He was invited to study at
many European music schools, but he refused them all.
He believed he could not endure a change of environment and decided not to become a concert pianist for the
same reason. He couldn't handle the touring life. After
he completed his studies, he said he wanted to be a composer.

I wasn't interested in what happened after that. I
was in the middle of puberty and had just discovered
swing and jazz music after the war. Now even more
fascinating music was arriving from the other side of the
Atlantic: rock and roll! While I was in the middle of this
music revolution, Ernst withdrew into his parents' melancholy house—which he never left—and began to
plunk out incomprehensible music on the piano.

"Atonality!" Bettan would say and roll her eyes.

I thought atonality was something obscene and was
wondering if cousin Ernst would turn out to be a homo-
sexual. No one ever saw any girls around him. He was
twenty-four then. According to Aunt Alice, he had a
girlfriend at the academy, but no one in the family had
ever met her. As the years went by, I became more and
more convinced that this girlfriend was fictional.

Ernst would be at the piano composing for days on

end. He would hardly leave the house. Heaps of sheet music grew around him. Aunt Alice was starting to worry about his mental health and finally had a chat with my father. My father believed it was time for Ernst to come out of his shell and meet people. He had a great number of contacts due to his work at the newspaper, and after pulling a few strings, he was able to arrange a performance of Ernst's brand new compositions.

The event was held at the music academy—one of the smallest concert spaces. The concert was advertised as "experimental," and I had a bad feeling about it. Only five musicians were on stage, including Ernst himself. The others were fellow former students from Ernst's academy days. All the relatives had been invited and we took up more than half of the seats. It was a good thing that we were there to fill the space, because only ten other people came. What we didn't know at the time was that one of the country's most famed music critics, the tastemaker Bertil Neanderthál from the newspaper Dagens Nyheter, was also there. He would go on to praise this concert to the skies and write things like "an epic breakthrough for contemporary music" and "world-class musical provocation" and his conclusion was that "a new musical artist has been born!"

With this article in DN, Ernst's future success was guaranteed. It was lucky that there was a professional music critic in the audience because after the concert, all the relatives were touchingly in agreement for a change: it was the worst throbbing and wailing thing any of us had ever heard. Naturally, we had no idea about modern music, and we weren't used to listening to it, my kind mother would say to smooth things over. Still, my sisters and I agreed totally: that stuff Ernst was composing could never be called music. Uncle

Kalle said, "I thought Judgment Day had come at last." He said this in such a serious mien that my father couldn't hold back his laughter any longer. He laughed so hard, tears started to stream down his face.

But Ernst would have the last laugh.

Ernst's star started to rise in the heavens of experimental music. A few years later, his name was well-known. He began to appear at various cultural events and hopeful young women began to appear at his side. None of them seemed to touch Ernst in any deep way, and he never talked about any of them. So when the news broke that he'd started a relationship with the actress Anna-Greta Lidman, it hit us like a bombshell. He hadn't told anyone in the family. My mother read about it in a tabloid. Old cousin Ernst began to rise in my estimation, while my mother and Aunt Alice moaned and groaned, and Uncle Hilding disappeared even more deeply into the world of snake nests. My father rubbed his hands in glee. As a newspaperman, he knew the value of having a front-page story within the family.

Anna-Greta Lidman was just over thirty when the two of them met, but she appeared much younger. At the time, people compared her appearance to a mix of Brigitte Bardot and Doris Day. As an actress, however, her talent was definitely on par with the likes of Ingrid Bergman. At the beginning of her career, she was advertised as "Sweden's Number One Sweater Girl," but soon the blonde, busty pinup queen showed she could really act. The director Ingmar Bergman put her into some of his films and from then on, her career was assured. She appeared in a great number of movies during the fifties and sixties, almost all of which became classics. Ernst and Anna-Greta met at the premiere of *one of her movies. It was a small, independent film influenced by Buñuel's* The Andalucian Dog: *a film the history of cinema has now forgotten. Anna-Greta played a pretty small part, "for the sake of an old friendship"— she and the director were good friends—and Ernst had composed the music for the movie, of course.*

They were married in 1958. The ceremony took place in Riddarholm Church, in the company of family, the Swedish cultural elite and a collection of reporters from the worldwide press. Ernst was so stylish in his tuxedo that the ladies felt faint and Anna-Greta's neckline had the same effect on the male guests—or at least something similar . . .

During the reception, the bride drank too much champagne and it came to light that she was pregnant. The press was jubilant. This was too good to be true!

They honeymooned in Italy, and the rest of the family could follow their adventures in the newspapers, which is how we found out Anna-Greta was in the hospital for acute blood loss. A few days later, her miscarriage was reported.

Her first miscarriage was followed by two more. The doctors told her to avoid getting pregnant again. Her last miscarriage was late in the pregnancy and almost cost her her life.

Anna-Greta had roles in some French and Italian films. Ernst was a productive composer and had reached cult status within a small circle of music experts. It appeared to be idyllic how both of them could continue their careers without any jealousy between them. Ernst never talked about his marriage with the family, but we speculated about it quite a bit. From the outside, it appeared harmonious, and we never noticed any major crisis during the first decade of their marriage.

My cousin didn't earn much money for his music,
but Anna-Greta earned a great deal for her acting.
They were in a secure financial state, especially since
Anna-Greta had been an only child in an extremely
wealthy Göteborg family that surprisingly supported her
despite her choice of career. They covered the expenses
of acting, dancing and singing lessons. You also have to
realize that she was gifted in languages and she had a
good education. She entered Kalle Flygares Theater
College, and the rest of her career went on from there,
as I've mentioned.

But in the seventies, the same thing happened to her
as happens to all sex symbols: it became apparent that
she was starting to age. Her childlessness had also dealt
a hard blow to her emotional life. She started to look for
solace in the bottle. Rumors began to fly. Her looks
began to show the signs of hard drinking. It didn't matter
if she was a good actress—offers for movie parts dried
up. Her parents also passed away. Her depression
became so great that she was placed in a mental institution for a while.

When she was released, she decided to move back
to Göteborg. She took over the mansion of her parents. To the surprise of everyone in our family,
including me, Ernst agreed to move with her. To be
blunt, he didn't have much of a choice. She was the one
with the real money. He'd have nothing at all and no
place to live if it wasn't for her. Otherwise, he'd have
had to move back in with his sister, Elsy, and his now-
all-but-senile father. Hilding died a few years later, and
it was at his funeral that I saw Ernst for the first time
after he'd left Stockholm for Göteborg. I also remember
that he was happy about his situation in the mansion in
the Änggården District. He told me that he had an

entire floor to himself, which he'd turned into various music rooms. His grand piano was the focal point in one room, and another room had become a recording studio.

A few months later, I was in Göteborg on business and decided to pay Ernst a visit. Everything he told me about his living circumstances was true. Unfortunately, the rumors of Anna-Greta's decline were also true. It was tragic to see the once great star turned into such a wreck of a human being in just a few years. One thing that the tabloids did not know was that she'd undergone an unsuccessful facelift. The operation wounds became infected, leaving ugly scars, and she'd also suffered nerve damage. Whenever she would eat or drink, the numbed nerve endings would prevent her from closing her mouth, so something was always dribbling out.

She could not speak without slurring, a catastrophe for an actress. The plastic surgeon was one of the most famous in Stockholm, and he had to pay her a huge amount in damages to keep her from going to court. But what did it matter, when her beautiful features were gone forever?

She spent most of her days in a drug-induced torpor. Whenever she was awake, she rushed back into her fog as quickly as possible. When I saw them, Anna-Greta was deeply depressed.

Ernst was his old self. He devoted himself to his music and, after encouragement from my sister Bettan, he hired a housekeeper to cook and clean. She was always called "Mrs. Larsson," and I never was able to ascertain whether she even had a given name. This woman was a real treasure. She stayed with Ernst until his death in 2002. I believe she must have been seventy when she retired after he passed away.

In 1977, we were shocked by another bombshell.

Ernst had met another woman—a twenty-year-old ballet dancer! And she was pregnant with his child! At the same time, I was wrestling with my own midlife crisis, and I may have been the only one in the family who halfway understood him. Once I saw a picture of beautiful Angelika, I understood him even better. I hadn't seen Anna-Greta in over seven years, but I had no illusions that the intervening years had done anything to improve her sorry condition. Cousin Ernst had had enough and realized that life was too short to let the years fly by. Trying to save Anna-Greta was a hopeless project. To tell the truth, I don't think he even tried. He was who he was. Ernst had always lived in his own little world; his music was the center of his life. He certainly would never be an ideal therapist for a woman with mental health issues and a drug problem.

Ernst and I kept in closer contact during those years. I was usually the one to give him a call, but at times he called me, which he'd never done before. I was in the middle of a messy divorce and perhaps we both needed some support. Since Anna-Greta was so sick—and she certainly wasn't going to get any better after she heard that Angelika was pregnant—Ernst had to endure a great deal of criticism for his actions. I believe, however, that for the first time in his life, Ernst was in love. He was able to handle all the accusations and stood fast in his decision to live with Angelika. Still, Ernst wouldn't be Ernst if he didn't have his own prerequisites.

He'd moved in with Angelika, who had a tiny apartment in the Kortedala District. He got up every morning at six A.M., had his breakfast and then took the streetcar to his former residence. Like the rest of the Malmborg family, Ernst had never bothered to get a driver's license. He would spend the entire day at Änggården *with his beloved grand piano, which obviously would never fit in the one-room apartment in Kortedala. So if the mountain could not come to Mohammed, Mohammed went to the mountain. "I have to work," Ernst would tell Angelika, and though she was against this arrangement and had temperamental outbursts, she couldn't come up with a better solution.*

Strangely enough, Anna-Greta did not attack Ernst with accusations when he was with her. She seemed to become calmer and more secure. She wouldn't speak much with Ernst, but she would come into the room when he worked and sit down in a chair by the door. She would sit for hours without speaking, which didn't disturb Ernst in the least. At times, she would doze off, but the main thing for her was just to be in his presence. Ernst would talk to me about this sometimes on the phone. He was grateful she'd not made a fuss.

Angelika, however, was the exact opposite. She seemed to enjoy the spotlight and her prominence in the tabloids. She would go out of her way to get more publicity. Relatively quickly, it was apparent that she was much too young and intellectually unable to understand such a complicated person as Ernst. Although, to tell the truth, Ernst was simple enough. Just leave him alone with his music and he'd be perfectly content. Angelika's desire to be out on the town and attending parties was something he didn't understand. A few months before the child was born, I noticed that Ernst was spending more and more time at his former residence. He only called me up from Änggården, never from Angelika's apartment.

And that's where he was when Angelika called him and said it was time to go to the maternity ward. She was on her way to Östra Hospital, so it was easy for

Ernst to hop on the streetcar for the hour-long ride there. He told me much later that he went to Anna-Greta and told her why he needed to leave. He said she looked at him and her expression showed her mind was clear. "So, it's time," she said, without a trace of her speech impediment. Ernst thought she meant it was time for the child's birth and agitatedly replied that it was. Later, he realized she was speaking of her own suicide.

So, at the same time Sophie was being born, Anna-Greta died. She took a huge handful of pills and washed them down with vodka. Then she put a plastic bag over her head. Apparently, her death was pain-free and peaceful. She fell asleep. I had to keep pointing this out to Ernst the next few days. He grieved for Anna-Greta although he was not plagued by any feelings of guilt. "Anna-Greta always used pills and alcohol to escape. Not me," he said.

His grief over Anna-Greta was tempered with his joy over Sophie. He was truly happy to have a daughter. At the same time, his relationship with Angelika began to improve now that Anna-Greta was out of the picture.

Strangely, neither Ernst nor Anna-Greta had ever discussed getting a divorce. Anna-Greta had not written a will, and since he was her only heir, as her surviving spouse he inherited everything. But again, he had to face the torrent of criticism that he was responsible for her death. I have to agree with Ernst, who said, "Anna-Greta spent fifteen years killing herself slowly." I encouraged him to accept his inheritance.

Of course, Angelika did, too. Her cute little nose had sniffed out a heap of money. She had no compunctions at all about moving into the mansion and becoming Mrs. Malmborg the Second. Ernst had his doubts, however. Although he appeared unable to cope with *everyday reality, he was not an idiot. He'd realized a thing or two about Angelika. So, for the sake of his beloved daughter, he agreed to marriage, but not before Angelika signed a prenuptial agreement.*

Sophie had barely reached her first birthday when the marriage began to crumble. Ernst found out that Angelika had been having an affair with a French dancer. She denied it, but Ernst refused to be convinced. He knew by then that she could not be trusted. Six months later, she met that dimwit Magnus Eriksson and declared that she wanted a divorce. Ernst said that at that moment he had felt nothing but relief. He was also sad for Sophie's sake, but decided to make sure that he would stay in the picture. I advised him to contact one of the best lawyers in Sweden, Antonio Bonetti, who was practicing in Göteborg.

There was a bitter court fight. Angelika insisted that she did not understand what she was doing when she signed the prenuptial agreement. She demanded that she receive half of the property. Ernst would then receive sole custody of Sophie. Ernst may have agreed to go along with it, but the lawyer Bonetti pointed out that a child always has the right to custody by both parents. He demolished Angelika's demands. The final judgment was split custody and not a single dime to Angelika. She was enraged, but there wasn't much she could do about it.

So things went along fine for a number of years after that. Angelika and her new husband lived on Linnégatan. It only took a few minutes by streetcar for Sophie to go to Ernst in Änggården. The problems only really began again once that blockhead Eriksson gambled away all the money the family had. They were forced to leave their nice apartment and move to that shack in the sticks—*far from the big lights of the city. Sophie had to change schools, and things weren't going well with the shared custody agreement. She couldn't stay with Ernst every other week, as she wouldn't be able to get to school. Finally, they worked out a situation where she spent every weekend with him. This is how things were up to the night of that fateful fire in 1989.*

I remember each and every word Ernst said when he called me up and, not even greeting me, exclaimed, "They think she did it!"

At first I didn't realize it was him. His voice was weak and trembling—not at all his usual calm demeanor.

"Who are they? And who is she?" I asked.

"The police! They think Sophie set fire to the house—on purpose!"

He was so upset, his voice failed him.

Once I calmed him down, I managed to coax out the story of what happened. You probably know more about this aspect of it than I do, but according to Ernst, Sophie had been called to the police station repeatedly. Angelika had accompanied her, as well as someone from the Children's Mental Health Department. Ernst was in despair. He had a long talk with his ex-wife for the first time since the divorce. According to her, the reason for the repeated questioning was that the house had caught fire shortly after Sophie had left it. Sophie refused to say a word. Ernst had said Sophie told him that she was not responsible for the fire.

A few weeks later, Sophie moved in with Ernst and changed schools. She visited Angelika and Frej every other weekend. Angelika complained loudly about this new arrangement, but after a while, she noticed it was working for her, too. She no longer had any costs relating to Sophie. It could be that mother and daughter were able to forge a better relationship via their mutual love of dance.

I would see Ernst and Sophie at irregular intervals. A year or two could pass between visits. Our phone calls also became more sporadic. Ernst no longer had the same need to talk with me. He was content in his life with Sophie. As far as women went, he had a few long-term relationships, but he never lived with another woman again. Mrs. Larsson took care of his household and Sophie was there for companionship. Things were going fairly well.

It must have been a shock for Sophie when she found out that Ernst was suffering from advanced colon cancer. He was doubtful of the outcome, but finally agreed to an operation. He refused any radiation or chemo treatments. "I can feel I'm close to the end, so there's no need to add any extra suffering," he told me.

The operation went well, but Ernst could not accept that he had to wear a colostomy bag. He thought it was disgusting. Sophie learned how to take care of him. She and Mrs. Larsson took care of Ernst during the last months of his life. A district nurse came to help them and made sure he had his injections and medicine. Ernst passed away peacefully in his own home on Midsummer Day in 2002. Sophie and Mrs. Larsson were by his side.

I went to the funeral, which was the last time I saw Sophie before that unfortunate evening last September at the Book Fair. I know you have my testimony regarding what happened that night. The last thing I remember about Sophie is how the ceiling lights made her black hair glisten as she walked toward the stairs. Then the elevator doors closed and I never saw her again.

Neither Sophie nor her father were easy to understand. Still, I believe I knew them better than most.
They weren't aggressive people. They reacted the same
way to conflicts: they pulled away.

Both you and I must believe that Sophie's murder is
connected to the fire that she was suspected of setting
fifteen years ago. Notice I write: "suspected of." I
believe wholeheartedly that she did not do it.

Therefore, I see no logical reason for her to have
been held captive and to be killed in cold blood because
of it. It could be interpreted as punishment for the
arson, but if she didn't set the fire, there would be
nothing to punish. Perhaps it will be shown that her
murder had nothing to do with that fire after all.

If you have any further questions, please contact me
whenever you need to talk. I know that Viktor Borgsten
has provided you with all my telephone numbers and
addresses.

Yours sincerely,
Max Franke

"ANGELIKA MALMBORG-ERIKSSON IS coming over at two," Tommy said.

"In that case, I'd like to sit in," Irene said, too quickly.

Tommy lifted an eyebrow and grinned provocatively. To her annoyance, Irene felt her face redden.

"Here. Read this. Max Franke just sent it to me. There's quite a bit about Angelika in there, too."

Tommy took the stack of paper and began to read.

It wasn't that she didn't trust Tommy; it was Angelika she didn't trust. No man should be allowed to be alone with her for any length of time. Irene knew she was being absolutely ridiculous, but she still remembered the pheromone-filled atmosphere of the office the last time Angelika laid eyes on Tommy. Of course, that was fifteen years ago, but Irene had no illusions about Tommy's vulnerability—he was recently divorced and so far he had no steady partner. Irene had no idea about any of Angelika's current romances besides the rumor she was involved with a high-level executive from Volvo. Irene knew, however, that that woman was always on the prowl.

Irene stood and decided to go to forensics to see if they had any new information about the fire.

Svante Malm's freckled face lit up when he saw Irene. "Hey there! You must be psychic. I was just going to give you a call. Now I won't have to," he said happily.

"Anything new?" asked Irene.

"Yes. As far as Sophie's clothing is concerned, we now know that she was wearing a studded leather jacket when she disappeared. We can say with absolute certainty that she was not wearing it when she died. We found these instead."

He pulled out the obligatory plastic bags from his desk drawer and laid them on the surface of his desk. Irene could see some long, small items, flat and irregular in form.

"What are those?" she asked.

"Don't know for sure, but they're not studs. They were found on the body and we believe they were decorations on a piece of clothing she was wearing. We are going to clean them so it will be easier to guess what kind of clothing they came from."

Irene tried to think. Clothing decorations? Jewelry? Something stirred in the back of her mind, but she wasn't able to catch it. She pushed that aside for the moment and instead said, "Perhaps it was a theatrical or dance costume. Her mother is coming this afternoon and she might know what kind of clothing Sophie was wearing."

"Yes, ask. The analysis of the rest of the scene is clear. Sophie was lying on a polyurethane mattress. The killer had piled a heap of paper and textiles over her. Probably he poured out some gasoline and set her on fire. The course of the fire was quick and explosive. He'd put a thick woolen fabric over the lower half of the body, which, thankfully, saved it from complete cremation. This fabric was badly burned, but parts of it that were beneath the body were not damaged. An authentic Persian-style carpet, actually, according to our carpet expert, Ahmed, extremely valuable. Let's see . . ."

Svante flipped through a notebook and his face lit up when he found the information he was looking for.

"Here it is! Probably an antique Karabagh. Worth

between twenty and thirty thousand kronor, depending on size."

"So our suspect set it on fire. But of course you use what you have. What other flammable material did you find?"

"Some woolen blankets. They are more difficult to burn than synthetics or cotton. Newspaper and the remains of patterned cotton. Curtains or sheets—most likely sheets."

"So, we have a quality carpet and expensive blankets. Simple, thin mattress. Cotton fragments that we don't know much about," Irene summarized.

"Exactly."

"Did the tire tracks give any leads?"

"No, unfortunately. We didn't discover the body until Monday afternoon. The weekend had been a busy one, so a case of arson in an old shed that was scheduled to be torn down anyway was not high on our priorities. The rain was pouring down on Sunday and Monday, so all possible tracks had disappeared in the mud."

"Too bad. I still need to find out where Sophie had been kept for almost three weeks. Even if she'd been drugged, where could a person be hidden for that long without the neighbors noticing?"

"Look for a place that's out of the way or abandoned. Preferably both."

The farm. It hadn't been searched because it was assumed Ingrid Hagberg was still living there. Not until Irene had talked to Frej had she learned that the place had been empty for three months. There was nothing but fields and forests around the house. Even if people were moving about in the village of Björkil, the house was set off from the road and difficult for the neighbors to see. Once it got dark, the killer could have easily driven to Högsbo Industrial Area with a drugged Sophie, carried her into the building and then set her on fire. And in the wee hours, no witnesses had seen anything suspicious in the area or even noticed the fire. The remains of the fire were discovered the next day.

"You could be right. We should take a look at the farm. The old woman who owned it has been hospitalized for three months. Someone else could have been using her house to keep Sophie prisoner," Irene said.

Frej. He'd said himself that he watched the place for his aunt. He had a car. What kind of motive would he have? Why would he keep his sister—half-sister—prisoner for three weeks? Why would he drug her and then kill her? At the time of the fire that killed his father, he and Sophie seemed to have a normal relationship. She'd even let him move into her mansion.

Sophie's murder had been terrible and full of hate. She'd been abused and drugged. Why would Frej do something like that? Money? No, he would not inherit her wealth. Angelika would.

Many people involved with the investigation had stated that Angelika was always on the lookout for money. Could Angelika be behind the murder of her own daughter? She had a car. She had a motive. Would she have been able to carry it out? Not likely unless Frej assisted her. Would he let her use his aunt's house to keep Sophie prisoner and eventually kill her? It seemed too bizarre, even for Irene, who had investigated a number of horrible cases over the years.

"Hello! Earth to Irene!" Svante said.

Irene started. "Sorry, I was thinking about what you said. I got lost in various theories," Irene excused herself.

"I'd be glad if I set you on the right course to solve this case. I hope we get this guy."

"We will. Absolutely."

Irene tried to sound more confident than she felt.

• • •

DURING LUNCH, IRENE and Tommy discussed what Svante Malm had found out. Absentmindedly, Tommy stirred his spoon in the cup of watery stuff the cafeteria served under the label "minestrone." His only comfort was the apple cake with vanilla sauce for dessert.

"An empty house available to several of the people involved. We definitely ought to investigate the farm. Do we need a search warrant?"

Irene thought about it. "That'll take some time. I have a better idea. But first, let's go get some baguettes. This stuff is not going to get us through the day."

IRENE WENT ONLINE and began to search through the names of real estate agents active in the Björkil area. The third agent hit a bull's-eye. Ingrid Hagberg's property was for sale and listed at the Berzén Agency. The advertisement included several color photographs and a description:

> Large horse farm. 18 ha pasture/fields, 5 ha forest. Hunting rights. Home built 1921 and thoroughly renovated 1972–74. 310 square meters living space. Landscaped. New heating system. Combi for wood/electricity installed 1998. Ground floor: spacious country kitchen, living room, dining room, TV room, bathroom including toilet. Additions in 1974 include scullery, storage closet, laundry, furnace room and sauna. Second floor: four bedrooms, large hallway with balcony, bathroom with toilet. Other buildings: 520 square meters. Stable with 10 stalls. Large, wonderful orchard. Quiet location close to bus stop and shops. Just 5 miles from Center. Must see! Price: 8 million kronor or best offer.

Ingrid Hagberg would be wealthy once her property was sold. In her present condition, however, she couldn't take much joy in the money. Frej would probably inherit it before long.

Irene called the real estate agency. A young man with an energetic voice picked up quickly. He introduced himself as Erik Johansson. His voice lost a great deal of its energy when he realized that Irene was not a potential customer. After a bit of negotiation and a little police jargon on Irene's side, he promised to show her the property. He would not be able to meet her until the next day at the earliest. They agreed on 9 A.M. at the house. "A real customer is going to be there at eleven."

AT FIRST GLANCE, Angelika did not appear to have aged a bit. She hadn't gained any weight and she moved as easily and gracefully as she had all those years ago. Perhaps her hair was just a shade darker—a shimmering mahogany—but that didn't necessarily mean she was dyeing grey strands. The color fit her perfectly and even matched her short brown leather jacket. All her other clothes were black. Her V-neck angora sweater revealed an elegant gold cross in the gap between her collarbones. She walked across the floor in boots with sky-high heels, keeping her eyes on Tommy the whole time. For Irene, she barely condescended to give a glance from the corner of her eye.

Tommy got up and smiled widely as he held out his hand. "Hello! Please, sit down."

Angelika smiled as well, but her smile no longer gave off the same sparks as fifteen years ago. There was exhaustion in her eyes that had not been there before.

"It's been many years since I last saw you, but you haven't changed a bit," Tommy reassured her.

"Kind of you to say so," Angelika said with the shadow of a smile.

As she sat down, she slipped out of her leather jacket to

set it across her knees. As she looked at Tommy, tears shone in her dark eyes. In an unsteady voice, she asked, "When will I be able to take her?"

Tommy floundered for half a second before he realized what she was asking. "Sophie's body?"

"Please."

"It could still take a week or two before all the tests are finished. Sometimes . . . a test has to be redone . . . Would you like me to find out when she will be released to you?"

"Yes, please. I've already contacted the funeral home."

Angelika fumbled in her purse and finally pulled out a package of paper tissues. She wiped her tears and discreetly blew her nose. Irene could see that Tommy was off-balance—this questioning had taken a turn he hadn't expected. As if Tommy were reading her mind, he cleared his throat and subconsciously straightened his back as he tried to take back control of the conversation.

"We talked on the phone the day after the body had been identified. You were naturally very upset and emotional, and I decided to wait to talk to you. Now we've made some progress in the investigation and we would like to ask you a few questions, if you don't mind."

"Of course not. It's just . . . it's incomprehensible that anyone would . . . murder her."

Tears began to stream down her face, and she pulled a handful of tissues from the package. She pressed one of them to her eyes, and her voice was barely audible. "Sorry . . . I'm just so upset . . . and the funeral home today . . . can't understand . . . that she's dead."

Irene could tell that Angelika's grief was deep and authentic. It was not difficult to understand her despair over the murder of her daughter. But at the same time, Irene remembered she hadn't shown nearly this level of grief when her former husband, Magnus Eriksson, had died. Then she had been more concerned about practical problems, such as the lack of insurance money.

Before Tommy began his questions, Irene slipped in one of her own, the one bothering her all these years. "Now that Sophie is deceased, can you give me an honest answer? Do you believe she set fire to the house all those years ago?"

Angelika swiftly wiped up all her tears. "Never. She was not the one who burned our house. That was Magnus! I am absolutely convinced. He was drunk and smoking . . . he'd done it before." Angelika began to gesture to underscore her point. Her eyes were now dry and she almost bobbed up off the chair she was sitting on. She said, "Sophie told me that she didn't even know Magnus was in the house! It was dark and quiet when she came home from school. She ate a sandwich and used the bathroom. She must have had some stomach trouble—she was in the bathroom for a long time. So then she had to bike as fast as she could to get to her ride on time. Tessan's mother always gave the girls a ride to the dance school, and she'd pick Sophie up at the convenience store."

Her story lined up with what Frej had said, as well as with the letter Max Franke had written saying Sophie had explained her innocence to her father. Obviously she'd been able to talk to her nearest and dearest about what she'd done that half hour she was home. She had just refused to talk to the child psychologist and the police. Why?

Without revealing her line of reasoning, Irene asked a follow-up question. "If Sophie had nothing to do with the fire at Björkil, why do you think she was burned to death fifteen years later?"

The tears returned as Angelika barely whispered, "I have no idea."

"You don't even have a theory?" Irene said, feeling a sting of conscience as she pressed Angelika.

"No, none."

Angelika shook her head, lowering face so it was hidden behind the curtain of her bangs. Angelika wanted to put up a shield. Or perhaps Irene was being unduly suspicious. Perhaps Angelika really had no idea what had happened to her daughter. Irene would have been able to accept that if the warning light of police instinct hadn't been blinking in her brain. Sophie's death and the death of her stepfather were much too similar to be coincidence.

Tommy ran through questions concerning Sophie's friends and acquaintances, as well as potential enemies, without stumbling upon anything they didn't already know. Still, it warmed Irene's heart to hear Angelika say, "I am very happy that Sophie and I had a much better relationship the past few years."

"Why did you have a bad relationship when she was younger?" asked Tommy.

"Well, I wouldn't exactly call it bad . . . she was a difficult child. I probably didn't understand her properly. Honestly, I was much too young when I got pregnant with her, and I conceived her with the wrong man. Ernst was even crazier than Sophie was!"

Irene decided to ask another question that had been on her mind since 1989. "How did you meet Ernst Malmborg?" Angelika jerked, as if she'd forgotten Irene was even in the room. She wrinkled her brow unhappily and appeared to reflect, then shrugged and said in a voice devoid of emotion, "I was still studying dance, but managed to get a job with a dance troupe. We performed in a festival of modern ballet and music. Ernst had written a piece for one of the numbers. A girl named Gisela and I performed it. The piece was called *Night and Day*, and Ernst thought we looked like night and day. Gisela is very light, almost an albino. And, as you see, I've always been a bit more, shall we say, brunette."

For the first time since she'd entered the room, she smiled

flirtatiously and gave Tommy a glance from behind her eye-lashes. Tommy's expression said he definitely preferred a girl with a bit more melanin. In order to dispel the attraction between the two, Irene asked a new question.

"Was that Gisela Bagge? The woman who is now the Director of Instruction at the House of Dance?"

Angelika seemed surprised. "Do you know her? Yes, she's the one."

How interesting that Gisela was back in the picture. Why hadn't Angelika mentioned her before? On the other hand, fifteen years ago Irene had been focusing on Sophie and not on Ernst or Angelika.

"I met her at the House of Dance this morning. She told me there would be a premiere of Sophie's ballet, *The Fire Dance*, soon."

Angelika nodded. "Yes, the first piece Sophie choreo-graphed. She called it 'A Saga in Dance.' I didn't go to any of the rehearsals because she told me she wanted to surprise me. Frej is in the ballet."

"Frej dances?" Irene exclaimed in surprise.

"Of course he does. He's been dancing since he was very young. Lately he's been studying photography instead. All he dances these days is capoeira. He doesn't have time for any-thing else."

"Capoeira? Is this a ballet done with capoeira?" Irene was confused.

"There is no such thing as a capoeira ballet. Capoeira is more like an exhibition." Angelika couldn't help smiling through her tears.

She dried her eyes and blew her nose again. Talking about dance seemed to calm her down. Perhaps because dance was her world and she felt more in control of the line of questioning.

"Of course, I was curious what she was up to and I tried to pump Frej for information. From what he said, there is some capoeira in this piece, as well as some daring new moves. I am really happy that they decided to go ahead with rehearsals so the premiere can go forward as planned. It certainly would be what Sophie would have wanted."

TOMMY AND IRENE sat together for a while after Angelika left. They discussed the case. Irene walked over to the map of Göteborg hanging on the wall. She tapped a spot with her forefinger and said, "Here is the crime scene. It is on the outskirts of the oldest part of the Högsbo Industrial Area. Nothing's going on here because the buildings are going to be demolished for the new pharmaceutical plant. The actual shed in question is especially deserted since it faces the Nature Reserve of Änggård Mountain. It's just two kilometers from Änggården."

She moved her finger and tapped another spot on the map. "Here's Angelika's apartment on Distansgatan. It's equally distant from the crime scene. Sophie disappeared from Park Aveny Hotel here."

Irene turned to Tommy. She ticked off her questions on her fingers.

"Why did Sophie leave Park? How did she disappear? Who met her? Where was she taken? Where was she kept for three weeks? Why was she transported to the industrial area? Why was she abused? Why was she drugged? And the most important question: Who did all this to her?"

Tommy leaned back in his chair and gave Irene a taunting look. "My dear Watson, we will have the answer to that question once we've found the killer, not before."

"I believe Sherlock needed to take cocaine to think. Right now I need a different kind of stimulant," Irene said and sighed.

She walked out of the office to get two cups of coffee from the machine.

KATARINA HAD NOTHING else to do, so she was happy to join Irene to go see capoeira. Their dog, Sammie, jumped into the back of their Combi. He loved taking car rides. In his old age, he preferred riding in the car to going on long walks. For his whole eleven-year lifespan, he'd always believed the car belonged to him. His owners were allowed to drive it due to his largesse. In the last few years, he even allowed the younger family members to drive, as long as he could ride along.

At his last veterinary appointment, Sammie was diagnosed with cataracts in both eyes. During the day, it didn't seem to bother him much, but in the evenings it did. He no longer wanted to go for walks once it got dark. The once-plucky terrier now would bark at imagined ghosts whenever the wind rustled the tree branches or shadows moved outside the shine of the streetlights. More and more often, he would bang into mailboxes and posts. With a pang of sorrow, Irene realized that her beloved dog was truly getting old.

They parked near a streetlight so that it wouldn't get too dark in the car. The temperature was nearing freezing, but Sammie would still be fine in the car for an hour or two. Irene wrapped him up in his blanket, and he sighed contentedly as he settled into his nest. It had been three months since his last professional grooming—his shaggy coat would help keep him warm.

There were many more people in the cafeteria than there had been that morning, and the air was filled with laughter and conversation. Irene caught sight of Frej's blond hair in the crowd. He was sitting next to the girl with pink braids, the girl Irene had watched earlier that morning as she practiced capoeira. Irene headed toward them.

"Hello again," she said, smiling.

Frej looked up. "Hello. What are you doing here?" he said, without enthusiasm.

"I'm going to talk to Marcelo Alves after the session, and Felipe Medina has promised to interpret for me. I brought my daughter Katarina along so she could take a look at capoeira. She's interested in the martial—"

Irene was stopped in the middle of the sentence by Katarina, who gently but firmly moved her aside. Katarina held out her hand to greet Frej and his female friend.

Frej smiled widely when he saw Katarina. Irene was again aware of how charming he could appear, in spite of that ugly soul patch. A style of the times, Irene thought. Was it rappers who started it? Hip-hop artists? Anyway, it was popular among the young men these days. Irene remembered seeing that tiny, square beard on some of the younger male reporters on television as well.

The pale capoeira dancer introduced herself as Lina.

"Do any of you have a key so we can get in there?" asked Irene, pointing at the glass doors closing off the hall to the rehearsal rooms.

"No, Marcelo has it. He lets us in half an hour before class so we can change," Frej replied.

"He's coming now," Lina said, rising.

As if his name summoned him, Marcelo appeared in the hall on the other side of the glass doors. Irene had never seen him in person before; she'd only read his name in the police reports. He was just a tad bit shorter than Irene. He was dressed the way the other male capoeira dancers had that morning: bare chest and wide, white pants. He had delicate features, but was still attractive in a masculine way. Dark eyes dominated his face with their long, thick lashes; a small smile played around his well-formed lips; and his long, dark brown hair sprang up in curly locks around his head. His way of moving reminded Irene of a sleek feline—control over every single muscle while still completely relaxed.

Both male and female faces turned toward the door when he opened it. From a separate table, the rest of the capoeira group got up. Irene remembered them from earlier that morning.

Irene went to Marcelo and introduced herself. Felipe Medina came over to them immediately.

"I've already told Marcelo you'd like to talk to him and I'd interpret," Felipe said.

Marcelo smiled and nodded in agreement, but he didn't say anything. Irene wondered how much Swedish he actually understood.

As Frej walked past her, Irene said, "Hey, Frej, I'd like to stop by and take a look at Sophie's apartment again."

"Why? The police have already gone through it more than once."

"I know, but my boss wanted me to take another look just in case there's anything we missed. Are you home tomorrow afternoon?"

Frej looked at her resentfully, then shrugged. "I'm done by two or three, so, like, three thirty."

"All right, I'll be there at three thirty."

Frej nodded and disappeared into the changing room.

KATARINA FOUND CAPOEIRA totally fascinating. She was as impressed by the acrobatics and sparring as Irene had been. Once the session was over, she said with determination, "I'm going to start taking capoeira."

"What? What about your jiujitsu?" Irene exclaimed, alarmed.

Katarina sighed and rolled her eyes. "That's *your* thing. You were the best in the world, not me. I'll never be as good as you. I want to go into something different."

"I wasn't the best in the world," Irene protested. "Just Europe."

Still, deep inside, Irene knew that Katarina was right. Her daughter had never enjoyed jiujitsu as much as Irene had. In her last year at school, she had trained every single day. The other side of the coin was that her grades weren't as good as they could have been. Still, the year after graduation, she'd won the European championship.

Katarina had been in the junior league, and she had placed well, but during the past six months, she'd been losing motivation. Perhaps she did need to try something new. Irene tried to look at it positively, but she had trouble swallowing the lump in her throat.

When the class ended, Katarina went over to talk to Frej and Lina while Irene moved toward Marcelo and Felipe.

"We need to take a shower first," Felipe said. "Let's meet back in fifteen minutes."

"That's fine," Irene said.

She walked back into the rehearsal room, which was now redolent with the smell of sweat. The ventilation in the ceiling was working full force and would soon clear the air. To tell the truth, Irene loved the smell of sweat in workout rooms. It spoke of people keeping their bodies in shape. She was a physical person, as her husband often said. Katarina and Frej were chatting in one corner, and Irene headed toward them, but when Frej noticed her approach, he quickly said goodbye to both of them and walked away.

"He's going for a shower," Katarina explained.

Katarina took a few tentative hops in front of the

floor-to-ceiling mirror. She whirled in a clumsy pirouette and came to a stop in front of Irene.

"A beginners' class is starting in January, and I'm going to register. This summer, they're going to have a three-week intensive, and I plan to go."

Irene still felt the lump of disappointment in her throat, so she could only nod. Katarina was eighteen, the age of adulthood in Sweden, and in the spring, she'd be nineteen. She could now marry whomever she pleased without permission from her parents. She had the right to vote. She was old enough to go to jail. Of course, Irene could not forbid her to take capoeira instead of jiujitsu. Katarina was free to train in any sport she wanted.

As if she could sense Irene's distress at her decision to change her martial arts focus, Katarina rested her hand on Irene's arm.

"I'm not going to stop jiujitsu completely. Capoeira is only twice a week, so I can, you know, keep doing jiujitsu once a week or so."

Marcelo and Felipe came back a few minutes later dressed in thin black jazz pants and tight white T-shirts. Felipe pulled out two mats and set them on the floor. As he moved, the wooden beads at the ends of his braids clicked.

"Go ahead and sit on this one," he said with a smile, pointing to one of the mats.

Irene and Katarina sat down opposite the two dancers. The aroma of men's body wash reached them.

"We only have half an hour. Marcelo has to teach a salsa class. I'm going to stick around to help get the class going. They're all a bunch of newbies. Maybe you'd like to stick around?" Felipe smiled encouragingly at both mother and daughter.

"Yes! I'd love that!" exclaimed Katarina. Her face shone like the sun.

"It would be fun, but my dog is in the car, and I don't want him to get too cold . . ." Irene started.

"But I'm staying," Katarina said.

The two young men smiled at her, and Irene felt a twinge of worry. Both of these men were extremely attractive—much too attractive.

To recapture the initiative, she said, "So, let's get right to it. My first question for Marcelo is very personal. Still, it's extremely important that I have an honest answer."

She paused to give Felipe the chance to interpret what she just said. Felipe spoke in swift Portuguese. Marcelo raised his eyebrows, but said nothing. He nodded as he looked over at Irene.

"Witnesses interviewed about the night Sophie disappeared had the impression that Marcelo and Sophie were together—a romantic couple. Is this true?"

Felipe's eyes widened a bit, but he quickly interpreted the question. Marcelo laughed softly, but then his expression sobered again. He looked directly at Irene and said something with great emphasis. Felipe did not have to finish interpreting for Irene to understand that he denied this.

"He says that they were, like, good friends, but they weren't a couple. No *bazza*. Sophie was a difficult and unusual person. Marcelo didn't understand her, but they had a good working relationship with *The Fire Dance*." Felipe smiled broadly. "Marcelo and I are both in *The Fire Dance*. You have to come on Wednesday and watch the premiere!"

This was the second invitation to the premiere Irene had received, and she nodded. Her curiosity had been awakened, and now she actually wanted to see it. She had never seen a live dance performance in her life; she'd only watched dance on TV.

"Wednesday? I'm going to skip jiujitsu and come with," Katarina exclaimed.

"Great! Lots of people will be there!" Felipe said with delight.

Irene wanted to steer the conversation back to the relationship between Marcelo and Sophie, but before she asked a follow-up question, she said to Katarina, "Why don't you go over to the cafeteria for now. I'll be done soon."

"Why?" Katarina protested but reluctantly stood up. Even though she'd enjoyed the capoeira class, she understood that her mother was at the House of Dance to work, nothing else.

Marcelo quickly said something to Felipe.

"Hey, Katarina," Felipe said. "Marcelo said you can borrow some salsa clothes from us so you don't have to go home in sweaty clothes."

"Thanks, that's really sweet of you."

She turned at the door and smiled. Her blue eyes were shining in enthusiasm, and Irene realized that her daughter was excited about dancing. Irene glanced back at Marcelo and saw that her daughter was not the only one who looked forward to her joining capoeira.

After the door closed behind Katarina, Irene started her line of questioning again. "A few witnesses stated that Marcelo and Sophie were so close at the table that it really looked like they were more than friends."

Felipe gave Irene a crooked smile. "You just don't know him . . ." Then he turned to the Brazilian and interpreted the question.

Marcelo sighed and his dark eyes looked into Irene's. He ran his fingers through his thick hair, looking worried. Irene sensed just how disturbing he could be to a woman's peace of mind. *Glad I'm not young anymore*, she thought. But a second later, the unwelcome thought came to mind: *But Katarina is*.

"He says he and Sophie were never in a relationship. They were just really good friends," Felipe said.

"Did Sophie think so? Did she think they were 'just friends'?"

Felipe looked at her in surprise, but interpreted the question without comment. Her stomach lurched as she noticed Marcelo's hesitation before he began to answer. *There's something here*, her police instincts told her.

Finally, Marcelo went into a long harangue and Felipe looked completely perplexed. Before he began translating, Irene interrupted to say, "Felipe, I hope you understand that you cannot repeat anything we are talking about in here. It's all confidential."

"Of course," Felipe said, a wounded tone in his voice. "Marcelo is one of my best friends," he added, as if that added extra weight.

Irene smiled and held up one of her hands in defense. "All right. I realize it was unnecessary for me to say it so directly, but it's important that I did. It's part of the regulations when dealing with an interpreter."

Felipe still looked offended at being accused of being unable to keep things confidential, but he began to interpret what Marcelo had just said.

"He said he never wanted to *bazza* with Sophie. She was his landlady, you know. They had a good working relationship. He noticed, though, that she wanted more than that. Two times he woke up to find her standing in his room. He never bothered to lock the door, and she'd just walked right in. Nothing happened, though. Both times, she turned and walked back out when she saw he was awake. He did notice that she liked to be, like, say, hugged and stuff."

"What did he think about it?"

Marcelo was watching her seriously as he answered her question. Even if she did not understand his words, she could tell he was trying to make her understand his complicated relationship with Sophie.

"It was really tough for him. He liked her but he didn't want . . . sex. She was attractive and everything, but he didn't want any trouble. But he could see that she needed . . . human contact. He believes that Sophie was a very lonely person," Felipe interpreted.

The door opened, and Irene could see Lina and her pink braids. "Can I let them in in five minutes?"

Marcelo held his thumb up and nodded. Irene realized that she was out of time. She thanked Marcelo and Felipe and left.

Katarina was in the cafeteria chattering with her new-found friends in the capoeira group. She didn't even look up as Irene walked past and out into the darkness.

Sammie was overjoyed when Irene opened the rear door of the car. She let him out for a short break before they drove home. The cold rain soon sent Sammie back into the car. It was definitely much cozier in his warm blanket nest.

THE MORNING FOG lay heavy on the fields. At times the fog was so thick the drivers had to creep along the narrow highway heading toward Björkland. Irene was ten minutes late to her meeting with the real estate agent. In spite of the fog, she had no trouble finding him—all she had to do was follow the sound. The Hives' latest album was blasting from the sporty black Toyota. Irene recognized the song and even though his windows were rolled up, she could make out the words perfectly.

Irene parked her Volvo and got out. She walked over to the Toyota and tapped on the window. The guy inside jumped and turned off his stereo at once. He opened his car door and jumped out. His hand was already stretched out to greet her, and he had an apologetic smile on his lips.

"Hi, I'm Erik Johansson. I didn't see you arrive. I was thinking you might have forgotten our appointment."

"Hello, Irene Huss. I never forget an appointment, but traffic was slowed by the fog."

Erik Johansson had a firm, quick handshake. His leather jacket was attractive, but not practical in the damp weather. His thin-soled loafers also were not suited for the soggy ground. Irene felt she was properly dressed in her raincoat and rubber boots. Dog owners always keep weatherproof gear close at hand.

Erik Johansson happily made some small talk as he stepped between the puddles. He was just over twenty and barely of average height. His feet were soon going to be soaking wet, a fact he mentioned himself as he happened to slip into a pool of water right in front of the entrance. He also let loose a few choice words, which he apologized for. Irene laughed and told him she'd heard much worse during the course of her career. She found she liked the good-humored young man, who looked new at his job.

Erik Johansson turned the key in the lock and held the door open for Irene. "Ladies first," he said.

Irene had a feeling of déjà vu immediately—everything was the same in the large country kitchen; it was even possible that the withered plants on the windowsill had been the same ones sitting there fifteen years ago. The stale, dusty odors of an empty house hit her.

"We haven't decorated the interior yet. We haven't had time. This afternoon we're going to freshen up the place."

"Does that mean you haven't cleaned it, either?"

"Well, of course it needs to be cleaned, too. Nobody buys a house with dead plants and old curtains. We can't do anything about the wallpaper, but these days the seventies are coming back in style, so maybe it'll be all right. The floor is in much worse shape. Check it out: scratches from dogs. We really should redo the floors, but the old lady doesn't want to, even if you'd get the money back after the sale. 'Just sell the place,' she told us with a grimace."

"I see. And how would you redo the interior?" Irene found herself truly curious. She'd never thought of any of this before.

The real estate agent reacted to her question with enthusiasm. He ran his fingers through his blond hair.

"It'll be a challenge! The old lady is going to have to pay for the cleaning and staging herself, but we'll take it off her share. The cleaners are coming this afternoon. I've gone through the wardrobes and I've found some really nice curtains that we can iron and put up. That is, the cleaners will do that. We're going to replace the broken sink in the bathroom . . . that might already have been done by now. Then we'll put some handwoven rugs on the floor. I found them here, too. And on the work counter by the window, I'm going to put a rustic wooden bowl filled with apples. Then the sweet aroma of apples will fill the kitchen and people will think: 'Oh! A real country kitchen!'" He gestured just like a contented client.

"That's wonderful!" Irene had to laugh.

"Yes, all that stuff is extremely important these days. In fact, I ended up re-booking the client who was supposed to have come at eleven today. He's going to come by tomorrow instead. He'll have a much better impression," Erik said with a smile.

Something told Irene that this young man would go far in the real estate business.

Before they started the tour of the house, Irene asked, "You haven't noticed anything odd or out of place here?"

He raised his eyebrows and looked at her, perplexed. "Odd? Like what?"

"Well, anything . . . unusually messy, or something that might indicate someone was staying here after the old woman was moved out. Or that just one room was especially clean and free of dust."

"Oh, I see. Like someone was living here without the old lady knowing about it and then tried to get rid of the traces." Erik appeared to think about this for a minute, but then he shook his head. "Nope, can't think of anything unusual in any of the rooms in here. The guy who inherited the place has been checking on it and making sure nothing's going on—like leaks or a break-in, stuff like that."

"So you've met Frej Eriksson," Irene stated.

"That's right, his name was Frej. Yes, he was the one who showed us—that is, my boss and me—the property in the first place. Nice guy. He has no say in what happens to the place because it still belongs to his aunt. He might have agreed to have the floors redone."

With Erik as her guide, Irene toured the large country home. The interior was characterized by inherited furniture and knickknacks from the early part of the previous century, as well as a major remodel during the seventies. Since then, time had stood still. Of course, medallion wallpaper was in style again, at least as far as trendy design magazines had it, but Irene was certain that she was not yet ready to see green velvet wallpaper with gilt impressions on the walls. Perhaps this was a sign that she really was getting older. Fashion and design are not as exciting the second or third time around.

The only item that appeared to be newer was a television. On the bookshelves, there were several photographs of long-dead ancestors standing stiffly straight in their best black clothes. In the center, there was a large wedding photograph, probably of Ingrid Hagberg and her husband, with the inscription *Gefa - 52* elegantly printed in a black flourish in one corner. A faded color photo of Ingrid and her husband in their middle age was framed in gold. Judging by the wide shoulder pads and the overflowing frill at her neck, Irene judged that the picture had been taken in the early eighties. The man at her side was tall and strong. Ingrid was smiling happily, while her husband glowered. He had died not long after, and Ingrid had been left to run the farm on her own. At the time of the fire in 1989, Ingrid had already been widowed for years.

Two large color photographs had been placed on the top shelf. One showed a drooling, happy baby and the other a much more serious Frej in his graduation cap.

Nowhere in the entire house was there any trace that Sophie might have been held against her will for three weeks.

The stable was large and had been kept in good shape, but the empty stalls gave a feeling of abandonment to the entire building. The other sheds were in much worse condition. There was no sign of anything out of the ordinary.

Irene thanked Erik Johansson for taking the time to show her the farm and wished him the best of luck in making the sale. His whole face lit up.

"It won't be a problem at all! We have lots of interested parties. We have showings booked for the entire weekend. We'll just have to hold out until we get the asking price. Or even more!"

"Do you really believe someone will pay eight million kronor for this house?" Irene couldn't help asking.

"Not for the house itself. It isn't worth much. But the property is zoned in the city, so the land is extraordinarily valuable. Just think of how many single family homes you could build on twenty-three hectares!"

ON THE WAY back to town, Irene stopped at the Pizzeria Napoli in Brunnsbo. She had two reasons: one, she was hungry and two, she wanted to check out Frej's alibi about buying pizza the evening that Sophie had died.

The place was small and the aroma of freshly baked pizza hit her the moment she stepped inside. Her stomach growled. There was a table with four high bar stools by the window. If you were a customer, you'd have your back turned to the pizza chefs and have a view of the traffic outside. At the moment, all four chairs were unoccupied. Pizzeria Napoli was not the place you went to enjoy the view. Most of the customers probably bought their pizzas to go.

A man who was twenty-five or so was shoving a pie into the oven with a large wooden paddle. He was as dark as the average Southern European, and he was wearing the typical pizza baker uniform: T-shirt and flour-covered jeans. PIZZERIA NAPOLI was printed on the T-shirt in large letters. He smiled widely as he greeted Irene. When Irene asked for the owner, the man yelled "Isthvan!" toward the back of the building.

A deep voice replied, and the pizza baker gave Irene a dazzling smile.

"My cousin. Owns here." He gestured to include the entire contents of the pizza joint.

The man who came out from the back was older and heftier. The man gave his name as Isthvan Gür as he shook hands with Irene. When Irene identified herself as a police officer, the two men exchanged rapid glances, but neither of them said anything.

Irene took out a photograph of Frej, an enlargement of his most recent passport picture. She showed it to the men and asked if they recognized him. Isthvan Gür glanced at the photo and shook his head. The cousin took a good long look and then smiled.

"Him I know. Peppe! It is Peppe!"

"Peppe?" Irene asked, confused.

"Him I joke with. He buy always pizza pepperoni. Him I joke and call Peppe, 'cause of pizza pepperoni."

The cousin's happy expression vanished as he caught sight of the owner's look. In this establishment it was obvious that one should never discuss the customers with the police under any circumstances. Irene decided to ignore the reason behind this attitude and instead get some answers to her questions.

"Do you know Peppe's real name?" she asked.

"No, I joke call him Peppe. But he tired of pizza now."

"Doesn't he come here any more?"

"Yes, but now he buy kebab special. Extra everything!" the cousin said, pointing proudly at the menu plastered to the wall.

Irene read: *large pita with extra kebab meat, lettuce, tomato, cucumber, pepperoni, onion, goat cheese. Choice of sauce. 60 kronor.* She felt her mouth start to water.

"I'd like to try one of those," Irene said.

Isthvan's gloomy expression eased up slightly. Without saying anything, he began to slice kebab meat from the rotating spit over the oven. He filled a large pita with the condiments promised on the menu. While he worked, Irene continued to question the younger cousin.

"Do you remember the last time he was here?"

The young man seemed to ponder this question before answering. "One, two weeks. Lots people come. Don't know." He shrugged in apology.

"But he must come here often if you're able to recognize him," Irene stated.

"Sure. Know him, sure. Usual he here, one, two time every week. He like pizza and kebab."

"Hope you like it, too," Isthvan interrupted them in his deep voice. He smiled slightly and handed Irene the warm kebab sandwich.

"Could I have a Ramlösa mineral water as well?" Irene asked.

Irene took her food to one of the bar stools by the window. A few customers had come in while she'd been talking to the pizza baker, and now the men were busy filling other orders.

Irene's cell phone rang after she'd barely eaten half of her sandwich. She saw Tommy's name on the display.

"Can you come directly to Högsbo?" he asked.

"Sure. What's up and where should we meet?"

"Let's meet where Sophie's remains were discovered. I've found out some interesting things about this area."

THE GREY LAYER of fog was still hanging heavily near the tops of the trees as Irene parked on the narrow road. She buttoned her jacket before she got out of the car. It seemed as if the fog was trying to sneak into her collar as it swirled around her neck. Perhaps it was just this dismal place that gave her the creeps. She stuck her hands deep into her pockets while she waited for Tommy. A few minutes later, he drove up and parked behind her car.

"Have you taken a look at the fire scene?" he asked as he jumped out.

"No, I was waiting for you."

They walked together around the abandoned tire manufacturing plant and over to the remains of the old ramshackle shed, now just a heap of blackened boards.

"Unbelievable that there was so much of her left," Tommy said.

There wasn't much to look at beyond the sorrowful sight. They stood silently for a minute and took in the desolate atmosphere.

"Now let me show you what else I've found," Tommy said.

He walked back toward the cars, then past them and turned onto a narrow side street. On one side, there was a short concrete building with tiny broken windows. On one of the walls, there was a faded sign: DANIELSSON BROS. CEMENT WORKS. Next to the building were piles of abandoned cement pipes.

Approximately ten meters from the former cement works lay the dilapidated remains of a wooden building.

Two of its outer walls were still standing, though they were covered in soot, much like the cement foundation.

"This building burned down!" exclaimed Irene.

"Yep. Beginning of June this year. The building had been abandoned years ago, and it was scheduled to be torn down like the other ones around here. Arson. No suspects. And there's more. Come with me."

Irene noticed a bulldozer parked alongside the burned building that would obviously soon be gone.

Tommy kept walking a few hundred meters along the narrow streets and stopped before a piece of land that had been scraped clean.

"They've already gotten rid of it, but this had been a wooden building. At one time, it was a car mechanic's shop. It burned down in April. That was also arson. No leads. Suspect unknown."

"Any more around here the past few years?"

"No, none. Other than the one in which Sophie died."

"Strange. Three arsons in the space of six months."

"Does this situation remind you of anything?" Tommy asked, his voice filled with urgency.

Irene tried to think what he was hinting at, but she couldn't figure it out. She shook her head.

"The arsons at Björkil! There were many other fires about then, and the papers were all writing about a possible pyromaniac," he said, with triumph.

"But . . . but it can't be the same arsonist," Irene objected, astonished.

"Maybe not. Still, I was thinking about the arsons at Björkil, and I decided to find out if there were others around here, and I found these two. Actually, there were also three container fires in August and September—not here exactly, but on Marklandsgatan. Three in one week. Perhaps they're not connected with these fires, but it's not

more than a kilometer from here." Tommy paused theatrically before saying, "They were *also* arson."

Irene nodded as she reflected on this new information.
Everything would have to be looked at anew. A thought
hit her.

"Do you think that Sophie's killer knew about these other
two fires in the area? Perhaps he set fire to the shed hoping
that her body would be totally consumed and never found.
The remains of the fire would be bulldozed away, just like
they've done here." Irene pointed to the empty property,
where the contours of a foundation were still visible.

"It's possible."

They walked back to their cars, each lost in thought.
They did not run into a single living being. They could
hear the noise from the midday traffic on the freeway, but
here everything was silent and deserted, waiting for the
bulldozers and the final obliteration.

A RELATIVELY NEW red Renault was parked next to the
sidewalk in front of Sophie's mansion. *Probably Frej's*, Irene
thought as she pushed open the squeaky front gate. *Or, I
should say, his aunt's*, she corrected herself.

A weak sun was bravely doing its best to shine through
the veils of clouds, but the last horizontal rays of sunshine
didn't lighten the sight of the mansion's decay. The paving
stones leading to the front door were treacherous from fallen
leaves and moss. The mansion seemed to loom in a melancholy way as she came nearer the entrance.

She pressed the doorbell by the entrance. The angry
sound of the signal echoed behind the door, and a long time
passed before she heard the sound of footsteps approaching.
Frej opened the door and could hardly be described as enthusiastic when he saw her. They greeted each other, and Irene
stepped over the threshold.

The mahogany chest-high dado rail and the sepia carpets gave the impression of twilight in the large entry hall. There were many doorways along the hall, and at the end was a grandfather clock and a chest of drawers made of dark wood. Immediately inside the entrance reigned an elegant floor-to-ceiling mirror, covered with a thick layer of grime that gave Irene's image a matte, indistinct appearance. To the immediate right of the entrance was a closed door leading to the basement—at least as far as the small, bronze sign could be believed. To the left, there was a large hat rack, and a few meters farther along, a staircase to the upper floors. All kinds of clothes were tossed at random onto the hat rack. Since just two men lived in the house now, Irene concluded that the brand new, elegant, light brown jacket with a faux fur collar must have belonged to Sophie. She must have also bought the pointed ankle boots with extra narrow low heels. They were carefully arranged beneath the shelf, waiting for their owner. The sight of the clothes made Irene feel a little sad. Perhaps Sophie had bought them to wear at the premiere of her *Fire Dance*.

The house smelled musty and Irene could hear grit crunch under her shoes. The parquet floor, much the worse for wear, creaked and was slightly springy as she walked across it.

"Where do you want to start?" asked Frej.

"You don't have to lead me around. I can take a look by myself," Irene replied.

"All right. I'll be in my apartment. Top floor."

Frej headed up the stairs, and Irene waited until she heard him close a door. Then she stepped to the basement door and opened it. The strong stench of mold and moisture swept up the staircase to her nose. She fumbled for the light switch on the inside of the basement wall. She found it, but when she pushed the button down, nothing happened. The lightbulb was out. She'd have to go back to her car for the flashlight in her glove compartment. Perhaps Frej had another lightbulb on hand, or maybe she could borrow a flashlight from him. She closed the basement door and walked into the kitchen visible through one of the doorways.

Irene stopped and looked the kitchen over. Without a doubt, this was the original kitchen from the time the house was built. The cabinets reached all the way to the ceiling and had beautifully carved edges and corners. They'd been lacquered in dirty beige, but chips had fallen off in many places. The stove and the refrigerator had been updated—at least the ochre color led to that conclusion. There was a smooth glass globe hanging from the ceiling and a similar lamp attached to the wall above the stove. There were no countertops and no dishwasher. A glance through the filthy windows showed Irene a few overgrown raspberry bushes straggling in front of a dark green hedge. The kitchen stank of leftovers and rotting food. A stack of dishes was piled in the sink.

Irene opened the refrigerator door and then closed it as fast as she could. It was empty, but it smelled like a moldy dishrag. Obviously neither Frej nor Marcelo used this kitchen.

Although it might be considered for landmark status, the kitchen needed to be scrubbed from floor to ceiling. Irene wasn't exactly a pedantic housekeeper herself, but this was probably the filthiest kitchen she had ever seen.

As she walked over the brown linoleum floor, the soles of her shoes stuck and made a smacking sound each time she lifted a foot.

The next door opened to a bathroom with a fairly new shower. The stench of ground-in dirt and urine made Irene gag. *How could a woman ever live in such a filthy environment?* Irene asked herself. She herself didn't mind a few dust bunnies or a few spills, but this was something else again. Her mother Gerd would declare it "a trash heap unfit for humans" and sniff. Then she'd get a bottle of bleach, a few huge washrags and a big bucket of steaming hot water.

The door after that revealed a large dining room aligned with the living room. Heavy oak furniture dominated the interior. Gloomy, brownish red carpets did not lessen the depressing effect. The entire room was covered in a thick layer of dust. The furniture must have been chosen by Anna-Greta Lindeman's parents when the house was new. Except for a few pieces of artwork that were more modern, it appeared that the entire arrangement had stood undisturbed for over a century.

The last doorway in the hall was beneath the stairs to the upper floors. It led to a spacious, well-lit room, which had probably once been a library since there were floor-to-ceiling built-in bookcases along three walls. The light from the corner window fell onto a large mahogany desk, on which there was a computer and a printer. Irene knew that the technicians had gone through the computer without finding anything of interest, but this room still gave her some things to explore. The shorter wall had an unmade bed—a simple pine bed from IKEA. The sheets were bright pea green with large yellow flowers, and Irene suspected they came from the same store as the bed. A sour smell, a vaguely familiar one, came from the bed, but it was hard to identify. Irene did not find the bed itself of much interest. But the bookshelf behind it was.

Sophie had cleared all the books from the shelves, except for the two uppermost ones. The reason those were left alone was probably because they were too high to reach, even standing on the bed.

Sophie had arranged all her belongings on these shelves. The lowermost one held all her shoes. There were a number of toe shoes in pink and white silk, as well as black and white ballet shoes in leather and a few pairs of sturdy shoes with heels. Irene realized that these latter shoes were also dance shoes. Closest to the door was a pair of huge black boots. Irene wondered if these were the ones that Sophie had been wearing when she met her fifteen years before. Considering the condition they were in, it was not out of the question.

Above the shoes was a shelf of knit leg warmers in various colors and thicknesses. In a clear plastic box, Irene could see hairbands and bobby pins. On the next shelf, Sophie had placed her tights and socks. Sweaters, leotards and other smaller articles of clothing were on the next level. At the top, there were jeans, pants and skirts.

Every item was neatly folded and stacked in orderly piles. Each pile of clothes was of a single color: a red pile, a white one, a black one, and so on. Irene contemplated the arrangement with admiration. The woman who couldn't even clean her toilet had a meticulous way of sorting her dance outfits and accessories.

But where were her other clothes? Irene looked around, but saw no dresser or wardrobe. On impulse, she walked over to the mahogany desk by the corner window and pulled open a drawer. Inside there was a heap of panties all jumbled together. The drawer next to it had bras and sports bras. Only one of the drawers had anything remotely connected to what people usually kept in their desks: pens and pencils, dirty erasers and an unusually long ruler at the bottom.

Irene raised her eyes to the wall next to the window, where Sophie had taped up large sheets of paper close together to form a surface of almost four square meters. Every sheet had five lines drawn straight across. Between and on the lines were marked points and tracks. The pattern was incomprehensible and appeared completely random. Sophie had placed a banner across the collection, where she'd carefully written *THE FIRE DANCE*. Obviously, this was part of Sophie's "saga in dance."

Perhaps Frej knew what the mysterious signs meant. She decided to head upstairs and visit Frej in his attic apartment.

The stairs creaked loudly beneath each step she took. On the second floor, she decided to go ahead and take a quick look around. The staircase opened up into a light, airy hallway. The only piece of furniture she saw there was an unusually long sofa placed against one wall that gave the hallway the look of a desolate waiting room in an abandoned train station. Across from the stairway, there was a balcony door between large windows.

There were six closed doors in the hallway. Irene opened the closest one on her left and saw that she'd ended up in Ernst Malmborg's studio. A huge control board with regulators and buttons, microphones, tape recorders and all kinds of instruments sat there untouched. If it hadn't been for the thick layer of dust over everything, one could imagine that the musicians had just stepped out for coffee and would be back soon.

The room next to it was smaller, but it held just one grand piano with its bench. The room was also extremely cold. There were no curtains on the windows or pictures on the walls. Perhaps Ernst thought it would disturb his concentration while composing.

She closed this door carefully and opened the door beside it. A large double bed with a faded pink cover dominated the room. Probably Ernst's bedroom. On one wall, there was a huge oil painting.

Irene took a few quick steps into the room to take a closer look and saw that it was a portrait of Anna-Greta Lidman in her glory days. The actress's long blonde hair cascaded down her shoulders with a lock of hair reaching down to one of her breasts. The painting ended just above where her nipples would be, and her upper body was nude. Her blue eyes glittered, hinting at the joy of life, and an elusive smile played on her sensual lips.

Alcohol, depression, pills and natural aging had broken her. Irene felt a strong sense of sympathy for the woman in the painting. No one can win the battle against age. It was lost from day one.

Irene nodded slightly both at the woman in the painting and at her own thoughts.

A voice from behind made her jump.

"I thought you were coming up to see me."

Irene whirled around and had difficultly hiding how startled she'd been.

"Did I scare you?" asked Frej, raising one of his eyebrows.

He was not able to conceal the pleased tone in his voice. Irene couldn't help but smile at him.

"I thought I'd take a look around as long as I was here. Then I wouldn't have to come back," she said.

"Okay. Have you looked at Marcelo's room yet?"

"No, I haven't."

He gestured for her to follow him. They walked across the hall. Frej pointed to the room beside the staircase and said, "Toilet's over there. Has a bathtub, too. The next room is a guest room, but, like, no one has stayed there in the past twenty years or so."

He continued to the door nearest the balcony and opened it. He swept his arm in an exaggerated gesture of welcome. Irene stayed put.

"Marcelo's not home, is he?"

"Who cares? He's almost never here." Frej gave Irene's back a slight nudge.

"Hello? Marcelo?" Irene called out to be on the safe side.

There was no answer, so as long as she had the chance, Irene decided to do a quick look through Marcelo's digs.

They stood in a large room functioning as a combination kitchen and living room. On the other side of the room, a door was half open.

The kitchen contained a three-in-one with two cabinets, a refrigerator and two stove plates. Irene recognized the setup since the police break room had one just like it. A small kitchen table and two chairs were set against the wall. The table was covered by a worn wax cloth with blue checks. Irene thought again of her mother. If Gerd could see this tablecloth, she'd immediately grab a dishcloth and a spray bottle.

The minimal countertop was covered in dirty cups and saucers, and crumbs crackled underfoot as they walked across the floor. Obviously, Sophie and Marcelo shared the same approach to house cleaning.

Next to the window were a sofa and two mismatched chairs around a coffee table. The table had no cloth to hide its scratched and worn surface. A candle stub had been jammed into a wine bottle there, and melted wax and water rings had permanently destroyed the finish. A number of cigarette burns marred the arms of both the sofa and the chairs.

"Does Marcelo smoke?" asked Irene. She pointed at the burns.

"Smoke? No, why? Oh, the holes. He didn't make them. That was Ernst's first wife. The one you saw in the painting. My mom said she used to forget she was smoking when she was drunk. Dangerous, of course. It could, like, set the house on fire . . ."

He stopped in the middle of his sentence and gave Irene a look from the corner of his eye, before he turned around and pushed the door open all the way.

"His bedroom," he said shortly.

The blinds had been pulled down to keep the room in darkness. Irene reached for the light switch. The faint light from a rice-paper lamp barely illuminated the room. The only furniture was the bed, the same kind Sophie had, a worn pine chair and a small dresser. As Irene expected, the bed wasn't made. A strong scent of after-shave hung in the room. Frej opened a wallpapered door to reveal a surprisingly large closet. All of Marcelo's clothes were hanging there. Shoes and random items were scattered on the floor. In the middle of the mess was a large cardboard box. Irene peered inside and saw miscellaneous papers and photographs. She would have liked to go through the box, but couldn't with Frej hanging over her shoulder.

As they were about to leave, some photographs pinned to the wall above Marcelo's bed caught Irene's attention. She stopped abruptly and Frej bumped into her back.

"What the hell?" he asked, surprised.

"Those pictures," Irene said. She strode toward the bed and carefully removed them from the wall.

Three photographs. All in color and all showing a large fire.

"What's this, Frej?" she asked in a sharper tone than she'd intended.

"What's what? Oh. Those. Pictures of the bonfires on Walpurgis Night. Sophie wanted some photos with fire blazing. For, like, inspiration."

"Inspiration?"

"For her dance. *The Fire Dance.* Marcelo had been helping her with those parts where the two of us dance . . . capoeira, you know."

"You're the one who took them, right?"

"Of course."

Irene looked more closely at the photographs. It could well be that these were from a Walpurgis Night bonfire. The pictures emphasized the flames shooting up, but on one of the pictures the silhouette of someone's head loomed in the foreground. Frej smiled at her as he said, "If you see *The Fire Dance*, you'll understand. The fire is the most important part of the entire dance."

Irene nodded as she stuffed the pictures into one of her jacket pockets. "I want to take a closer look at these. Let Marcelo know that he'll get them back."

"Okay, though he really doesn't need them any longer. We've finished choreographing the dance. And I have copies in case he does need them."

Frej walked out of Marcelo's bedroom and through the filthy main room to hold open the door chivalrously for Irene. Darkness had fallen and the hallway no longer looked at all welcoming—just deserted.

Frej moved to the stairs and hit a switch. Irene felt relieved when the darkness was chased away. This old house made her irrationally fearful of ghosts. Ridiculous. She'd never been afraid of the supernatural before. It was probably just the realization that Anna-Greta Lidman had lived here during the last years of her life and had also died in the house. This house was filled with her tragic fate.

"This way," Frej said, as he opened the last door in the hallway.

A small attic staircase was hiding behind it. It was steep, but there were railings on both sides.

They went up into a narrow hallway with three doors. Frej pointed at the one of the left and said, "My darkroom." Then he pointed at the one straight ahead. "My bathroom. And here's the door to my apartment."

With a smile of pride, he opened the last door.

They entered a short hall with wardrobes on both sides. Then they stepped into a large living room with a slanted ceiling. A large window and a balcony door were across the room.

"Faces west," Frej said, gesturing to the balcony.

"What a delightful apartment!" Irene couldn't help exclaiming.

"The kitchen is to the right and the sleeping alcove to the left," Frej said, not concealing his pride.

Although the ceiling slanted down on both sides, there was enough room to stand upright almost all the way to the walls. In the kitchen, there was the same three-in-one combination as in Marcelo's apartment, but there was a small kitchen counter with drawers beside it. The entire floor in the apartment had been recently sanded and painted a light color. The windows had no curtains, and there were no plants on the windowsills. The walls were a light lavender blue and all the furniture was black, including the bed in the alcove. Even the bedclothes were black, Irene noticed. The small sofa and the low armchairs had been draped with black covers and he'd lacquered the coffee table in shining black. Black and white photographs were on the walls, and in the sleeping alcove hung an enlarged color photograph of the Walpurgis Night bonfire.

"Did you fix it up all by yourself?" asked Irene.

"Yep. The walls and the furniture," he said.

"Even the floor?"

"Well . . . Felipe and his cousin Mats helped me there. Mats is a carpenter. He fixed up the kitchen benches, too."

The effect was aesthetically pleasing and functional in a strict and slightly cool manner. What Irene noticed above all was how clean it was. She didn't mention that, but asked instead, "Did you carve out this apartment from the attic?"

"Nah. It's been here since the house was built. For, like, the servants. Sophie and her dad had some kind of house-keeper living here until the old man died."

"I've heard something about her . . . Mrs. Larsson, I believe her name was. Do you know where she moved?"

"No idea." He sounded completely uninterested.

"Was it her furniture that you fixed up?"

"Nah, she took her stuff with her. Sophie and I put what-ever she left behind in the basement."

"Oh, the basement. I wanted to take a look at it. The bulb over the stairs was out. Do you have another bulb?"

Frej shrugged. "I imagine there's a flashlight in Sophie's kitchen," he said.

Irene suddenly remembered the strange pictures Sophie had set up in her room. She asked Frej if he knew what they were. He smiled crookedly as he replied, "Ask my mom. I can hear her coming now."

Irene listened and also heard the quick steps heading up the creaking stairs.

Without knocking, Angelika pushed the door open and breezed into her son's apartment.

"Frej, whose car is . . . ?" She stopped when she caught sight of Irene. "Oh, it's you," she said.

"Hello. I had to check Sophie's apartment one last time, and Frej was kind enough to give me a tour of the house," Irene said, trying to look as friendly as possible.

If you don't have a search warrant, you don't have one, she thought.

Angelika didn't say anything in response, but instead looked at Frej, who wouldn't meet her gaze. His face had closed up, and he had a morose look to his mouth. Was he angry with his mother?

Angelika frowned and looked sharply at Irene. "Good thing you came today. The workmen will be here soon to rip out the entire interior. Not Frej's apartment, but the rest of the house."

"Are you moving in here?" Irene asked in surprise.

"I'm coming back into my *own* house," Angelika answered.

By the look she gave Frej, Irene realized her comment was meant for him. Probably Frej was not at all enthusiastic about his mother moving into the house. *But the house does belong to her now,* Irene reminded herself, *even if the estate isn't fully settled yet.*

Angelika smiled her pale smile as she said to Irene, "Staffan and I were considering moving in together anyway. We've been living apart for quite some time now. The Änggården mansion fits our needs, and he would enjoy helping me renovate this fine old building. His brother is a master carpenter and . . ."

BOOM! Irene jumped as the door slammed behind her back. She hadn't noticed Frej leaving.

Angelika sighed loudly and gave Irene one of those between-us-mothers look, "Frej thinks he's going to lose some freedom, but I've explained to him over and over again . . ." She paused a moment. "I've also promised Marcelo he can take over my apartment on Distansgatan. It's a great two-bedroom. However, if Frej doesn't like my arrangements, he can move there, and we'll let Marcelo stay here."

She gestured to include the space around them. Irene could understand Frej. He'd put his heart and soul into renovating this apartment. The thought that he would have to leave it must be unbearable.

"As long as you're here, could you explain what those signs are on the paper Sophie put on the wall in her bedroom?" Irene asked.

"It's called Benesh notation. It's a way to make choreography notes. The notations are then written below the score so that the music and the dance movements can be read simultaneously.

"So it's a way to write down dance steps?"

"You could say that. I never use Benesh in my work, myself. I use a video camera or I write down stick figures."

"Do you know if Sophie always used this kind of notation?"

"I would imagine. It fit her . . . mindset."

In the silence that followed, they could hear a car drive up on the gravel outside. Angelika lit up.

"Oh, Staffan's here!" she exclaimed happily.

She turned on her heel and held the door open for Irene, who couldn't think of any reason to stay. They walked down the stairs together and reached the ground floor just as the doorbell rang. Angelika rushed to the door with light steps. With a whoop of joy, she flung her arms around the neck of the man standing outside. They kissed and embraced for a long time. The man laughed as he finally loosened himself from Angelika's arms and came into the house.

"This is a police officer who's just leaving," Angelika said, staring hard at Irene.

Irene smiled at the tall man and held out her hand in greeting. The man had a firm handshake and introduced himself as Staffan Östberg. Without a doubt, he fit the stereotype of the head of Volvo. She could glimpse his suit beneath his dark blue ulster. It was a sober medium brown with a matching nougat shirt and a wine red tie. His hair was steel grey and thin at the top. All in all, he was a proper man who had passed his use-by date and, as far as Irene could tell, would be nearing retirement shortly. Angelika still preferred older men.

"We're going to spend the entire weekend figuring out what the workmen are going to do here—or at least where they'll begin," Angelika twittered as she gazed, starstruck, at her new live-in companion.

He smiled tenderly and looked at her the way one looks at an overenthusiastic child. "Of course, my dear. We already know what needs to be done here, but Kenneth will stop by and give us some advice."

"Kenneth?" Angelika asked.

"My brother. His men will take care of everything. Disposal, plumbing, woodwork, painting . . . everything."

Staffan Östberg said this so evenly and calmly that Irene almost wanted to jump in and ask if Kenneth could stop by her house as well. She had a few rotting roof boards where the attic met the gutters . . . But she stopped herself in time, when it dawned on her that this wonderful man certainly didn't work for free, and handymen charge an arm and a leg. Obviously, Staffan Östberg could afford it. Angelika did like her guys to come with money.

Perhaps she always searched for economic security in her choice of men. Now she was coming into a great deal of money from her daughter, who certainly hadn't been a spendthrift.

"Are you going to start your renovations on the ground floor?" Irene asked.

"No. First we're going to look into the drainage around the building as well as replacing the water main. Then we'll make sure the roof is sound. Once that's done, we can move on to the house itself."

Irene could tell Angelika wanted to protest, but held her tongue. It was obvious who was going to be paying for the party.

"So we will still have a few months if we need another look at Sophie's things," Irene said.

"Of course," Staffan said. "We won't be getting started inside until after Christmas."

Angelika looked disappointed, but again she said nothing. Irene knew it wasn't easy for her to refrain from speaking.

She said goodbye to the lovebirds and began her treacherous journey across the paving stones, which were still as slippery as soap.

She hadn't seen Frej on her way out, and once she reached the street, she knew why.

His red Mégan was gone.

"I'm going to dance this evening, too!" Katarina happily told Irene.

Irene was not taken by surprise. When she'd heard her daughter singing as she walked down the stairs, she'd suspected the worst. It was Saturday morning, and the only reason that Irene was up this early was that she needed to drive downtown to run some errands.

"Going to the House of Dance?" she asked.

"Yep."

"What's the dance class this evening?"

"South American. It's going to be great!"

"A beginner class?"

"No, it's a student party. And each student can bring a guest. And I was, like, invited!"

Katarina smiled and her eyes lit up. Irene felt her mood sink into the joints of her toes. She recognized these symptoms. Her daughter was falling in love.

Things had been calm on the guy front since August, when Katarina and Johan broke up. Katarina had said then that she planned to stay single for the rest of her secondary education, and even, perhaps, for the rest of her life.

But now it was happening again. Gisela Bagge was right. Marcelo Alves was a danger for the hearts of every woman out there. He'd take whomever he pleased. Marcelo with his glittering eyes and sensual mouth. His hair, which begged for fingers to run through it. A perfect body over which he had complete control. But poor as a church mouse and just about to be thrown out of his filthy apartment. Marcelo was not a mother-in-law's dream. His love lasted as long as the carbonation from champagne. Should she warn Katarina? After quick deliberation, Irene decided not to say a word. Anything she said would have the opposite effect. At any rate, the best thing to do for now was to wait and see how things developed. This great love was hardly more than twenty-four hours old.

"Just think! I never knew how fantastic it was to dance," Katarina said, as she poured milk and cornflakes into a bowl.

"Better late than never," Irene said. She tried to smile as encouragingly as she could.

She could feel the strain in her facial muscles, but it seemed Katarina was not aware of it. Katarina eagerly whirled her spoon around for emphasis.

"I want to sign up for capoeira after New Year's, but I have the chance for some private lessons right now. So from this day forward, I am only going to go to jiujitsu one day a week. And after New Year's, I'm going to quit."

"But, sweetie, please reconsider . . . why quit after putting in all those years of effort?" Irene realized she was stammering.

"That's right. After all those years. It's boring! I'm never going to get any better than I am now. I'd like to try something different. I want to dance!"

Her last sentence was so determined that Irene realized argument was useless. She remembered Katarina's earlier words: *you were the best in the world, not me.* Deep down, she knew Katarina was right. Jiujitsu had been *her* thing, not Katarina's. Her daughters needed the freedom to develop their own interests.

When she heard Jenny thumping down the stairs, Irene

really became nervous. It was just nine o'clock and her girls hadn't come to breakfast so early in almost ten years.

"Hello, sweetie. You're already up!" she said to her other daughter.

"Yep."

Jenny walked over to the counter and sliced a French roll in half. She'd gotten dressed in black baggy jeans and a tight turquoise sweater with a boat collar. She wore a black camisole beneath it. Between her shoulder blades was a small tattoo. She wore no makeup, and her dyed black hair made her face seem pale and washed out. She headed over to the fridge to get a jar of olive paste. Jenny was a faithful vegan, and she never ate cheese or any other animal product. The French rolls had been baked with olive oil and water instead of milk. Jenny always knew what was in her rolls because she baked them herself.

Irene realized it was too late. The girls were already grown. She couldn't really influence them any longer. There's so much that could go wrong in a young person's life, but they have to go out into the world and make their own way.

Irene wanted to plead: *Please, Katarina, don't mess with Marcelo! He'll leave you brokenhearted. And, Jenny, please just try to be a young girl and don't waste your energy on aping pop stars!* She knew she wouldn't say anything. If the girls made a bad decision, they would learn from it because people only learn from the mistakes they make themselves.

"Are you girls going to come downtown with me? I need to do some shopping," Irene said.

Jenny just shook her head.

Katarina said, "I'll come. I need to buy a pair of dance shoes."

"I see you're hot for that Latino guy." Jenny gave her sister a teasing look.

"*Sí, sí!*" Katarina said, laughing as she danced out of the kitchen—a salsa step judging from the swing of her hips.

Jenny rolled her eyes and sighed. "She's such a nerd." She plopped down on her chair and poured herself a cup of tea.

"Why are you up so early?" asked Irene.

"I have to study. Got a test on Tuesday. And I have to write a plan for my senior project."

"What's it on?"

"We're going to make a recording."

"A recording?" Irene echoed.

"Yep. Polo is going to record a demo, and I plan to document it on video and with photographs. I'm going to write about it as well. It'll be, like, a documentary of the entire process from when we start writing the songs until we have a finished CD for sale. Though I have to say, we've already written most of the songs."

"That's a wonderful idea!" Irene exclaimed with honest admiration.

"Well . . . we do want to do a good job," Jenny said with a smile and a wink.

For a second, Irene was reminded of the scatterbrained fifteen-year-old Jenny had once been. Irene felt the warmth in her heart spread to her entire body. Her wonderful, stubborn, risk-taking, beautiful—not to mention good-hearted—daughter! She got up and gave Jenny a big hug and a kiss on the forehead.

"You get that from me," she said.

THEY HAD A hectic morning downtown. Irene and Katarina ran in and out of the stores, taking a coffee break standing at a coffee bar before rushing on. Irene felt stressed because she didn't want to miss her jiujitsu training that afternoon. Just to be on the safe side, she'd packed her bag with her uniform in the trunk of her car. She'd been wise. One glance at her watch after they'd finished and she realized she had no time to go home.

"Don't worry, I'll take the express bus from Drottning-torget. You'll take all the shopping bags in the car, so it'll be easy enough for me."

"Are you sure you'll be fine? I mean . . ."

"Of course, I'll be fine."

Katarina got out of the car and waved happily. She disappeared into the crowd in front of the Nordstan shopping mall entrance. Irene felt guilty, but also relieved. Now she would have no trouble getting to the dojo on time, but she wouldn't have an opportunity to bring up the subject of dance and the possible new boyfriend.

Irene sighed loudly and raised the volume on the radio. "Angie" by The Rolling Stones filled the car, and she felt a bit better.

WHEN IRENE ARRIVED home, a wonderful aroma met her. Her stomach leapt with joy since she'd eaten nothing all day but a cinnamon roll with her lunchtime coffee.

Sammie came rushing up to her, wanting hugs and pets. She hadn't paid any attention to him all day, so it was right to treat him to a lot now.

"Mamma, can you take Sammie out?" Jenny called from the kitchen.

"Of course. Isn't Pappa home yet?"

"He just called and said he was going to be late. A huge group came without a reservation. So I started dinner."

"Vegan food, I assume?"

"Of course."

Irene felt her mood sink. She was starving and had been expecting a good dinner made by her in-house gourmet chef. She felt grouchy as she unhooked Sammie's leash from its hook by the hat rack and headed outside into the autumn darkness with her dog.

• • •

WHEN THEY RETURNED a half-hour later, Krister had just arrived home. First he greeted an overenthusiastic Sammie and then his wife. The kiss he gave her had the unmistakable scent of damp dog.

The wonderful aromas from the kitchen were even stronger, and, in spite of everything, Irene's mouth began to water. She had to admit that Jenny was getting good at her vegan cooking.

When they walked into the kitchen, Irene noticed that the table had been set for five. It was not unusual for one of the twins' friends to stop by and have dinner with them, but Irene hadn't been told they were expecting someone today. Before she had time to ask who was coming, the doorbell rang.

"He was alone this evening, and he thinks it's boring to make dinner, so I invited him over. He was going to be driving here to pick me up anyway," Katarina said, somewhat defensively.

Her cheeks flushed. Stars danced in her eyes. Irene felt both hungry and irritated as she went to the front door. Then she realized what her daughter had just said: *he was going to be driving.* Marcelo Alves didn't have a car. If this wasn't Marcelo, who was standing on the other side of the door? Frej? It would have to be Frej. She'd misunderstood everything. Frej also danced capoeira. Irene was not sure that things would be much better with Frej as the presumptive boyfriend, but she had no time to think about that now. She opened the door.

"Hi, there!"

The outdoor light revealed the bright colors of a huge Rasta cap. Beneath it, Felipe Medina's wide smile shone.

FELIPE PROVED HIMSELF to be a pleasant and open young man. He happily chatted away on anything and everything during dinner, which turned out to be surprisingly good. Jenny had roasted root vegetables, tomatoes, garlic and olives in the oven. She served herbed chickpeas in garlic as a side. When Irene pointed out that this meal contained quite a bit of garlic, she replied with a smile, "Flu season is starting! Garlic is the best thing to help your immune system. It helps cure colds and keeps potential disease carriers away."

There was something to what she said. Irene took a large helping of the root vegetables. To be on the safe side, Krister had added a large chunk of cheddar and some smoked ham to the table to go on the freshly baked bread. Irene and Krister shared a bottle of white wine. Neither the twins nor Felipe drank anything other than water. Felipe was going to be driving, Katarina wanted to make sure she had enough fluids before dancing, and Jenny never drank alcohol. Jenny was a pure-living person all the way down to her fingertips. She never used drugs, and she didn't smoke, either. It was reassuring for Irene. As a police officer, she knew how drugs circulated in the music scene. One thing she did worry about was that Jenny refused to take any kind of medication at all. Jenny felt that the body should handle all of its troubles on its own. Thank God she hadn't yet gotten seriously ill. Irene knew she'd have a problem with her idealism if that day came.

"Are you planning to become a professional dancer?" asked Krister.

Felipe smiled and shrugged. "I'm already a professional. I've been dancing since I was, like, three. Mostly I work freelance. I also train groups in capoeira. But I don't want to dance until my joints are trashed, like my father."

"Is he retired? Gisela Bagge said that dancers retire early," Irene added with hesitation.

"He stopped dancing fifteen years ago. Now he's an insurance salesman."

"What do you want to do when you're done dancing?" asked Krister, continuing his informal investigation. He certainly could interrogate someone gently after all these years of living with a policewoman.

"I want to be an architect, but my grades weren't high enough to get in. I'm on the waiting list—number thirty-three this fall."

"Isn't there high unemployment among architects?"

Felipe smiled and his braids rustled. "It depends on how you draw."

There was something to what he said. Katarina's expression showed she thought this was the cleverest thing she'd heard in years. Irene strangled a sigh as she realized her daughter was hopelessly in love. Still, it was much better that Felipe, and not Marcelo, was the object of her romantic dreams.

THE FIRST MONDAY morning in November was exactly as one would expect from the first Monday morning in November. Damp haze stuck to the windshield like glue, and the entire city was dripping moisture. It was just above freezing, but the Weather Service predicted a change in the afternoon. A high was coming in from the east, bringing clear skies and cold temperatures for the next few days. It would be pleasant to have a change from the dismal grey rain they'd endured during the past week.

Felipe had given Katarina two free tickets to *The Fire Dance*, and she'd asked her uncultured mother to the premiere. She didn't have to ask twice, as Irene was already curious about Sophie's saga in dance. *Always something to look forward to*, Irene thought, as she turned the wipers on high.

THE DAY STARTED with a bang: a gruesome case of assault connected to a case the papers had already started calling "The Gang Killing." The week before, the leader of the Gårdsten gang was knifed outside the Central Train Station. The victim's name was Roberto Oliviera, and he called his gang the Pumas. The suspect belonged to a rival gang, and the teenage witness who had fingered him lay unconscious with a fractured skull at Östra Hospital. The suspect, unfortunately, had a watertight alibi for the time of both the murder and the attack on the witness. Problematically, the alibi came from his relatives: his grandparents, siblings and cousins, some of whom were also members of the gang. The police would have to interrogate a huge number of witnesses; some would need interpreters, and others would not only because they absolutely refused to speak at all. The investigation took more and more time, until most of the week had gone by.

Every once in a while, Irene would call Ingrid Hagberg to try to arrange a meeting for Friday, but no one would pick up the phone. It would have to wait until the following week. Irene was too busy with the investigation of the gang murder and the intimidation of a witness.

ON WEDNESDAY, IRENE brought home three takeout pizzas for dinner. She and her daughters ate them quickly right from the carton. Jenny, of course, had ordered a vegan pizza without cheese.

Irene had counted all the different kinds of pizza while she was waiting for her order. It turned out there were 111. Imagine being as boring as Frej, ordering the same pizza week after week, though he seemed to have gone over to Kebab Extra Everything to get some variation.

"Do you want to come with us and see *The Fire Dance?*" Katarina asked her sister.

"No, I have to study English," Jenny replied.

It was easy to tell by her tone of voice that she didn't think she was missing much.

Jenny went to her room, and after a few minutes they could hear the pop music of Mando Diao floating back down the stairs. Irene looked at Katarina.

"When did Jenny start listening to that kind of music?" she asked.

"A couple months ago," Katarina replied. "I believe his name is Anders."

"Anders?"

"He's a bass player for a band. They played at that Slottsskogen festival last summer. He and Jenny have been kind of hanging out since then."

"Has she told you about him?"

"Not really, but the music . . ." Katarina nodded toward the stairs where the refrain of "Clean Town" drifted down. "Seems to be serious," she said. She smiled meaningfully.

Irene had to bite her tongue to keep from asking Katarina how *her* love life was going. Better to wait and see what developed and let her daughter come to her.

One look at the clock told them it was time to get going to the House of Dance.

Every seat was filled in the hall. The world premiere of a dance choreographed by a young woman who had recently died under mysterious circumstances certainly had the power to draw an audience, not to mention a whole gang of reporters.

A faded woven cloth in all sorts of shades of red hung in front of the stage, and the fabric moved slightly as dancers parted it to peek at the audience. The seats mostly were filled with dance students and teachers, friends and parents, as well as a number of specially invited dance professionals. Irene felt like the proverbial cat among the ermines.

To her surprise, Irene saw two firemen in complete gear climb onto the stage and disappear behind the curtain. The thought that there were now three people in the audience who knew nothing about modern dance gave her a bit of comfort.

Irene looked over the program she'd received when she entered. It was a simple sheet of paper folded in half.

WELCOME TO
THE WORLD PREMIERE OF
THE FIRE DANCE
A saga in dance by Sophie Malmborg, choreographer.
Sophie never saw her work performed.
Her tragic death has touched us deeply.
The ensemble would like to dedicate this performance to
her memory.

Music:	ERNST MALMBORG
Direction:	GISELA BAGGE
Set Design:	MARCUS ANDERSSON from the Eldsjälarna Theater
Costume Design:	IDA JÄRNBERG
Dancers:	
The King	DANIEL NILSSON
The Queen	SANDRA BRUHNSKOG
The Princess	LINA GUSTAFSSON
The Prince	TOBIAS FALK
The Guardian	ISOLDE WERNER
The Fire	MARCELO ALVES
	FELIPE MEDINA
	FREJ ERIKSSON
The Guests	EVITA MEDINA
	KAROLIN ÖSTMAN
	VIKTORIA KJELLBERG
Other Participants	
	MARKUS ANDERSSON and TINA JONASDOTTER From ELDSJÄLARNA THEATER

THE LIGHTS WENT down and the curtain parted.
The entire stage was dark. Then one musical note swept
over the audience and increased in intensity as morning

dawned behind the silhouette of a circular tower. Around this tower were three six-foot U-shaped narrow steel rods. Irene couldn't figure out what they were supposed to represent. The tower was gloomy and threatening. Slowly, full daylight came as the music changed to a line of melody that could hardly be called pleasant to the ear. Irene now understood what Max Franke meant when he described Ernst Malmborg's music. *Atonal*, as Ernst's sister had called it, rolling her eyes.

Several figures danced onto the stage. They all wore black, but it was still easy to distinguish who was who. The Queen was the first to appear. She was dressed in a wide, long dress with a golden tiara glittering on her head. The Prince and the Princess swirled in, hand in hand. Each wore a simple gold band around their foreheads. They had on tight leotards, and the princess's skirt was short and wispy. Her long, rose-dyed hair stood out against all the black costumes. Irene recognized Lina from capoeira.

The Guardian entered after them. She wore a rough cape and came to stand with bent legs in front of the dark castle tower. The Queen and the two royal children crawled across the floor in an odd dance, but Irene could tell that they were at least following the music.

Suddenly, the music stopped, and the dancers stood as if petrified on stage. One lone drum began to beat. It increased its tempo until it neared a frantic crescendo. From backstage, a dancer leapt out. This figure wore a gold crown clearly signifying the King. He moved across the stage with hunched leaps and wild but rhythmic gestures. In one hand, the King held a bottle and would take large swigs. The Queen and the children huddled in fear as the King captured the entire stage for himself. He swaggered and gesticulated for a long while.

The music calmed down, and the King began to yawn. He

lumbered over toward the tower. The Guardian let him in and then locked the door behind him, before going back to her spread-legged stance. The Prince and the Princess dared to come forward again to dance together. Irene interpreted it as some kind of game of hide and seek. At times, one of them would try to sneak into the tower, but then the Guardian would chase him or her away in a friendly but determined manner.

The audience jumped at an unexpected trumpet blast. The Queen came rushing in with a picnic basket. With the help of her children, she spread a large blanket on the ground, and then they placed bottles, dishes and food upon it. Their colorfully dressed guests arrived and began to enjoy the party, dancing and eating. They encouraged the sulking Guardian to join the festivities. Although she was hesitant at first, she took a few swigs from a bottle and was soon right in the middle of all the frolicking.

Listening so intently to the music was exhausting, and Irene wished that it would soon be over. At that moment, the music faded to one solo flute, and Irene felt her prayers were answered.

The party guests began to yawn, and one after another they lay down to sleep. The light dimmed and soon it appeared to be twilight. Only the Prince was still awake. He'd found a bottle from which he drank. On unsteady legs, he staggered toward the tower. Since the Guardian was not at her post, he had no trouble opening the door.

When the door was completely open, all the lights went off at once. Three masked men with burning torches leapt out of the tower. They whooped and yelled, and the effect was both dramatic and frightening. Pounding drums began to beat, over which a lone violin could be heard. The music resembled the music Irene had heard at the capoeira class. The three men wore ski masks with only their eyes visible.

They wore wide, black pants. Their torches were blazing on both ends, and the dancers swung them frenetically as they yelled and leaped, attacking one another with kicks. Their sweaty bare chests shone in the light of the fire, and their eyes glittered in the dark holes of their masks. Irene held her breath.

The wild music abruptly ended, and although slower music began, the effect was even more threatening. The men slowly walked to the U-shaped steel rods, where two more black figures had appeared. The capoeira dancers held their torches to the rods simultaneously, and fire burst out as if the tower truly were on fire. The five dancers began to dance, partnered with the flames, their forms casting black shadows against the bright fire in the background.

A shriek was heard. The King appeared at the top of the tower. He fought helplessly against the flames and then fell back into the tower.

The fire went out just as quickly as it had come. The stage was now silent and dark.

The audience didn't stir.

The lone flute began to play as dawn returned. The party guests began to awaken. They stretched and started to get to their feet. It took some time before the Guardian realized what had happened. She began to run in despair around the tower, and soon the other guests searched with her. The Guardian found the Prince, sleeping peacefully, still clutching his bottle. Resolutely, she pulled him to his feet. She hid him beneath the Queen's wide dress, and then the Guardian hung her large cape over the Queen as well. Their trick seemed to work, as none of the other guests noticed how the Prince was brought away.

A few moments later, the two women returned with the Prince between them.

The guests brought out colorful shawls and hung them

around the royal family members. Everyone danced, their shawls swirling. The atmosphere was almost ecstatic.

One by one, the dancers left the stage until only the Princess remained. Lina then danced a solo. Her rose hair and her multicolored shawl whirled over the stage. She radiated enormous strength and energy. Although Irene had never been to a ballet performance before, even she could see that Lina was a brilliant dancer.

The light went out again. The three capoeira dancers ran in with lit torches and went down on their knees in the middle of the stage. Lina was in front of them with her arms over her head and her leg high to the side. She appeared as a silhouette against the fire. The dancers were motionless as the music died away. Behind the capoeira dancers, the two black figures came and put the fires out. The stage was plunged into darkness.

For a few moments, the audience was breathless. Then the applause broke out. Everyone was clapping, whistling and stamping their feet. The stage lights came on, and the dancers bowed. They had to bow again and again, as the applause seemed unending.

"That was absolutely magnificent!" exclaimed Katarina. She was clapping enthusiastically while gazing at the stage in rapture.

The house lights came up to the audience's standing ovation.

Irene happened to glance at the exit and saw Angelika leaving. For a moment Angelika turned back, and Irene could see her face. It had drained of color, and she looked like she would faint at any moment. She fumbled with the door before finally pushing it open and rushing out.

KATARINA STAYED FOR the party after the performance, but Irene hadn't been invited and had no intention of going.

She drove home in the November darkness. It was good that the traffic was light, because she had difficulty concentrating on her driving.

She was still lost in the performance. It had been as far from a lacy, traditional ballet as it could get. Obviously the fire in Björkil had been the inspiration behind the story. Even if the main characters and the place were not identical, the basic chain of events in real life was the same. Angelika was the Queen, and Sophie and Frej were the royal children. That much was obvious. The fire was the one that had killed Magnus Eriksson. The Guardian and the party guests were add-ons that Sophie had created for color and contrast.

Nevertheless, there were elements of the story that Irene found noteworthy. The Queen and the children were in black *before* the fire. Only after the King was dead were they dressed in colorful clothes. Even if Irene wasn't an expert in interpreting dance, she could see that the family, shown as unhappy before the fire, became happier afterward, when Magnus Eriksson was dead. But was that true?

Sophie had certainly seemed happier afterward. She had been able to move in with her father and seemed to have been content with that arrangement.

Angelika had griped about money after her husband's death, but even before, she'd had financial problems. As Irene went over it in her mind, she remembered that Angelika had been mostly concerned about the lack of insurance. She had been freed from her drunken and gambling husband. Still, she didn't have to wait for his death to be free. She simply could have asked for a divorce.

Frej had lost his father. How had the relationship been between father and son? Irene realized that she had no idea. Angelika had said once that Frej had had emotional difficulties after his father's death, and so it had been a good idea for Sophie to move to Ernst's.

Irene contemplated Angelika's reaction after the performance. It would have been understandable if she'd been moved to tears watching her dead daughter's work performed. Still, Angelika hadn't acted the part of a bereaved mother. Her eyes had been wide with fear; there was no grief in them. Her fingers had been stiff from terror, as she'd grappled with the door handle. She'd looked like she'd just seen a ghost.

At Thursday's morning prayer, Irene brought up the issue of the probe into Sophie's murder. The superintendent wrinkled his forehead and said sternly, "We have a number of ongoing investigations right now. We have to work on the murder of Roberto Oliviera immediately. We've got the suspect in jail, and we don't have much time to break his alibi."

"Good luck with that," Jonny muttered.

"What the hell do you mean?" Andersson growled.

"I mean that this Milan guy is one tough devil. We couldn't lock him up for the knifing last summer. And this ridiculous alibi—a family party with over thirty people in attendance—yeah, try and break that one." Jonny's grin was more a grimace.

Andersson glared darkly at him, but it didn't help. Jonny was right. It was tough to prove Milan hadn't been at the family party. Any witnesses to what had really gone down that night wouldn't spill to the police. Most people have a good sense of self-preservation.

"We still have to try. The more time passes, the easier it will be for that son of a bitch to get away with it," the superintendent said glumly.

"But we have him on the Central Station security cameras the night of the murder," Birgitta protested.

"Sure, but he never denied that he and his gang were at

the train station. We don't have any pictures with Milan and the murder victim in the same shot. We can't even prove that they ran into each other that night," Fredrik Stridh said.

"Milan states that at eleven thirty he went straight from Central Station to the party. The murder happened a half-hour later. Milan was with his thirty witnesses by then," Tommy added.

"His whole damned family! Right! They're all having dinner after midnight . . . their religious festival . . . Ramada . . . what is it called?" Jonny asked.

"Ramadan," Tommy said.

"The assault took place right outside the victim's residence. No witnesses," Birgitta said.

"One and a half weeks after the murder. Five days since the assault. The trail is starting to get cold. We're going to put everyone on it today and tomorrow. Except for you, Irene. You have until next week to solve the Sophie murder. Do you have any idea where you're going to go from here?"

Irene thought about it, then said, "We haven't talked to Ingrid Hagberg. I think that's past due."

"All right, go talk to the old lady. The rest of us are going to be busy with this damn foreign gang and all their relatives."

The superintendent got up to demonstrate that it was time to get to work. Irene watched him go. Would he call Felipe a "damn foreigner"? Probably. Neither Marcelo nor Felipe were very dark-skinned, but they were definitely darker than the average Swede. Irene had no illusions. They were foreigners, and their children would be foreigners even if they were born in Sweden. Because of the color of their skin, they would always be seen as foreigners.

IRENE STILL DIDN'T get an answer when she called Ingrid Hagberg. She decided to drive out to the assisted living facility in Torslanda. According to the phone book, the place was called Happy River Assisted Living. Judging by the address, it was not far from the abandoned airfield.

The identical six-story yellow brick buildings looked brand new. The surrounding area was still mostly countryside, but there was a great deal of construction activity. The politicians had rezoned the area and planned a new center with shops, apartment buildings and social services. The area around Göteborg was expanding quickly, and Torslanda was attractive with its access to the ocean.

Irene parked in a visitor's spot. She could see small rose bushes huddling in the flowerbeds. They would need a few more years to really come into their own. Narrow sticks that would be trees were planted here and there, held upright by props thicker than their skinny trunks. The entire area had a cold, abandoned look in the November fog. The sound of the foghorns near the sea made a somber chorus.

Irene had a bag of treats she'd bought at the bakery on the way. She buttoned up her jacket to protect against the chill before she got out of the car.

Ingrid Hagberg lived in building 4C. The entrance was on the other side of the building from the parking lot, and it was was locked. All visitors had to use the entrance telephone. Irene found Ingrid's name on the sign and pressed the button. It took a few minutes and a number of tries before a weak voice came through the speaker.

"Is that you, Frej?"

The shaky voice of an old lady was hard to peg to the image of the strong woman Irene had met fifteen years earlier. After everything Ingrid had gone through, it was not so strange that her voice had changed.

"It's Irene Huss here. I'm a police officer. Do you remember me? We've met before," Irene said, using her most warm, trust-inspiring voice.

"You are? I see."

There was a buzzing sound from the door, and Irene pushed it open. The entrance lobby was inviting. Along one of the walls was a large window with open curtains and numerous plants on the windowsill. In front of the window was a small vinyl sofa. *How thoughtful to have somewhere for the old folks to sit while waiting for a ride*, Irene thought.

She entered the elevator and pressed the button. The elevator began to rise slowly and then came to a gentle stop. Irene jumped in surprise as a man's voice said, "Fourth floor. Fourth floor."

When her heart stopped pounding, Irene realized that the elevator had been fitted with a mechanical voice to help those who had trouble seeing. *They ought to warn you about stuff like that*, Irene thought. *Maybe with a sign or something.*

She had no time to think about this further, as a door across the hall cracked open.

"Are you the policewoman?" a shaky voice asked through the gap.

"Yes, I am, Mrs. Hagberg. I'm Detective Inspector Irene Huss."

"So many police officers have talked to me. I don't want to talk anymore. There's no point. He's never going to jail."

"Who's never going to jail?" Irene asked, confused, while noticing that the door was starting to close.

"That drunk who crashed into me."

Irene thought as fast as she could. Apparently Ingrid Hagberg assumed Irene's visit was about the accident last summer, when she'd been hit by a driver under the influence. "This is not about the accident. I'm here to talk about Magnus and Frej."

There was no sound of the metal lock being turned in place. Instead, Ingrid pushed the door back open.

"Well, come in, then," she said.

Irene stepped inside.

She knew that Ingrid would have changed, but she was still shocked by how much. The thin, bent woman clutching a walker hadn't the slightest resemblance to the hefty farmwoman who'd invited her for coffee fifteen years earlier. The only thing that hadn't changed was her large hands, although they had grown thinner and more claw-like. Perhaps her hair would have been just as thick, but it was hard to imagine now, as it had all been cut short. Two large scars from an operation ran across her skull. The only hint of her former heft was the loose flaps of skin hanging from her throat and arms. Her weight loss must have happened very fast. Even her short-sleeve zippered tunic was much too large for her, as were her black pants, which hung like sacks around her legs. Long traces of oatmeal ran down her tunic and onto her pants.

Clumsily, Ingrid turned around and, with the help of her walker, began to limp away from the door and into a large living room/kitchen combination. The furniture was brand new and pleasant. The only item that seemed to have traveled from the farm was a huge fir sideboard. The drop leaf was down and was crowded with photographs and knick-knacks. Irene could spy a bed through another open door. In spite of the fact that the place was clean, the smell of urine hung in the air.

"Sit down," Ingrid said, and pointed with a trembling finger at the kitchen table.

Irene chose the chair without the upholstered booster pillow.

Ingrid swayed back and forth as she slowly lowered herself onto the corduroy-covered booster. She exhaled loudly.

"So what do you want to know about Magnus? He's dead," Ingrid said gruffly.

"I know. I talked with you shortly after he died. Do you

remember? You were kind enough to offer me coffee and freshly baked cinnamon rolls . . ."

"You were poking around where you had no business. Snooping," Ingrid grumbled.

"I was part of the investigation of the fire. We didn't know what caused it . . ."

"My brother died."

To Irene's distress, tears began to roll down Ingrid's cheeks. In order to distract her, Irene said, "Should I turn on the coffee pot? I brought something to go with coffee."

She put the bag of bakery items on the table and began to rustle the paper. Ingrid stopped crying immediately.

"The coffeemaker is on the counter. Filters and coffee are in the cupboard above it. The coffee cups are right there next to them." Ingrid spoke clearly without a trace of tremor in her voice.

Irene got up and went to the kitchen counter. She filled the coffeemaker and, just to be on the safe side, added a little extra coffee. She wanted the old lady to be as energetic as possible. She discreetly washed the coffee cups and dried them before setting them on the table. It appeared Ingrid hadn't bothered washing them before putting them back on the shelf.

"You don't happen to have any sugar, do you?" asked Ingrid hopefully.

"No."

"I just thought . . . you see, I've run out of it. But I have some of this artificial stuff here on the table. It'll have to do."

"Would you like milk in your coffee?" Irene asked.

"No," Ingrid said.

Ingrid's bad mood had lifted with the prospect of coffee and something sweet to go with it. *She's just like a child getting a bag of candy,* Irene thought. *Not much to look forward to in a place like this, even if it is fresh and clean.*

Just to say something, Irene began, "The apartments here are really laid out well. Everything seems so nice and well-maintained. They even have flowers on the windowsill and a little sofa—"

"All the flowers are from residents who've died. And the vinyl is just in case someone pees on the sofa. It's disgusting," Ingrid said.

An unhappy tone had crept back into her voice, and Irene wondered how to get her back into a good mood. With nothing better to say, Irene asked, "Do you have a plate I can set these on?"

"Top shelf in the same cupboard as the coffee cups," Ingrid replied promptly.

Irene pulled down a rose-colored, pressed-glass plate and arranged the chocolate cookies, raspberry muffins and cream puffs on it. She'd bought three of each, so that Ingrid could have some left for her evening coffee.

"The coffee's ready," Irene said.

She poured it into the mugs. Ingrid took some artificial sugar from a plastic holder and shook it into her coffee. Irene handed her the plate of cookies, and Ingrid grabbed a cream puff. Her eyes were shining as she chewed it.

Irene was glad that she'd thought to bring some sweets with her. "Does Frej often come to visit you?" she began.

"Sometimes."

"I understand you were close. I remember he was wearing a light blue sweater the day I met him. He told me you'd knitted it for him and that he really liked it."

Ingrid paused in her chewing and nodded. "The flat-knit one. Gave it to him for Christmas."

Ingrid pushed in the last bite of the cream puff. She began to eye the plate again greedily. A large drop of vanilla cream had landed on her sweater, but Irene held her tongue for now. Perhaps she'd say something when she was ready to go.

"Have you been in touch with Angelika or Sophie since the fire fifteen years ago?" Irene asked.

"No, why would I be?"

"Well, Angelika was Frej's mother and . . ."

"I've always hated that monkey. And that girl was the one who set fire to my cottage. I'm sure of it!"

Ingrid was so upset that she drew her hand back from the plate without taking anything.

As calmly as she could, Irene said encouragingly, "So you say Sophie set fire to the cottage on purpose. Are you absolutely sure about this?"

"Yes, I am!"

"How do you know? Did Sophie tell you anything?"

"No, but it was her!"

A stubborn look crept across the old woman's face. Irene felt that she should change the subject, but she also knew she had to get as much information as possible about the fire in Björkil. She let her thoughts tumble about in her mind as she drank her coffee and ate her cream puff. Meanwhile, Ingrid had recovered enough to take a raspberry muffin. She bit into it with obvious pleasure, thrusting her tongue into the jelly. She smacked her lips contentedly as she pulled back her tongue into her mouth.

Irene decided to go for it. She stood up and asked, "Would you like some more coffee?"

"Yes." Ingrid was busy eating the rest of the muffin. As Irene came to the table with the coffee pot, Ingrid already had another cream puff in her hand. Irene poured the refill. When she sat back down at the table, she asked in as neutral a tone as she could, "Why did Frej sleep so long that afternoon?"

Ingrid stopped in the middle of chewing. "Frej? Which afternoon? He never napped."

Ingrid's grouchy voice was back.

"The afternoon Magnus died. You said you couldn't get to the fire right away because Frej was napping after dinner. He slept for three hours. You arrived on the scene at a quarter to nine in the evening. Why did he sleep for so long?"

"Kids sleep. He was tired. Now I want you to leave."

She said this quite clearly. She stood up unsteadily and reached for her walker.

"Go right now!"

Ingrid's entire body shook, and she glared at Irene.

"There's the door," she snapped, pointing determinedly with a trembling finger.

Irene realized there was nothing she could do but obey. She left the sweets on the table, and as she reached the door, she smiled at Ingrid and said, "I can stop by next week if that's a better time. And I can bring something good to go with the coffee."

At first it seemed that Ingrid had not heard her, but just as Irene was going to give up and shut the door behind her, she heard Ingrid say, "In that case, I want more raspberry muffins!"

As Irene was about to turn onto the road, a white Fiat swung into the parking lot so quickly Irene had to hit the brakes to avoid it. The driver of the other car didn't even bother to look at her, and sped into the handicapped spot closest to the entrance, tires squealing. As the driver hopped out, Irene was surprised to see Angelika.

What is she doing here? According to Ingrid, they never got together, but perhaps it was just as Frej said: the elevator didn't stop at the top floor. Sometimes Ingrid sounded lucid. Other times, she was like a grouchy five-year-old. *Or is she just playing at being confused when it fits her purposes? Hard to tell.*

Irene decided to wait until Angelika came out again. She drove to a side street and parked behind a garbage truck so that her car would not easily be seen. From there, she could keep her eye on the exit from the parking lot.

Just a few minutes later, Angelika came back outside. She was hurrying, and her shoulders were hunched. She opened her car door and jumped inside. She backed out of the parking spot and without pausing, hurtled onto the road. Irene followed, keeping a few car lengths between her and Angelika.

Thanks to the hilly roads, it was not difficult to keep an eye on Angelika's car. They drove past the convenience store and to Ingrid's driveway. The Fiat's turn signal indicated it was going to make a left turn, and Irene passed it on the right.

Angelika was going to the place where Magnus Eriksson was buried. *Why?* There was nothing there but an empty lot.

Irene turned around in a school parking lot and headed back to the driveway. She turned in and drove her Volvo down the gravel road, now covered in weeds. The rain of the past few weeks made the road soft and muddy. The Fiat must have had some difficulty maneuvering over it.

Irene pulled in next to Angelika's white car. It was so covered with mud it almost appeared camouflaged. Angelika was standing with her back to Irene. The withered tufts of grass reached to her knees. She did not move, and her hands were deep in her pockets as if she were freezing. From a distance, she looked like a lost little girl.

Irene got out of the car and inhaled the scent of wet earth and rotting plants.

"Why are you spying on me?" asked Angelika. Her voice was sharp and hostile. Perhaps she thought it would mask the fact that she'd been crying.

"I'm not spying on you. I was in the parking lot by Happy River when I saw you racing past like a car thief. I needed to talk to you anyway, so I followed you," Irene said.

"You must have been spying on me. How else would you have found me here?" Angelika asked suspiciously.

Irene decided to tell it like it was. Ingrid would certainly mention that she'd been visited by a policewoman named Irene Huss who'd offered her coffee treats.

"I had gone to see Ingrid to talk about what happened here." Irene gestured to indicate the whole empty lot.

When she glanced back at Angelika, she had a shock. Angelika looked positively terrified. Her dark brown eyes looked unnaturally small in her tiny face, which had lost all color. She sank down onto the ground, still staring at Irene and saying nothing. Her resemblance to Sophie was uncanny.

Irene wasn't sure how to proceed. In order to break the silence, she asked, "Were you able to reach Ingrid?"

Angelika shook her head. She swallowed a few times before she rasped out, "No. She did not want to see me."

"Did you speak over the house telephone?"

"Yes."

"Ingrid said that she'd had no contact with you since the fire. Is that true?"

Angelika nodded and looked away.

"Why did you suddenly want to see her, then?"

Irene's question came out more sharply than she'd intended, and it had the same effect as cracking a whip. Angelika jerked and gave Irene a quick, fearful glance. Then she looked away at the grass covering the empty lot. She said nothing for a long time. Finally, she replied.

"Two days from now it will be exactly fifteen years since Magnus died. He is buried here at Björlanda Cemetery. I was wondering if Ingrid wanted to come with me to visit the grave. Bring some flowers. Something. I don't have time on Saturday, so it had to be today. But she didn't even want to speak to me. We . . . we never did get along, exactly. I thought I'd try to mend our relationship now that she's old and sick."

She looked up at Irene with clear eyes and an open smile like a little girl who wanted to be believed. Irene might have gone along with her story if it weren't for the act, but now she knew Angelika was lying. This was not the place to pressure her, but Irene made a mental note for the future.

"Couldn't you have phoned ahead?" Irene asked innocently.

"No use in that. I've called her before, you know, just to see if Frej was there, but she always slams down the receiver."

"Why are you and Ingrid on such bad terms?"

Angelika gave a short, raspy laugh. "She's hated me from the first minute she saw me. It's nothing personal. She would have hated any woman who got too close to her beloved little brother. He was her surrogate child. And now she's moved her affection to Frej. Thank God he has a strong personality and can resist her. Magnus was too weak to handle her."

She stopped talking and Irene could see the emotion drain from her eyes.

"Do you still miss him?" Irene asked impulsively.

Irene realized she'd asked the question before thinking how to phrase it. A long silence hung in the air until Angelika finally responded.

"It was such a long time ago. So much water under the bridge since then. And now all this with Sophie . . . it's hard. But he was Frej's pappa, and we were married for almost nine years. I can still feel the empty space he left behind. I felt so alone then, so . . . abandoned."

Irene took a few more steps toward the huddled figure before she asked her next question. "What exactly happened fifteen years ago?"

Tears streamed down Angelika's face. "No one really knows. Perhaps Sophie . . . but I don't think even she knew for sure. Sophie was incapable of lying. She may not have spoken about something . . . deliberately . . . but she never lied. She told me the truth when she said that she didn't know Magnus was sleeping in the bedroom when she came home that afternoon. The house was not on fire when she rode off on her bike. She said she didn't smell any smoke."

"So what do you believe happened?"

"I'm convinced that Magnus fell asleep smoking. He had a habit of smoking in bed . . . especially when he'd been drinking."

She said this last bit in a defiant tone. During previous questioning, she'd always denied that he'd had a drinking problem. Irene nodded as if she understood and left it at that.

"Why do you think Frej slept so long that afternoon at Ingrid's house?" she asked in her most neutral tone.

Angelika stiffened. "What did she say when you talked to her?"

"She wasn't clear . . ."

Angelika seemed to relax. The tense look in her face softened, and she even smiled slightly. She dried her tears with a tissue from one of her pockets and blew her nose. Then she cleared her throat before she answered.

"She always babied Frej. He had a cold that day, and he was tired. So she put him to bed and let him sleep. She didn't know that you're not supposed to let an eight-year-old sleep for so long."

"Still, she saw all those fire trucks and the ambulance and the police cars. She'd even called in the alarm herself. It wasn't exactly a normal afternoon."

"No, it wasn't, but Ingrid was a strange bird. I don't believe she thought things through. Nowadays she's really cuckoo. At least, that's what Frej told me. You can't trust anything she says."

Irene could tell Angelika was fishing for something.

Angelika gave her a hasty glance. *Why is she so nervous about something Ingrid might have said?*

Angelika got to her feet and brushed at the dampness on her pants. "Now I really need to get going. I have to teach all afternoon. It's great that your daughter has started capoeira. You have to be in fantastic shape to be able to do it, and Frej says she is."

Before Irene could think up another question, Angelika swept past her. Without a backward glance, she got in her Fiat and drove off. Irene watched her rear lights disappear behind a cascade of water kicked up by her tires.

IRENE WOULD NEED a search warrant. Otherwise it would not be possible to get into the basement of the Änggården mansion. It would also be a good idea to check into Frej's darkroom. Not that she suspected Frej could hold his sister captive in that room without Marcelo noticing. She just wanted to take a closer look at what Frej was up to.

Did she really suspect Frej of killing his sister? Irene thought long and hard. He had no direct benefit if his sister was out of the picture. The reverse was true. Now his mother inherited the house, and she was making Frej's life much more difficult than when he'd lived with Sophie. Frej seemed to be an open and uncomplicated kind of guy. He had many friends and a number of interests. Frej had no motive for killing his sister, or, to be more accurate, his half-sister. In fact, it seemed that they'd had a good relationship over the years. Extremely close, in fact, considering that they'd been raised in separate households.

Marcelo had even less of a motive. He'd be kicked out of an apartment that he felt comfortable in. There was no sexual motive, either, and it appeared that he and Sophie had been good friends, even if Sophie's nightly appearances in his bedroom indicated she had hoped for something more.

Was there anything more? Sophie appeared to have been an unusually asexual young woman. Where did she fit in on the sexual spectrum? Did she have a place? Irene's experience told her that everyone has something that turns them on, but in all of Sophie's twenty-six years, there was no indication that she'd ever been in love or in a relationship with either a man or a woman. Nor were there any indications of any other, more unusual, tendencies. All she had was dance: her life and her passion. It seemed that dance had replaced all human relationships in Sophie's life. Perhaps that was indeed the case. It was through dance that Sophie could reach others even though it seemed she'd never gotten close to anyone, with the possible exception of her teacher Gisela Bagge. Gisela had called herself "something of a mentor" for Sophie, and she and Angelika had been dancing together when Angelika met Ernst Malmborg. Later on, Gisela had seen Sophie's talent as well as the strained relationship between mother and daughter. She'd also said that she'd been Sophie's closest friend.

Still, even to Gisela, Sophie had been a mystery. According to the psychologist at Child Protective Services, she'd had a genetic personality disorder that made it impossible for her to form attachments to other people. This made the entire speculation go in circles: Was there ever a person Sophie felt close to at all?

The only one Irene could think of was Ernst Malmborg. Still, could their relationship be described as "deep"? Perhaps they just got along because they were so similar. It didn't mean that they were close—just that they'd let themselves be at peace in each other's company.

Angelika had an economic interest in Sophie's death, but no other motives. Why would she keep Sophie hidden for three weeks? If she'd had a hiding place, where would it have been? And how could she have dragged her daughter to the

shed and then set it on fire? It didn't seem plausible. Angelika was a greedy liar, but it was hard to imagine her killing
a family member in cold blood.

If Sophie had not been hidden in the mansion basement, where should she search? The answer was defeatist:
anywhere at all. The killer might not be anyone in Sophie's
circle. Considering the abuse Sophie had suffered as well as
the fact that she'd been drugged, it was more than likely
that the killer was outside that circle. The only hope for
the investigation was that there was a clue somewhere: a
person, a contact, a coincidence, perhaps a secret relationship. There had to be a lead to the killer. She would just
have to find it. Perhaps she'd already run into it without
knowing it. Right now, she felt as if she were searching in the
dark.

The truth was they had nothing concrete to go on. For
the first time, Irene wondered if it was a drawback to have
been on the arson investigation all those years ago. Perhaps
the old, unsolved case was preventing her from seeing this
one clearly. She would just have to keep going forward one
step at a time. Perhaps that would drive the killer out of his
hiding place.

Irene sighed. Her speculations were not bringing her any
further. She decided to convince Superintendent Andersson
to ask the prosecutor for a search warrant for the Änggården
mansion. It was the only thing she could think of right now.

WHEN IRENE WALKED into the conference room for the Friday morning prayer, she realized there was an unusual tension in the room. Everyone's eyes turned to her, and Andersson glared at her darkly.

"You're late!" he barked.

"There was an accident in the Gnistäng Tunnel . . ." Irene started to explain.

"And you've been reported for attempted murder!" the superintendent cut her off.

Irene's mouth fell open as she tried to make sense of his statement. All that came out was a "Whaa . . . ?"

"The nurse at Ingrid Hagberg's assisted living facility phoned us, absolutely furious. She'd already called Frej and accused him of bringing sweets to her, but he denied it. Then they called his mother and she knew that you'd been there. So they put two and two together, and it came out you tried to off the old lady!"

"What? How? What . . . what do they mean?" Irene stammered.

"Ingrid Hagberg has a severe case of diabetes. After you filled her up with sugar, she wound up in a diabetic coma and is in intensive care right now!"

Ingrid's greedy look at the bakery bag. The way she'd shoveled the cream puffs into her mouth. How her hands shook just like a dry alcoholic who'd gotten a free bottle of the hard stuff. Irene replayed the scene in her mind and cursed her own idiocy.

"Oh, good Lord, give me strength!" she moaned.

"You could certainly use it," Andersson replied drily.

"She didn't tell me she had diabetes," Irene tried to defend herself.

"No, after her brain damage, she is apparently unable to recognize her own illness. The nurse says that they regularly search her apartment to make sure there are no sugary things in it. Everyone who visits has firm orders not to bring anything with sugar." Andersson took a deep breath as his fingers drummed the table. "Let me remind everyone here that this unit does not ever—and I mean *ever*—take anything sweet to anyone we want to interrogate!"

Irene kept her mouth shut. Of course, the sweets had been a bribe to get Ingrid in the mood to talk. Still, Irene had thought it would be nice for an old lady to have treats with her coffee even though she had to admit that she'd had an ulterior motive. She'd never considered that Ingrid could have diabetes. Irene felt absolutely awful.

"I'm going to take you off the Sophie case for a while. You've gotten nowhere with it anyway. We'll take it from the top next week."

The superintendent gave Irene a harsh look before he stretched to his full height and looked over his entire team.

"And now for the good news. It appears that the investigation of the so-called Gang Murder has gotten somewhere."

The superintendent's expression brightened as he turned toward Birgitta, who stood up. The large screen on the wall blinked on to reveal an enlargement of a photograph obviously taken at night.

"These photographs came in a padded envelope in the mail last night. Anonymously. However, we have found a fingerprint on the inside flap of the envelope. I'll get back to that in a minute."

Birgitta turned to look at the picture on the screen. The resolution was sharp, so it was easy to tell who and what was in it.

The photograph seemed to have been taken on a slant with a telephoto lens. In the background were two shimmering white taxis and a sign indicating it was taken in front of the Nils Ericson bus terminal at the Central Train Station. In the foreground, a large man was pressing a relatively thin young man against a brick wall. His left hand was around the young man's throat. Both were wearing black leather jackets and baggy jeans. The large man had his hood up, but his victim's face was easily visible. Without a doubt, it was gang leader Roberto Oliviera. He looked as if he were trying to defend himself by kicking his assailant.

Birgitta clicked to the next picture. It was an enlargement of the previous photo. In his right hand, the larger man was holding a stiletto knife. Both his hand and the knife were bloody. Roberto had sustained five knife wounds, including in the liver and one severing an artery. He was dead when the ambulance arrived ten minutes after the call went in.

The last photograph showed the suspect straight on. The top of his hoodie was still up, but his face could clearly be seen. It was Milan. No doubt about it. He still held the bloody stiletto knife. In his other hand, he had a white plastic bag. Apparently, he'd folded the knife and dropped it into the bag just seconds after this photo was taken. Perhaps he'd wrapped the bag around his hand earlier so that his clothes wouldn't be covered with blood.

In the background, his victim was sinking to the ground. The date and time for the murder of Roberto Oliviera were stamped on the bottom left-hand corner of the photo.

"Milan's fried," Jonny said contentedly.

"Yeah, we got him all right, but the most interesting thing is who was behind getting him there," Birgitta said calmly. She shifted back to the first picture. "Our technicians have gone over these and determined that they weren't Photoshopped. Just to be on the safe side, we're going to send them to England and have their experts make absolutely sure. These photos are consistent with what we thought happened. Roberto left his five companions to go to the bathroom. He had to search to find an empty stall, so he went over to the Nils Ericsson Terminal. His friends were still hanging around the Pocket Shop in the Central Station, talking to some girls. When Roberto came out to rejoin his friends, he ran into Milan. Perhaps Milan had been shadowing him. There are no witnesses to the murder itself—at least, not any who have come forward. The only one who talked to us, Victor Fernandez, is now in the hospital after being assaulted. He was part of Roberto's gang, and he was the first one to find his boss. He stated that he'd seen Milan running away from the scene. Milan had turned around, and Victor recognized him. According to Victor, Milan was jumping into a black car on the other end of the parking lot. Unfortunately, no witnesses saw the car, either."

"Now Victor can't testify. He has come out of his coma, but he can't remember the past few years at all. The doctors don't think he will ever regain his memory," Tommy informed them.

"Without the photos, we'd never have had any evidence against Milan. But now we do," Birgitta said.

"So, spit it out, woman! Who sent them?" Jonny exclaimed impatiently.

Birgitta smiled at him spitefully and said, "The thumbprint is clear and has shown the sender of the envelope to be . . ." She let her glittering brown eyes sweep across the room to make sure everyone was paying attention before she dropped the bomb: "Glenn 'Hoffa' Strömberg."

The room was so quiet they could have heard a pin drop. Everyone except Andersson and Hannu had the same expression: complete surprise.

"Impossible! That devil had been sent up the river permanently!" Jonny said.

"That was years ago. They've let him out."

Irene felt a shiver all the way to the marrow of her bones. This was not going to be one of her better days. First this business with the diabetic coma and now Glenn "Hoffa" Strömberg reappearing like an evil jack-in-the-box. She had done everything in her power to drive the fat vice president of the Hell's Angels from her memory, which had been difficult right after she'd confronted him. The past few years, things had gotten better. Sometimes she would still dream of the assault and the humiliation she and her young colleague, Jimmy Ohlsson, had suffered during the incident. Jimmy had been permanently injured by kicks to the vertebrae of his spine. Irene's physical injuries had healed, but the mental scars were still there.

"Why did Hoffa send these pictures to us?" Jonny began excitedly. "And how the hell did he get them in the first place? How did he or one of his MC bandits just happen to be in the area with a camera the moment Milan attacked Roberto? It seems . . ."

"Drugs," Hannu said quietly.

"Drugs?" Jonny repeated, as if he'd never run across narcotics before.

"Of course. Hell's Angels have been running drugs throughout Western Sweden. Milan is supported by gangs from the Balkans and Poland who work with the Banditos. According to the Narcotics Division, the Hell's Angels are angry that the Eastern Mafia is dumping cheaper drugs into the market and grabbing a larger share."

"What the hell . . . Hell's Angels and the Eastern Mafia . . . Why would Milan kill little Roberto if the battle is on that level? He was just a little fish," Jonny protested.

"That's right," Hannu said. "A little fish who didn't know his place. Milan was boastful and was attracting attention to himself. Twenty years old and feeling like he's king of the hill. Sold drugs in an area he thought was his. Milan wanted to set an example and make sure the other small kings got the message that the Eastern Mafia was nothing to mess with. So Roberto was killed."

"Okay, but that means that we are now back to square one. Why was a Hell's Angels member photographing Roberto's murder?" Jonny asked stubbornly.

"They wanted to get rid of Milan. Perhaps they were just following him to kill him later. But then they had a better idea when they managed to get a picture of Milan at just the right moment. It's much easier to have us send him up the river than to get involved themselves."

"Milan fell into his own trap," the superintendent said contentedly.

"With just a little help from our friends, the Hell's Angels," Birgitta added.

Her comment resulted in a sour look from her boss, but he didn't say anything. Instead, he clapped his hands energetically and said, "All of you know what to do next. Let's conclude this investigation."

Everyone in the room started to get up from their

chairs, but Andersson looked directly at Irene. When she caught his eye, he said, "Irene, you stay here. I need to have a little chat with you."

Jonny turned in the doorway and said in a stage whisper, "Someone's gonna get a spanking!"

With a sneer, he walked out.

"One of these days I'm going to wring that bastard's neck," Irene hissed so quietly that only Tommy could hear her.

He nodded thoughtfully. "Yep. All we need is a place to bury the body."

IRENE SPENT FRIDAY afternoon writing a report about her fateful coffee klatch with Ingrid Hagberg. When she was finished, she had to write reports about her meetings with the women in Milan's family. It would be late before she could go home for the evening. A few days earlier, she'd promised her mother that she would take her to the cemetery to put lights on her father's grave. "You can at least visit your pappa one day a year. At the very least on All Saints' Day," her mother, Gerd, had said. Irene realized that she would not be able to make it. After a great deal of calling around, she finally reached Krister, who promised to bring his mother-in-law to the cemetery before lunch. He was going to work the evening shift, and then he had the rest of the weekend off.

Irene had spent the entire previous day phoning people. Angelika was not all that upset, but seemed distracted as she listened to Irene's apology about what had happened at Ingrid's apartment. Frej, on the other hand, ranted about "the fascist police" and was actually pretty nasty about it. On the other hand, compared to the nurse at the assisted living facility, he was fairly easygoing. The nurse was quite clear about her opinion.

Irene also had little to say when she was alone with her boss. It did not seem to be the right time to mention the visit fifteen years before at Ingrid's home. She simply reiterated

that she'd just hoped to make the afternoon a bit more
pleasant for an old lady by having an old-fashioned coffee
date. Andersson snorted and told her very clearly just what
he thought about her idea.

After that, to Irene's relief, he'd changed the subject to
the gang murder. He decided that she and Birgitta would go
interview Milan's female relatives who had attended the
Ramadan party the night of the murder. Hannu and Jonny
would go interview the male relatives. Meanwhile, Fredrik
Stridh was assigned to a new case, which had come in the
day before. It was high priority since it dealt with an
underage boy of about eight or ten and his sports trainer. The
newspapers had already gotten wind of the story and had run
a headline in large letters: PEDO TRAINER! Irene could
not help but wonder if the headline writers actually double-
checked what they wrote. It certainly had an unfortunate
double meaning.

On Friday morning, then, Birgitta and Irene were joined
by a female interpreter, and they all headed to an apartment
building in the district of Hammarkullen.

Milan's relatives were all Bosnian Muslims. He had
moved to Sweden with his mother and four siblings during
the war that followed the breakup of Yugoslavia. The father
of the family had disappeared during the war. The family
arrived with two of the mother's brothers and their families.
The uncles had started a greengrocery, which became successful as the years went by. As far as the police could
determine, they were honest, hardworking small busi-
nessmen. Unfortunately, they were probably going to be
charged with perjury and had already been informed of the
possibility. Both uncles had blanched behind their rather
large mustaches, but neither of them changed their testimony. None of the women did, either.

Milan had been twelve when he arrived at his new

homeland. His classmates were afraid of him because he was strong and aggressive. He was "respected" right away. According to his teachers, he was intelligent, but not a scholar. During his last year of formal schooling, he rarely showed up in class.

He'd started with petty theft and vandalism. Before too long, he and his friends became true gangsters and began to bring in some real money for the first time in their lives. Milan was clever and could think quickly, a plus in his line of work. He took to his new profession like a fish to water. Now he had money, excitement and respect.

For the past few years, he'd been one of the major players in the Göteborg narcotics scene. He rose quickly in the ranks, especially after he'd made good contacts during a stint in prison. He'd served eight years for assault and battery, and behind bars, he met Slobodon Polanski. They were both let out at about the same time, and their business association took off. In fact, they were much too successful in the eyes of their rivals, the Hell's Angels, whose dominance in the narcotics market was threatened. The Angels must have decided it was high time they did something about it.

Hannu's theory was that the Hell's Angels had started to monitor Milan's movements, and it was only by chance that their man had found himself at the station at midnight when Roberto was killed. Since there were no witnesses or pictures from the station cameras, they'd decided to take things into their own hands. Perhaps it was Hoffa himself who sent in the photos when, reading the media reports, he realized that Milan was going to be released for lack of evidence.

Glenn "Hoffa" Strömberg seemed to have disappeared in a puff of smoke. No one knew where he was. Rumor had it that he'd been seen near the Karlstad clubhouse, but the undermanned Värmland police force had not been able to confirm the rumors. On the other hand, it was not illegal to give the police a tip about a murder, so they weren't exactly searching for him all that hard. As Birgitta pointed out, it was probably the first time Hoffa had ever cooperated with the police voluntarily.

It was just about nine in the evening when Irene left the police station. Jenny had reassured Irene that she would be home to take care of Sammie. She had to study. It was amazing how her daughter had suddenly decided to strive for good grades. How her other daughter was doing in school was much less certain now. At breakfast she'd mentioned something about "going to a party" with Felipe. Irene had no idea where this party was supposed to be taking place since she hadn't listened closely.

Irene couldn't drive her usual route home, since it was closed. The big tunnel-building project had been causing traffic and chaos in Göteborg for the past few years. The routes changed from one day to the next. Somehow, she missed her turnoff and found herself on Göteborg's main drag, Avenyn. She noticed lanterns by all the entrances to the pubs and restaurants. Many people had carved pumpkins with grinning faces that smiled at pedestrians, lit up from the candles burning inside them. The dreary November dampness drove folks into the warm, cozy pubs. It was the evening before the Day of the Dead, and many restaurants had signs declaring a Halloween party in English. Numerous pedestrians wore costumes, monster masks or witches' dresses, although the dresses might just be part of a teenager's normal Goth wardrobe. It looked to Irene like Morticia Adams was their favorite fashion designer.

In Sweden, All Saints' Day was celebrated on the first Saturday of November. This year the date fell on the same day as King Gustav Adolf's Day, which is especially celebrated in Göteborg, since Gustav Adolf was seen as the founder of the city. A special pastry was baked that day, and a torchlight parade was part of the celebrations.

It was also fifteen years since the day of the fire in Björkil.

The evening suddenly seemed particularly grim to Irene. She longed for home. She turned onto Sprängkullsgatan and drove past Skanstorget. She would have to take Dag Hammerskjöldsleden to western Göteborg this evening.

As she neared the exit for Änggården, she was hit by an impulse. She had not yet had the chance to ask her boss to request a search warrant. It could take until the end of next week to get one, if she was going to be unusually unlucky. Without following her train of thought to its conclusion, she turned onto Storängsgatan and made her way down the side streets until she reached Sophie's house.

THERE WERE CARS lining the streets all around, and she had to circle until she found a parking spot a few blocks away. Before she got out of her car, she took her flashlight from the glove compartment and stuffed it into the inner pocket of her jacket.

As she started to walk toward the house, she could hear loud, pounding music. As she got closer, she heard voices shouting over the music. She was surprised to see bicycles of all kinds against the stone wall.

The gates were wide open. Irene stood in the shadow of the garage to assess the situation.

Whatever she had been expecting was nothing like what greeted her. The whole house was filled with light, and there were candles leading up to the front door. The loud music and the sound of laughter and conversation streamed out of all the open windows.

There was a party going on at Sophie's house.

Irene shivered, and not just because of the damp weather. She felt deep inside that Sophie's memory was being dishonored on All Saints' Day. The poor girl had not even been buried yet and people were celebrating in her home.

Irene shook off the sentimental feeling. Perhaps she could make use of this situation to get into the basement. It seemed like the perfect opportunity.

She buttoned up her jacket and began to walk across the slippery flagstones. She could see a crowd of people right up to the front door. Most of them were dressed up in Halloween costumes: vampires and witches. As she entered the house, she looked around and smiled happily as if she were sending a greeting to the other end of the hallway. Only a few of the young women gave her uninterested glances. Then they moved as one toward the kitchen.

Irene saw her chance and took it. She held her hands behind her and surreptitiously pressed down the door handle to the basement. She walked backwards through the doorway and then carefully closed the door behind her. She held her breath and listened to the darkness. After a few seconds, she dared to breathe again, and she turned on her flashlight.

She tried to move as quietly as possible, but she also didn't want to get her clothes too dirty. The sound of music and laughter was diminished down here, but she could hear the floors creaking overhead. The basement was filthy.

She began to search methodically. Although she had no idea what she was hoping to find, she hoped there might be a clue to Sophie's death. Perhaps all she really wanted to do was make sure that Sophie had not been kept in the basement.

There was one large room crammed with old furniture and tons of cardboard boxes. A strong stench of rat turds hung in the air. Generations of spiders had woven webs over the furniture. It looked like the set of a horror film.

The laundry room had been abandoned for decades. The machines were hardly modern, and the smell of mold came from their plumbing. Next to the laundry room was a door unlike the others. It was carved from boards of fir. Elegant handwriting on a sign proclaimed SAUNA. There was one more door with a sign that read W.C. Irene opened it but shut it again immediately. The stench was unbearable. Instead, she pushed open the door to the sauna and stepped inside.

From the light of her flashlight, she could see it was a good size. There were grey tiles on the floor and white tiles on all the walls. There was a shower at one end. The sauna itself was made of wood and had a small door in the middle as well as a tiny glass window. Irene walked up to the window and shone the beam of her flashlight through.

She almost screamed aloud. On one end of the sauna bench was a pile of clothes that appeared to be a human body. Her heartbeat sped up until blood started to pound in her ears. She stood still for a minute, her hand on the door handle, and took a few deep breaths to calm herself before she pushed the door open.

The aroma was indescribable. It was mixed with the smell of unwashed body and dirty clothing. From the bundle at the end of the bench came loud snoring.

Irene stepped quietly up to the sleeping human being. She saw that matted grey hair covered the face in a full beard. The man was on his back, and his hands were resting over his stomach. He looked fat, but that could be all the layers he was wearing under his down jacket. He'd used some garden furniture pillows to make his bed more comfortable.

Irene recognized a homeless person when she saw one. For the past decade, they'd gotten more numerous. Well, here was a homeless man living in Sophie's basement. Perhaps he'd done the same thing she had, and sneaked in after the party started. Irene decided to talk to the man.

She aimed her flashlight at the ceiling so that she

wouldn't blind him as she gently shook one of his shoulders. It was a while before he began to mumble and shift around, and even longer before he opened his eyes.

"Who the hell are you?" he asked angrily.

His breath filled the small sauna, and Irene tried to breathe through her mouth.

"My name's Irene. It's all right if you want to sleep here," she said calmly.

"Is it? Then get the hell away. Go on, get out!"

He turned over on his side as if he were going to go back to sleep. Irene shook him again and said, "I have to ask you a few questions. If you can't answer them, I'll tell the owners of the house that you're down here."

He blinked at her with red, swollen eyes and croaked, "Do you have to?"

"Yes, but if you answer my questions, I'll stay mum." She was friendly but firm.

He sighed heavily and rustled as he sat up. He coughed so that something loosened deep in his bronchial tubes. He cleared his throat and spit a huge wad of gunk onto the floor. It landed close to Irene's shoes. She pretended to ignore it.

"What's your name?"

"Hasse."

"More than Hasse?"

"It's just Hasse."

His voice had an aggressive undertone, so Irene decided to skip the business about a last name and go on.

"Have you been sleeping here for a while?"

"Sometimes."

"How often? Every night or just once or twice a week?"

"What the hell business is it of yours?"

"You promised you'd answer my questions or I'd tell the owners about you."

His red eyes glared at her for a while. Finally, he nodded

and grumbled something that Irene didn't catch, and that was probably a good thing. She asked her question again, and Hasse sullenly replied, "Couple times a week. When it's really cold."

"How long have you been doing it?"

He stared at her, then coughed out, "Doing what?"

"Sleeping here in this basement?"

"Couple years. Last winter. Otherwise I'd have frozen to death."

Irene looked more closely at him and realized he was not as old as she'd thought at first. His grey hair had made her think that he was well over fifty, but he was not much beyond forty. His hands were covered with black and blue bruises. He had a pair of old Graninge boots and he'd stuffed the bottoms of his blue jeans into them. At least his feet were protected. His down jacket was torn and much too large, but it was certainly warm. He had several shirts on underneath. They were all kinds of colors and material. The basement was certainly not a warm and dry place. He'd needed extra layers to keep from freezing.

"How do you get into this basement?"

"Door at the back. Never locked."

He seemed content with this arrangement.

"Have you been here often the past two months?"

"Sure, really often, because it's been raining all the time. Shitty weather!"

Irene calmly asked her follow-up question, the most important one of all. She could feel her heart rate increase in expectation. "Did you notice anything unusual the past few months?"

He was starting to shake his matted, hairy head, but stopped himself. "Yeah. The girl is gone."

"Which girl?" Irene asked, although she knew the answer.

"The girl who danced. I'd often hide in the garden and

watch her. She danced in a weird way, but . . ." He stopped for a moment to release a loud burp. ". . . really good." He didn't bother to excuse himself.

"Did you ever see her down here in the basement?"

"Nah, she never came down here. Nobody ever does. Lucky for me!" He laughed out loud and revealed teeth that would make all the dentists in Göteborg weep. He interrupted his laugh to look at her skeptically. "Nobody ever comes down here, but here *you* are. Who the hell *are* you?"

"A friend. If you say nothing about me, I'll say nothing about you. Well, good night. Sleep tight," she said, and turned to go. As she was about to press down on the door handle, Hasse asked, "Is there a party going on? That girl has never had a party before . . ."

Irene stepped quietly out of the sauna and then out of the room. As the door closed behind her, she remembered that Hasse had mentioned an unlocked door. She headed toward the back side of the house and easily found the unlocked door. It was heavy and hard to push open. The hinges groaned when she pushed, but there was no risk that anyone could hear it. The party was going full blast.

Fresh air was a relief, and Irene took several deep breaths to cleanse herself of the bad air from the sauna. The encounter with Hasse had cleared up one important question: Sophie had never been kept prisoner in her own basement. With that theory eliminated, the question remained—where had she been those three weeks?

Irene stood still for a moment and listened to the revelry in the house. It was incomprehensible that Angelika could be having a party so soon after the death of her daughter. And tomorrow would be the fifteenth anniversary since the death of her husband as well. *I wonder how Frej is dealing with all this*, Irene thought, feeling some sympathy toward him.

Irene had to admit that she would never be able to

understand a woman like Angelika. She hadn't fifteen years ago after the fire, and she certainly didn't understand her now. She began to walk slowly around the house. It was not difficult to see her way since light flowed from each and every window and illuminated the garden behind the house. She took only a few steps before she heard the sound of running feet and hushed giggles. She drew back into the shadow behind a large bush and stood completely still.

A couple came running past, hand in hand. The woman let herself be pushed against the outside wall, panting, and they kissed hot and eagerly. Their breath hovered above them like a cloud of smoke. The woman wore a knit sweater against the cold, but he had on just a short-sleeved T-shirt. He lifted her shiny black skirt and pulled down her panties. She eagerly kicked them away, unbuttoning his jeans. She cupped his enlarged penis and led it between her thighs. Then she curled one of her legs around his hip. He was panting hard and quickly. Their excited moans were covered by the loud music.

The woman was Angelika.

The man was Marcelo Alves.

He lifted her up by her ass and she wrapped her other leg around his other hip. She hid her mouth in his hair, and he burrowed his face between her breasts. They were in that pose for some time. Slowly, Angelika's feet returned to the ground, and she let her dress drop back into place. Marcelo buttoned his pants. They kissed once more, and then they headed in different directions. Angelika walked past Irene's hiding place, but her focus was straight ahead and a smile curled her lips.

Irene felt like a voyeur, but she also realized this was another complication to the case. *Would this information lead to something in the murder investigation?* Sophie had shown interest in Marcelo and had even attempted to seduce him.

Was this a murder fed by passion? This couldn't be about jealousy on Sophie's part—then Sophie would have murdered her mother, not the other way around. *How long have Marcelo and Angelika been hooking up? She's just about to move in with the wealthy and much older Staffan Östberg!*

Irene made another attempt to head around the house. She'd almost gotten to the gate, but just as she was about to make her escape, she heard a voice behind her exclaim: "Mamma! What are you doing here?"

Katarina's voice. Irene's heart sped up yet again. She was able to put a smile on her face before she finished turning around.

"So there you are! I didn't see you, so I thought you weren't here!" Irene said. She saw Felipe and nodded a greeting with a wide smile.

"Were you looking for me?" asked Katarina.

"Yes, but I didn't want to go in. I'm not invited, after all. I looked in the windows and doors, but I didn't see you . . . there's a real crowd in there."

"Why did you want me?"

"I have to borrow your house key. I left mine at home."

"But Jenny was supposed to be home tonight . . ."

"I know, but I was working late. It was already nine thirty when I left the station. We're just finishing up on the murder of that guy two weeks ago, the one at the Central Station, and in the car I saw I had my car keys but not my house keys. I called Jenny's cell phone, but she didn't answer, and neither did your pappa. He must be busy at the restaurant this evening. Then I remembered you said something about a party . . . and I thought maybe I'd be able to run into you, if I was lucky."

Katarina gave her a long look, but said nothing. Irene had the feeling that her daughter had seen through her lie, but didn't want to say anything in front of Felipe. Even if Irene could lie—she liked to call them white lies—as part of her job, she'd never lied to one of her family members. And she didn't feel good about lying now, either, but necessity knows no law. She couldn't tell her daughter that she'd been in the basement without a search warrant.

Katarina opened her purse and began to rummage around. While she was looking for the house keys, a figure came along the sidewalk toward them. Irene recognized Frej at once. He stopped to greet them. Although he was standing beneath a streetlight, Irene couldn't read the expression on his face because the brim of his hat put his face into shadow. He asked the natural question: "What are you doing here?"

Irene repeated the story about the forgotten keys, and it seemed as if Frej believed her. He nodded toward the house and did not even try to hide his bitterness. "She's fucking crazy."

He did not have to say her name. He continued in a falsetto: "I always have a party on Halloween. This year I'll do it in honor of Sophie! She received such wonderful reviews for her *Fire Dance*."

The expert imitation of his mother was uncanny. Irene had no doubt that she'd said exactly those words. They looked back at the house for a while in silence. Then Frej cleared his throat and said to Felipe, "Could you come inside with me? I'd feel better than going in by myself."

"Sure." Felipe smiled at his friend.

They turned to say goodbye to Irene. Felipe laid his arm over Katarina's shoulder, and they followed Frej. They walked into the house and were sucked into the whirling mass of celebrating party guests.

Irene stood on the sidewalk not knowing what to do. After a moment, she decided to go back into the house herself. She had a good reason. Katarina had actually forgotten to give her the keys.

Irene took off her jacket and draped it over her arm as she passed through the door. She almost ran into an older couple on their way out. The woman looked surly, and the man was unsteady on his feet. Both Irene and the woman said "excuse me" at the same time and smiled at each other. The man leaned toward Irene and stage-whispered, "Don't go in there! It's full of hippies!"

His breath had the same smell as Hasse's. He was wearing an elegant black suit and a white shirt. His red silk tie was held in place by a gold tie clasp. Irene guessed he was about sixty, and the woman was the same age. She was well-dressed in a black velvet suit jacket over a red top and a black skirt. The colors suited her silver hair, which was in a long page cut. Diamonds glittered on her fingers whenever she gestured.

"We don't really know anyone here . . . just my brother Staffan, of course. And my other brother Kenneth, but he's already gone . . ."

Irene smiled at Staffan Östberg's obviously upset older sister. "I've actually met Staffan once."

"Are you a friend of . . . her . . . Angelika?"

"Nooo, I wouldn't say that. Our children hang out together," Irene replied.

"Yes, well . . . we hadn't met Angelika before, or any of her friends . . . but now we really have to get going. Pelle is tired."

Judging by the fact that he was leaning against the doorpost with his eyes closed, she was probably right. With a determined look on her attractively made-up face, the short woman took one of her husband's arms and helped him down the stairs. He began to speak loudly.

"Can you believe they were openly smoking hash in the living room? I really ought to call the police! I wonder how Staffan found himself among people like these?"

His wife shushed him and pulled him toward the gate. They had trouble keeping their balance on the still-slippery flagstones.

Irene turned back to the house, but she couldn't see either Katarina or the two boys. For a second, she was tempted to turn around and go straight home, but her curiosity got the better of her yet again. She headed into the hallway and began to look around discreetly.

First she looked into Sophie's room. A cluster of young people was inside, looking at Sophie's dance notations on the wall. Irene recognized Lina's pink braids, but she had difficulty placing the others. She could tell by their analytical comments that they were all dancers. She gently backed out of the room.

The smell of hash, which Staffan's brother-in-law had protested about, wafted from the living room. Irene followed it and tried to sidle in without being seen. But she awkwardly bumped into a middle-aged woman coming out. The woman's black upsweep had come loose, and a clump of hair hung over one of her ears as if it were a Jamaican hat set askew. All her eye shadow had smeared beneath her eyes in black and blue lines. It didn't look like she'd intended to wear Halloween makeup, but it certainly looked like she was now. Her heavy breasts were generously exposed in the deep décolletage on a silver-embroidered black kaftan. She was holding a joint between her fingers. She turned her runny red eyes toward Irene and said, "Don't bother going in here. All the guys are over thirty." She pressed a lilac-painted fingernail onto Irene's collarbone and, confiding in a low, intimate tone, she said, "I like 'em young and fresh. My last one was just twenty-two . . ." She laughed hoarsely and winked conspiratorially at Irene, before an entirely different expression crossed her face. She muttered, "Gotta find the bathroom . . ." as she swept away, her kaftan billowing around her corpulent body.

Obviously, she shared her preference with Angelika. Irene spied Angelika herself sitting on a sofa, chatting with two men much younger than she was. One of them was Marcelo, but Irene did not recognize the other one. They sat on either side of Angelika and looked like they were enjoying themselves. Everyone else in the living room seemed to be having fun, too, except for Staffan Östberg, who was in a recliner by the fireplace. He was sipping red wine from a cocktail glass, but his stiff smile seemed plastered on. For some reason, he was wearing a pair of dark blue suit trousers, a white shirt and, instead of the customary jacket, a blue embroidered vest. A young woman with red hair had fallen asleep with her head in his lap. Every once in a while, he stroked her hair as if she were a cat or twirled a lock of it and let it slip through his fingers. His eyes were staring at a painting on the other side of the room.

Irene moved closer and confirmed her suspicions. The Volvo CEO was completely stoned. Once he finished his red wine, he'd probably be unaware of what went on around him for hours. Angelika would have plenty of time for more fun before the night was through.

Irene slipped back out of the living room. It seemed as if Angelika hadn't even noticed she'd been there.

In the dining room, a dance party was in full swing. The furniture had been pushed aside, and the rugs had been rolled up. There was a stereo on the large table. Robbie Williams's song "Radio" was going full blast. Vampires and witches were packed tightly together on the dance floor. No one noticed Irene. She might as well have been invisible.

She decided to climb the stairs to the second floor. She tried the door to Ernst's music room, but it was locked. So was the room with the grand piano. For some reason she couldn't put her finger on, Irene was relieved. She didn't think it had to do with preserving a sacred space if the partygoers had gotten access to the rooms, but rather preventing destruction.

Irene pushed open the door to the guest room, but heard a noise that made her quickly shut it again. The bed was occupied.

Guitar music and singing came from Marcelo's room. Someone was singing "In the Ghetto" in a way that would make Elvis roll over in his grave.

She found herself in the deserted hallway of the upper floor. As quietly as she could, she went to the door hiding the stairway to Frej's attic apartment.

She knocked on the door. When no one answered after three times, she tried the door. It was locked. She looked in the tiny bathroom. It was empty. The remaining door was the one to Frej's darkroom. She knocked loudly, and there was no response. To her surprise, she found the door slid open when she tried it. She hesitated on the threshold, and then decided to go in. She quietly closed the door behind her.

On the wall over a workbench, a light bulb cast a dim, reddish glow. Irene turned on her flashlight and let the beam play over the room. The brighter light revealed a rather large but Spartan space. There were a number of bowls and tubs on the counter below the red light. She could see some photographs hung on a line to dry. There was a huge black curtain he could draw shut if he wanted to block out all the light from the window. In front of the huge gaveled window was a large table, and above it, a long strip of fluorescent light. Probably Frej needed that when he wanted to inspect his photographs more carefully. A computer desk complete with a Mac was along one of the walls. There was also a color printer and a scanner. But Irene's attention was caught by the photographs set up along the other long wall.

Fires. In all the photographs, fires were burning. These

were not small, controlled bonfires, as found on Walpurgis Night, but huge flames—true fires, and at least three of them were coming from houses.

She heard a sound behind her back and instinctively threw herself forward. The kick went over her head.

If she hadn't moved, she would have been knocked unconscious. Perhaps even killed.

He must have been hidden behind the drapes, the thought shot through her mind as she dropped lightning fast to the floor and thrust her upper leg into her opponent's stomach while swinging her lower leg behind the leg he was balancing on. With all her power, she knocked his leg out from under him. He fell, and she scrambled up to get some distance between them. She could see his eyes glare with anger, and he was already coming up back to his feet.

"Frej! Cut it out! You're messing with a police officer!" she said as sharply as she could.

He seemed not to hear, but was getting ready for another attack.

Then the door opened.

"Mamma! What are you doing?"

Neither Irene nor Frej broke their gaze, but Katarina's voice stopped Frej cold.

"What am *I* doing! Why don't you ask Frej what *he's* doing?" Irene said as indignantly as she could.

"What *I'm* doing!" Frej was so angry his voice broke. "You've got to be kidding me. You're snooping around in my house!"

Irene decided to change tactics. She smiled as if she were asking forgiveness. She said in her most friendly manner, "I really didn't mean to snoop, as you put it. I was looking for Katarina. She forgot to give me a key. I thought she might have gone up here. But it must have been you I saw going up the stairs."

"You came in here! Into my darkroom!"

"Well, the door was open. Since the door to your apartment was locked, I thought she must have gone in here. And, just by the by, you ought to think twice before you use a capoeira kick. You could kill someone with that force," Irene said in a mild reproach.

"You had a flashlight, and you were sneaking around in here, like, I don't know, like a thief! How was I supposed to know who you were?" Frej glared at her with fury.

"I couldn't find the light switch," Irene said simply. She turned toward her daughter. "Please, Katarina, please just give me the key so I can go home. I've really had a terrible day."

Without saying a word or even looking at her, Katarina took the house key from her key ring and handed it to Irene.

"I'll hang it back on the inside door of the garbage room," Irene said as she tried to catch her daughter's eye.

"Sure," Katarina said without emotion. She took Felipe's arm and practically pushed him out of the room.

Irene turned back to Frej. "I'm sorry things have come to this. But as a matter of fact, I *am* investigating the death of your sister. You have to accept that part of my job is snooping around, as you put it."

"Like it's part of your job to put diabetics into comas? Is it part of your job to enter a house where there's a private party? Is it? Is it?"

"No, that was . . . unfortunate." Irene swallowed, uncomfortable with the turn the conversation was taking. To change the subject, she nodded toward the photographs. "So, you like fires?"

Frej stared at her with hostility. It seemed he didn't intend to answer, but then he surprised her by turning to look at his photographs and saying, after a moment, "No, that was Sophie. She wanted inspiration for her *Fire Dance*."

"Where did you take them?"

"Here and there. Walpurgis Night. Some real fires." He shrugged as if he weren't interested in where they were taken.

"How did you locate the real fires?"

"Followed fire trucks and stuff."

"You must have put in lots of time for it. Most often when fire trucks are called out, it's for false alarms," Irene said, thinking out loud.

Frej shrugged again without saying anything else.

"Well, it's time I should be going home," Irene said and headed for the door.

"I certainly think so, too," Frej said sarcastically behind her back.

I can really understand his indignation, Irene thought as she walked down the stairs. She had forced herself into his domain uninvited and "snooped." Strange. That was the same word his aunt had used.

On the ground floor, the party was still going strong. Irene pushed her way through the crowd toward the front door. As she passed the kitchen, she was brought to a stop when she heard a rough voice she recognized.

"I don't have a single damned painting left," he was saying. "I sold each and every one at my last exhibition . . . Do you have any more wine?"

Her mouth dropped open when she saw Hasse from the sauna enthroned in majesty at the kitchen table. He had a heaping plate of roast beef and mashed potatoes in front of him. He stretched his empty glass toward a witch in white face paint, who pressed the spout of the boxed wine to his glass and said, "Oh, yes, there's a little left." As she handed him the filled glass, she asked, "Where was your exhibition?"

"What? What exhibition?" Hasse's mouth was full of potatoes, and he concentrated completely on his glass of wine.

"The one you had last summer. When you sold all your paintings." The witch was patient.

No one saw Irene as she sneaked out the door and into the November night.

"YOU LIED!" KATARINA accused Irene.

Katarina looked furious. The two of them were the only ones sitting at the breakfast table. Krister was out walking Sammie in the morning's clear weather. Jenny had not yet dragged herself out of bed.

"What do you mean by that?" Irene replied, feeling uncomfortable.

"How did you know I was going to be at that party?"

"You mentioned going to a party . . ." Irene said evasively.

"No, I did not. I said that Felipe said maybe we'd go to a party. Yesterday morning I had no idea where this party would be. He didn't tell me until he came to pick me up yesterday evening!"

"I see . . ." Irene did not know what to say.

"And Jenny was home all evening. She was working on a song they're going to record today. She was still up when I got home."

"Maybe she was out with Sammie when I called," Irene tried.

Katarina's glare darkened, and she jumped up from her chair. "What are you really up to? Are you looking for a reason to send Frej to jail? He's a really great guy!" A tone almost of hatred came into her voice.

Irene sighed and decided to lay her cards on the table. At least most of them. "All right, here's what's really going on.

My colleagues and I are trying to find out who murdered Frej's sister. It was a particularly gruesome killing! She was kept prisoner, abused and eventually burned alive. Naturally, our investigation must include the family of a murder victim, and in this case that means Frej and Angelika. I admit I used that bit about the key as a cover. But I did find out some things of vital importance to the case, and I will need to follow up on them."

"What kinds of things?" Katarina was not placated.

"I . . . I . . . can't tell you because of the investigation."

"Oh God! The investigation! You always have to be super cop! You can never relax and be just like any other human being! Good God. How embarrassing it must be to sneak into a party just to spy on a suspect!" Katarina was so upset that she started to choke on her own voice. Her cheeks glowed bright red.

"Please believe me when I tell you that going to the Änggården mansion that night was very productive," Irene defended herself lamely.

At least that was true. Katarina gave her a last, mistrustful look and then walked out.

Yes, indeed, her uninvited visit to the mansion had been very productive. Now she needed to find out how long Angelika and Marcelo had been in a relationship. Secondly, she had to really inspect all those photographs of fires. There had been a fire at Björkil fifteen years ago, and there were now a number of fires involved in this investigation as well. Also, the same people were involved. Was there someone else in the periphery she'd missed?

Irene poured her fifth cup of coffee for the morning and stayed at the breakfast table deep in thought. She could hear thumping drums from upstairs, which meant that Jenny was awake. Jenny turned on her CD player the minute her eyes opened. Irene would never be able to do that. She was much too tired in the morning even to choose a song, and her fuzzy brain would never let her find the button. It was odd how the buttons on these machines kept getting smaller as the years went by. The text above them was even more microscopic. Krister had already gotten reading glasses. Maybe it was time she looked into it—except that she didn't want to need reading glasses. They were for old people. Still, she wished this trend toward tiny print would stop.

Irene sighed aloud. She would just have to make an appointment with the optician. But that would have to wait. She had too much work at the moment.

MONDAY WENT BY in a blur. Everyone was busy with all the ongoing cases. Irene had no chance to discuss the first stage of Sophie's murder investigation with the superintendent. She was happy that she'd impulsively gone to the Halloween party. It had spared her a great deal of work, and she'd gotten important information. Thanks to Hasse, she now knew that Sophie had never been held captive in the basement.

ON TUESDAY MORNING, Irene went right to Svante Malm at the lab. She found him wearing magnifying glasses and concentrating on a heap of glass splinters that were in a plastic bowl with a low rim. He was using a long tweezers to push the glass around.

"Hello, Svante," Irene said to get his attention.

He startled and looked up at Irene through his odd glasses. He yanked them off in irritation, but he smiled as soon as he saw who had come in.

"So great you've stopped by! You must have a sixth sense about when it's time to contact me! Now I don't have to try and reach you by phone."

He stood up and beckoned her to follow him. They

walked into the room next door. Svante began to search through the small, red plastic boxes standing on one of the shelves.

"Here! Look at these! They're real silver. I've cleaned them up." He set the open box on the bench in front of Irene.

The ornate pattern on the clasps reminded Irene of something . . . *What was Sophie wearing when she died?*

"Three of them are hooks and three are eyes, so there were three clasps on the piece of clothing in question," Svante said.

Irene nodded and took a good, long look at the silver clasps before she turned to the technician and asked him the question she'd actually come for. "Did you have a chance to look at the three photographs I sent you?"

"The ones with the fires?"

"Yes." Irene had brought the photos she'd taken from Marcelo's room right to Svante.

"Jens was the one who inspected them. I think he's in right now. Let's go."

They walked down the hallway to the last room. Svante tapped a pattern with his fingertips on the door and then opened it before anyone on the other side had a chance to react.

Jens was new; Irene had not yet met him. His shoulder-length black hair reminded Irene of a Beatles haircut, but his baggy jeans and T-shirt put him in the hip-hop trend of the day. He seemed to be very young for the job, but these days all the new employees seemed young. When Irene had brought her mother for an X-ray, she'd thought that the doctor in the X-ray department was fresh from graduation. Another sign that she was getting older.

Jens began to search through his computer files.

"Here we have the fires." He clicked on three pictures.

Then he clicked a few times on the first picture so it enlarged and filled the whole screen. "Check this shine," he said and pointed with a pen.

In the background was a metal reflection unnoticeable on the smaller image. Jens clicked a few more times, and the area around it enlarged to show the silhouette of a man wearing a helmet and loose pants and jacket.

"A fireman," Jens said.

"So this photo was taken at a real fire and not a Walpurgis Night bonfire," Irene said.

"Obviously," Jens said.

"Can you print a copy for me?" asked Irene.

"Certainly," Jens replied. "You probably want the others as well. I'll take care of it."

The screen blinked, and they were back at the original three photographs. Jens clicked on the second picture.

At first, all Irene could see were the flames of a raging inferno. Again, Jens pointed with his pen toward the screen.

"Check this space between the flames. Do you see what's there? Look closely and you will see a corner."

He enlarged the area of the corner, and Irene could tell what it was.

"That's a window frame. This is a house fire."

"Exactly," Jens said.

Jens brought up the third picture. Irene could see the fuzzy silhouette of a human head in the foreground while she looked. There was a huge fire behind it.

"On the enlargement, you can see that it's a girl's face. I've worked on it a bit and this is the result," Jens said.

The screen shimmered for a second and then it was possible to see individual features.

The girl had her face half in profile toward the camera. The smile on her lips was easy to see. Beyond a doubt Sophie was the girl in the picture.

Irene studied the picture for a long time. Although the face was half in shadow, the expression in Sophie's eyes could be easily made out. She wasn't concerned or troubled. Her eyes showed absolute joy and something else. Life force? Then Irene realized what it was: desire. For the first time, Irene saw a visible emotion in Sophie's expression, and she had no trouble interpreting it. Sophie was not hiding her feelings. She was showing her brother, the photographer, the face of a woman who felt deep inner release and lustful joy.

"God give me strength. I believe she's a pyromaniac!" Irene exclaimed.

"Why do you think that?" asked Svante.

"Look at her expression. Especially the eyes. I dealt with Sophie fifteen years ago and she was a master at keeping other people in the dark. She had a stone face that revealed nothing—absolutely nothing! But in this picture, she's almost ecstatic in her happiness."

"That could be. She does look happy," Svante agreed as he took another look.

"As a matter of fact, there were a number of fires out at Björkil before the one that killed Magnus Eriksson. Sophie was eleven years old at the time. She could have been the pyromaniac in Björlund. And there were a number of fires around Änggården this past summer."

Jens had been sitting quietly while he looked at Sophie's face. "One thing bothers me," he said thoughtfully. "She's not the one taking the photographs."

"No, that's her brother. He told us he took them. She gave him the job of photographing fires, which were supposed to serve as inspiration for a dance she was working on," Irene replied.

"Isn't it odd, though? If the girl was a pyromaniac and liked to set fire to houses and the like, isn't it strange that her brother just hung around taking pictures? Or what?"

"Absolutely. You have a point. I don't have an answer yet."

But I'm going to find one, Irene thought. *Frej has some explaining to do.*

JUST AS SHE had done previously, Irene left a message at the office at the School of Photography. When Frej called her back, he did not hide his irritation.

"What do you want now?" he asked brusquely.

"I must talk to you again. It would be good if we could meet at your darkroom."

"Why?"

"Because it's about the photos. Plus there's more we need to discuss."

"What's the big deal about the photos?"

Was she imagining it, or did Frej's voice sound nervous?

"They're very interesting. And they were important to Sophie. You were the one who took them, right?"

"Of course, but . . . she was the one who demanded I do it." Now there was a trace of whining in his voice. He sounded like a little boy who did not want to fess up to what he'd done wrong, but tried to blame someone else.

"Do you have a cell phone I can reach you on?"

"No, I lost mine."

"How can a young man of today get by without a cell phone?"

"I haven't had time . . . I haven't had enough money . . ." he mumbled.

"So, when can I see you this afternoon?" Irene asked without giving him a chance to find an excuse.

"After five," he said petulantly.

"All right then, I'll be there after five."

He didn't hear her last words as he'd already hung up the phone.

• • •

THE NEXT PERSON Irene sought was Angelika. She answered on her home phone and she, too, was not enthusiastic.

"I don't have time today. I work until eight P.M.," she said.

"But that means you don't start until after lunch. I can be there in half an hour," Irene determined.

"But . . . I have to go shopping . . ." Angelika protested.

"You can go shopping later. This concerns the murder of your daughter." Irene settled the matter with that. She knew she was turning the screws, but there was nothing Angelika could say against that argument.

Irene headed into Sven Andersson's office after her conversation with Angelika. Andersson was at his desk yelling into the telephone. When he slammed down the receiver, he complained half to himself. "Damn bureaucrats. They just don't get it! Must have inherited their jobs."

The deep red of his face forbade bringing up any sensitive matter, but Irene decided to make the attempt anyway. She smiled at her boss and said, "Do you have time for a cup of coffee?"

"Well . . ." The idea seemed to please him, and his anger began to dissipate as he thought about it. "That's not a bad idea at all."

"I'll go get you one," Irene said, and hurried back into the hallway.

When she returned a few minutes later, his face had faded to its normal tone. Irene set a steaming cup before him and the other in front of the visitor's chair, which she took.

"So what's happening on your end?" Andersson asked after he'd taken a few sips.

Irene took a deep breath before she decided to plunge in. "It's the Sophie murder. I've found a lot of new information."

"What kind?" the superintendent asked, displeased. He had given direct orders to put the gang murder first, and he wanted to finish up the work to hand it over to the prosecutor.

"Actually, quite a bit. The technicians examined the photographs Frej had taken at several large fires and were able to find Sophie in one of them. In it, Sophie was not the closed, emotionless person you and I knew. She was a sunny, smiling girl. I believe she was a pyromaniac."

"A . . . what? A pyromaniac? So she set fire to that cottage after all? The one where that . . . what was that idiot's name . . . ?"

"Magnus Eriksson, her stepfather, yes. It's possible that she was behind it after all. I will see Frej this afternoon at his darkroom in the Änggården mansion. Before then, I've arranged to meet Angelika Malmborg-Eriksson half an hour from now. More like twenty minutes."

"Why?"

"Because I want to find out what she might know about her daughter's possible pyromania. Also, I need to question her about her relationship to Marcelo Alves."

"That black guy who dances? Who might have been sleeping with Sophie? Was he sleeping with the mother, too?"

The superintendent raised an eyebrow, appearing a little more interested. Irene swallowed her discomfort and replied, "Yes, that appears to be the case."

"That is all f—" Andersson stopped in the middle of a sentence. He looked toward the door. Someone had just knocked.

Fredrik Stridh poked his head in and said, "Hi, there. Hannu asked me to inform you that another man has been knifed. He belonged to Milan's gang. They found him in a shopping mall staircase. He's been badly injured, but he's not dead. At least, not yet. It looks like a gang war is breaking out."

Before Irene or the superintendent had a chance to reply, Fredrik's blond tousled hair was withdrawn and the door closed.

For Irene, this was the worst possible news. Everyone would be put on the gang war investigation . . . Andersson interrupted her thoughts.

"All right. You have today to work on these new leads in the Sophie case. Tomorrow I want you working whole-heartedly on the Milan-Roberto gang case."

Irene leapt up from the chair, gave a Girl Scout salute and said, "I do promise—"

"Oh, just get out of here!" Andersson interrupted her, as he lifted his coffee mug to slurp the last of it. The coffee was still hot enough to burn his tongue. He began to mumble something nasty, sticking out his tongue to cool it. Irene decided to leave quickly. She stopped for a second at the doorway to ask, "Would you like me to get you a glass of cold water?"

"Get out!"

ANGELIKA COULD HARDLY be said to be happy about Irene's visit. In fact, she was downright surly and made no attempt to be polite. She let Irene in without a greeting. Irene was about to take off her shoes before she realized from whom Sophie had inherited her ideas about cleaning. She saw dust bunnies and dirt all over the hallway and decided to keep her shoes on.

Angelika had on thin leather ballet shoes. There was a hole in one of the toes, and Irene could spy a toenail with bright red polish. A number of runs streaked her black tights. Her long knitted cardigan was in great shape, striped in all the colors of the rainbow, and it reached just past her rump.

She had apparently just gotten out of the shower, because
her hair was dripping wet. She gestured to Irene to make her
way through the hall to the living room. She took a hair
dryer out of a dresser in the hallway and began to dry her
hair in front of the mirror.

Three doors lined the hallway. One went to a bathroom,
and the other two were half open. Irene would not be the
person she was if she didn't glance into the rooms as she
walked past.

The bedroom had a large unmade double bed. Both sides
looked slept in. The walls were painted a dull red right over
the wallpaper. Above the headboard hung a painting of a
couple making love. On the floor there was a shaggy rug,
which had been white once upon a time. White tulle was
used in place of curtains, and Irene had the feeling they were
simply wrapped around the curtain rods. In one corner, there
was a chair hidden by a huge pile of clothing.

She glanced into the kitchen. It was large and bright, not
necessarily a good thing, as the sunshine mercilessly revealed
a sticky floor and crumbs all over the countertops and the
stove. The kitchen cabinets were painted a bright orange,
which stirred a memory in Irene: her mother had had a coffee
pot that color. She had won it at a Red Cross Christmas raffle,
and she'd hated it from the moment she won it. She'd
returned it for the next year's Christmas raffle, and the woman
who had donated it recognized it and gotten angry. This was
over thirty-five years ago, and the two women still didn't
speak even though they lived on the same street.

Irene stopped at the entrance to the living room with the
strong feeling she had just stepped back into the seventies.
Here again, the walls were painted right over the wallpaper,
though this time the color was forest green. On the floor was
a deep red geometrically-patterned rug. At one time, it had
probably been brighter. The coffee table was unusually low,

but that was practical because the only furniture was a low-slung green divan and a thick mattress placed directly on the floor. The divan had a shiny silk cover with a tapestry pattern, and it seemed to be brand new. The mattress was covered with a bright yellow fabric with dark green flowers. Each cushion was either green or yellow. Everything matched, but it still made Irene feel slightly seasick.

She went over to the mattress and sat down. She had no idea how to sit on the divan. Perhaps it was intended for lying down. She pulled her long legs into the familiar position where she sat on her heels with her legs beneath her, a pose she often used when she visited Mokuso at the dojo. She had taken off her shoes and decided not to worry about the hole in her sock. She was certainly in good company there.

All the walls were covered with photographs and paintings. Her heart leapt when she saw a black and white picture nailed to the wall over the television. It was an enlargement of the photograph with Sophie's face in the foreground and the flames shooting up behind her. Without the technical touchup from the police force, it was difficult to recognize Sophie. It was perfect for Irene's purposes that just that particular photograph was displayed on the wall. She had the police copy of the enlargement in her purse.

Angelika took her time drying her hair, making sure that Irene knew she was in no hurry. Irene didn't let it get to her. It was fascinating to study all the pictures on the wall. There were shots of dance performances and theater performances in all sizes and styles. Probably Frej had taken a number of them. Irene also recognized Frej's graduation photo. It was the same one she'd seen at Ingrid Hagberg's home. There were no other photos of Sophie besides the one over the television set.

The hair dryer stopped, and Angelika came into the room. Gracefully, she sat down on the divan with her legs crisscrossed.

"So what's so important?" she asked guardedly. She appeared nervous, although she tried to hide it with her sullen tone. Irene could understand why, so she went right to the point.

"I was at the Änggården house last Friday night. I knew that my daughter was going there with Frej and Felipe. I had the bad luck to forget my keys, so I had to find Katarina. It was very late at night when I arrived, and the party was in full swing. I didn't know whether I should go in or not. I walked around the house to see if I could get a glimpse of my daughter through the windows. I happened upon a couple making love behind the house: you and Marcelo. You didn't see me."

Irene expected Angelika to become angry, but instead her face lit up and she smiled.

"Oh, that," she said.

"Have you been in this relationship with Marcelo for a while?"

"Relationship? Not at all." Angelika laughed. She looked at Irene with amusement.

Her reaction surprised Irene. Angelika showed no signs of guilt—she didn't even find it embarrassing that Irene had seen them.

"But you have sex," Irene said.

"Yes, we do." Her eyes had a naughty shine.

"How often?"

"It just happens. Not that often. Neither of us takes it seriously. It's just for fun."

"What does Staffan say?"

"It's none of his business." The warm look left Angelika's face. She turned ice cold. "We're adults."

"Actually, I'm not interested in your relationship with Staffan. I want to know about you and Marcelo. We know that Sophie was also interested in him. Did she know that you and Marcelo were sleeping together?"

"While she was alive, we didn't have any kind of 'relationship,' as you call it." Angelika sighed, then fell silent for a moment and looked out the windowpane on the balcony door. "And Sophie and Marcelo were never together. He didn't want to deal with someone so . . . complicated."

"So how long have you and Marcelo had a relationship?"

"You keep calling it a relationship . . . what a ridiculous word! We fuck when we want, that's all. The first time was . . ." She trailed off and swallowed. "It was the same evening . . . Sophie was killed. There was a party on Saturday night for a friend who was moving to Copenhagen. I went to it. Of course I was worried about Sophie, but I didn't know she would die that very night! That she would be . . . burning . . ." Tears came to Angelika's eyes.

"So the first time you and Marcelo were together sexually was that Saturday night."

"Yes," Angelika whispered.

"And then you've had sex a few times since then."

"Yes."

Angelika seemed to have no problem with this. How would this influence her relationship with Staffan Östberg? Perhaps not at all. They were, as Angelika had pointed out, all adults. Irene thought it was odd that they were even considering moving in together. Angelika had a lover thirty years younger than her next companion. Still, that was between Angelika and Staffan. Irene couldn't see how it impacted the murder investigation.

She decided to set aside the lovemaking between Marcelo and Angelika and go back to Sophie herself. She nodded at the picture over the television. "Frej told me he'd taken that picture."

"Yes."

"Do you know where it was taken?"

"No."

"Why does he take so many photographs of fires?"

Angelika gave her a quick side-glance and shifted nervously on the silk-covered divan. "Sophie wanted pictures of fire. She wanted them as inspiration for her work, *The Fire Dance*. I know she used them. If you recall the movements during the performance . . . when the tower burned. The dancers are moving like tongues of flame."

Angelika made some serpent-like movements with her hands and arms in order to illustrate the dance of the flames. Irene didn't remember any special fire-like movements, but perhaps she simply needed more education in the meaning of movement in dance. She went on with her questions.

"In this specific picture, there's a blurry human head in the foreground. Do you know who that might be?"

"No," Angelika replied, uninterested.

"Our technicians down at the station are quite good. They've run this exact photograph through their computer to see what they could make out. This is what they came up with." Irene pulled the photograph from her purse.

She handed it to Angelika, who seemed, again, suddenly nervous. When she clearly saw the person in the photograph, she blanched as if she'd seen a ghost. *On some level, she is seeing a ghost*, Irene thought. For a few seconds, she worried that Angelika might faint, as all the color drained from her face. Angelika stared at the photograph and swallowed a few times, but no words managed to come out.

"As you can see, Sophie is the one in the photograph. She seems very happy. I've never seen her like this," Irene said.

Angelika did not seem to hear what Irene had said. She kept staring at the photo.

"Did you know that Sophie was fond of fire? That she really loved fire? That she was, in fact, a pyromaniac?" Irene asked.

It was a bold statement, but her words sunk in. Angelika

screamed and flung the picture away. It slid over the glass table surface and landed on the rug. She kept swallowing, trying to form words. Finally, she was able to speak. "I didn't *know* . . . at times I *thought* . . . something!"

She started to cry and covered her face with her hands. Irene said nothing, but let her sit like that for a time. Finally, Angelika slid her hands away and gave Irene a tired look. "She was very little when it . . . started. I noticed she loved to play with matches. She liked the flame."

"How old was she when you noticed this?"

"About five or six. But that she was a pyromaniac . . . no! I never noticed that!"

"A few fires broke out in the area the summer of nineteen eighty-nine. Did you ever suspect that Sophie might have been setting them?"

"Never," Angelika said without emotion.

"Did you ever suspect that Sophie might have set fire to your home fifteen years ago?"

"No!"

Her exclamation seemed like a cry for help. Perhaps that's just what it was. Her eyes were filled with fear . . . or terror. For a second, the women stared at each other. Then Irene noticed tears brimming again in Angelika's eyes as sorrow replaced the fear. She looked away from Irene as she quietly said, "Yes, of course, the suspicion was there. But I never wanted to believe that Sophie . . ." She didn't finish the sentence, just bowed her head.

"Sophie never said anything which might hint that she was behind the fire?"

"No. What she told me, I told you."

According to what you said, Sophie was incapable of lying, Irene thought. *But perhaps she could lie when important things were on the line.*

Angelika raised her head and straightened to regain some

balance and her poise. She looked Irene right in the eye and said, "Frej knew nothing. He only did what Sophie asked him to. That's all he did, take pictures."

"I understand," Irene said, reassuringly.

She intended to take this up with Frej later that day.

FREJ CAME JUST before five thirty.

While she waited for him, Irene had used the time to reconnoiter the area. First she made a round through the yard with her flashlight to light her path. The strong wind rustled the tops of the old fruit trees and whirled the fallen leaves around her. At the back of the house, she saw Angelika's panties still in the wet grass, but left them there. Instead, she opened the back door to the basement and went in. A brief look into the sauna showed that Hasse was not at home. He had left behind some paper bags; the smell from them indicated leftovers from the Halloween party. He also had a few wine boxes lined up, with maybe a drop or two left in each. Irene touched nothing and left the same way she'd come in.

It had started to pour while she was in the basement. She hurried back to her car as fast as she could without slipping on the wet grass. She sat and waited for another ten minutes before the red Mégan arrived.

They stepped out of their respective vehicles at the same time and greeted each other. Frej led the way. The entire house was dark. He unlocked the door and switched on the outside light as well as the one in the hallway. Irene paused before stepping inside.

No one had cleaned up after the party. There were paper cups strewn about the floor. Cigarette butts were everywhere. All sorts of garbage was pushed into piles. The stench of sour wine and cigarette smoke hung over the entire mess. Irene thought she could also smell the slightly sweeter odor of marijuana, but perhaps that was just her imagination, since she'd seen people smoking it there. Frej stepped over a pile of garbage and headed directly to the stairs.

When they reached his attic apartment, he unlocked the door to his darkroom and said, "Wait here. I'm just going to put my bag in my apartment and use the bathroom."

With an exaggerated gesture, he bowed Irene into the room. He turned on the ceiling light before he left.

The room hadn't changed. Irene noticed yet again how neat and orderly everything was. Perhaps it was necessary so he could locate what he needed when he was working in the dark. The fire pictures were still up. The picture with Sophie's blurry face was also there.

Irene heard the flush of the toilet. A minute later, Frej entered the room. He'd taken off his down jacket, and he had on the light blue sweater Ingrid Hagberg had given him for Christmas. She would certainly be happy to know he was so fond of it.

"I'm in a hurry. I have to be back at the House of Dance in an hour," Frej said.

"This will be fast. There's just one thing I need to check with you," Irene replied calmly. She turned her head toward the photographs. "Why do you only take pictures of fires?"

"I don't just take pictures of fires!"

"You don't? I don't see anything else here," Irene stated.

"No, well, I haven't taken down Sophie's pictures yet."

"These are all Sophie's pictures?"

"Yes. She wanted them up. She wanted to come here and look at them whenever she needed, for inspiration." His voice was defiant with a noticeably aggressive undertone. He was obviously on the defensive.

"Was Sophie inspired only by fire?"

"Yes . . . well . . . as far as *The Fire Dance* was concerned.

She had to look at the pictures to see, like, how to describe the movement of the flames."

It was the same explanation Angelika had given. It was more than likely that Angelika and Frej had compared notes after Irene's visit to Angelika's apartment.

Irene walked over to the picture showing Sophie's half-profile. She pointed at the figure. "Do you know who this is?"

"Sophie, of course," he replied calmly.

He was, in fact, much too calm. He'd been ready for that question. Frej had definitely talked to his mother earlier that day.

"Why is she at this fire?"

"Why . . . she wanted to be there."

"Why did she want to be there?" Irene insisted.

Frej looked at her in irritation. "Because she wanted to be there!"

"Answer my question, or you'll have to go through all of this down at the police station. You'll be talking to my other colleagues and not me."

She let her words sink in. It was apparent that Frej was not taken with the idea of going to the police station to talk to other officers. Right now he had the upper hand in his own space.

"All right, then. Ask me the question again."

"Why did Sophie want to be with you when you went to photograph this fire?"

"She wanted to see fires live. To get, like, the proper feeling."

He shrugged and attempted nonchalance, but Irene could tell he was upset. All her police instincts told her there was much more to these pictures than Frej wanted to confess.

"Did she often go with you when you were taking pictures of fires?"

"Nah . . . just once."

For the first time, Irene could hear a touch of fear in his voice. He walked over to the large table on the other side of the room and leaned against the edge, crossing his arms as if he were relaxed. His eyes betrayed him. He did not want to look at Irene.

"You said she wanted to see the fires live. That must have meant she went with you fairly often," Irene said. She fixed him with her gaze.

"Yeah, all right, sure . . . she came more than once. It was important for her dance," he confessed lamely.

"Isn't it true that she was fascinated by fire? Perhaps unusually fascinated?"

Frej gave her a hasty glance but looked away again almost immediately. Irene let the silence take up space, and finally it became too much for him. He muttered, "Maybe. Maybe so."

Irene chose her next words carefully. "Did you ever suspect that she set things on fire on purpose? That she might be a pyromaniac?"

He jumped as if she'd slapped him across the face. "Pyromaniac!" he exclaimed. Now he was looking at her directly with naked fear.

"Look at this picture. Our technicians cleaned it up in their lab. Look at Sophie's expression," Irene said, and handed him the photograph.

He looked at the picture of his sister for a long time, then gave a deep sigh and handed it back to Irene. "She really did like to watch things burn. She used to say things like 'fire purifies.' But a pyro . . . I doubt it." He shook his head slightly.

The sharp sound of a telephone cut through the silence in the house. Frej stood up and headed to his living quarters. The ringing stopped. A minute or so later, he returned to his darkroom.

"I have to get going. That was Felipe. His car broke down and he needs a ride. It takes at least fifteen minutes to get to his place."

He opened the door as wide as possible. Irene had no choice but to leave. Nevertheless, she felt she had confirmation of her suspicions. Sophie had been fascinated by fire, and perhaps she was a pyromaniac. The asexual young woman had an unusual turn-on—fire was her passion.

THE FOLLOWING DAY, Irene and all her colleagues had to work on the latest knifing. Everything pointed to someone in Roberto's gang wanting revenge for the attack on Victor Fernandez. The new victim had pulled through the worst of his medical crisis, but he was not up to being questioned yet.

The investigation was slow and made more difficult because no one wanted to testify or snitch on a gang member. The police were unable to provide witness protection, so the only safe thing to do was to keep as silent as a wall. Or perhaps give false testimony—as long as everyone cooperated, like Milan's relatives.

The gang killings were beginning to feel like one long, nightmarish investigation with the certainty that these were not the first incidents, and were definitely not going to be the last. Gang criminal activity was on the rise. It cost time and real money to conduct these difficult investigations, during which neither side was going to help the police. Instead, the gangs carried out their own justice. Now there was the risk that more young men would be injured or killed.

One light in the darkness was the new 24-hour hotline that the social services had set up with the local police in the districts of Bergsjön, Gunnared and Biskopgården. The aim was to break the gangs' recruiting cycle. At-risk young people would be counseled to try to keep them from starting down a path of crime. The boys and girls were between the ages of twelve and eighteen; they'd been caught with drugs or were suspected of theft and breaking and entering. Each one caught was brought into the group with a plan that would help them return to society. The head of the local police had already expressed his surprise that so many young people had been brought in—many of them quite young indeed.

On Thursday, everything began to happen at once.

Irene's phone rang at a quarter past eight. She almost knocked over her cup of coffee as she reached for the receiver. Before she could speak, a sharp female voice trumpeted over the line: "Nurse Ulla at Happy River Assisted Living here. Are you the policewoman who visited Ingrid Hagberg last week? Who brought the sweets?"

"Yes . . . I'm Detective Inspector Irene—"

"Were you here again?"

Irene was confused. "What do you mean? You think I've come and visited Ingrid Hagberg again?"

"That's exactly what I mean. Did you?"

"No, I didn't. I've been much too busy here. I—"

"She's back in the hospital. Same reason. Someone has given her sweets. This time it was a box of Viennese nougat candy."

"Wha . . ." was the most intelligent thing Irene could manage to say.

"Viennese nougat. Someone gave her a big box of candy. We found the box, and it was completely empty."

Before Irene could say anything else, the nurse continued, "Ingrid was released last Saturday despite the fact that her blood sugar levels were still high. They are always high, but this time catastrophically so. Her diabetes is in its last stages.

One reason is that, especially after her head injury, she can't manage her diet. I found her this morning in a diabetic coma again when I came to check her blood sugar levels."

"Is the box the candy came in still there?" asked Irene when the nurse paused to take a breath.

"Yes, it's still on her kitchen table."

"Please don't touch it. And please don't let a cleaning person into the room."

"I'll tell them to wait if her room is scheduled to be cleaned today."

"Good. I'll be there in about an hour. Could you let me and a police technician into her apartment?"

"Sure. You have my cell phone number. Call me when you get here."

Irene called down to the lab and reached Svante Malm. He promised to come with her to Torslanda.

Tommy walked into the room and Irene was just about to give him the whole spiel about the Sophie case, from the Halloween party to the box of candy, when the phone rang again.

"Detective Inspector Irene Huss."

"Hi, Erik Johansson here!" a young male voice trumpeted.

"I see," Irene said uncertainly. She couldn't place the voice right away.

"From Berzén Real Estate Agency. We met last Friday at the farm."

"Yes, yes, of course." The coin dropped. "Sorry I didn't recognize your voice."

"Not to worry. I've just sold the farm. And when the new owner and I were going through the place really thoroughly, I happened to remember what you told me. Like, if a room stood out in any way. If it was messier or something. I didn't think of anything when you were here. Mostly I was thinking about the house itself. It was just messy all over. But the owner and I went through the barn, too. You know there was a riding school there, right?"

"Yes, I know about that."

"The riding club rented the place from the old lady for years. But then they didn't renew the lease."

"Yes, I heard they built their own place."

"Exactly. They moved on two years ago, according to the papers I have in front of me. The riding club had a changing room and an office built in the barn. It has been abandoned since they left. When the new owner and I went in, it hit me that the office was sparkling clean. In fact, unnaturally clean."

"Unnaturally clean?" Irene echoed.

"Yes. You can eat off the floor. Not even a dead fly, so to speak. And the toilet is squeaky clean, and the water has not evaporated out of the bowl and . . ."

"Erik, could you let me and a police technician into the barn today?" Irene could hear the tension in her own voice. All signals were go. This was definitely something.

"Sure. I can meet you there at one P.M. Right now I have a showing."

"After one is fine. Thank you very much for calling."

Tommy was giving Irene a questioning look. She smiled back, suddenly full of energy. "Get more coffee. This is going to take a while. Then let's go over to Sven, so I don't have to say everything twice."

Nurse Ulla unlocked the door to Ingrid Hagberg's apartment. The smell of an old, sick person hit Irene as they entered, just like the previous time she had been there. When Irene stuck her head briefly into the bedroom, she smelled ammonia. She couldn't explain why. Maybe it was her imagination.

An open box sat in the middle of the kitchen table. It was empty. They could see the square niches for the missing nougat. The cover showed a couple dancing a Viennese waltz—Viennese nougat, of course. The sweetest candy ever made. And easiest to eat, too, as far as the wrappers strewn about the table revealed. Only one piece was left. Ingrid had eaten each and every piece except this last one. Hardly a healthy thing to do for a diabetic, especially if she'd gobbled them all at once.

"I can't understand who would give her candy," Nurse Ulla said indignantly.

Irene thought that the nurse was giving her a distrustful look, but perhaps she was just imagining it.

"Did anyone visit her yesterday?" asked Irene.

"Not that I know of. Ingrid is fairly solitary. She almost never has visitors. Just that young man who comes around sometimes." Nurse Ulla pointed to Frej's graduation picture.

Svante Malm placed the empty nougat box and all the wrappers into a plastic bag. He had already put on full protective covering so he would not contaminate anything as he searched for evidence. Irene and Nurse Ulla wore only paper shoe covers and paper head coverings. They had strict orders from Svante not to touch anything and to move as little as possible while in the apartment.

"No indication the candy came through the mail," Svante said. His voice was muffled as he was on his knees with his head under the countertop. "There's no mailing envelope in the garbage. But there is this."

He held a plastic bag from a convenience store with a pair of tweezers. There was no Pressbyrå anywhere near Happy River, which showed that Ingrid Hagberg *did* have a visitor yesterday.

OPERATION KNOCK-ON-DOORS DID not yield any results. None of Ingrid's neighbors had seen or heard anyone visit Ingrid. Irene figured out that her neighbors did not have much contact with Ingrid.

The neighbor next door was a tiny woman who boasted that she was about to turn ninety-four next month. She kept telling Irene this. She seemed very glad to have a visitor—a person who, most importantly, listened to everything she had to say. After twenty minutes, Irene was exhausted. Nevertheless, she was able to confirm that the talkative old lady had neither seen nor heard anyone come to Ingrid's apartment yesterday. Of course, as she put it herself, her hearing and sight were not what they'd been, but since she was just about to turn ninety-four, that could be overlooked.

The woman reminded Irene of a porcelain doll, but she had tough opinions about her neighbor. Ingrid had been "antisocial" and "unpleasant," and she never wanted to participate in any activities the assisted living center arranged for the residents.

All the other residents Irene talked to confirmed this description of Ingrid as "antisocial." She was not exactly well-liked.

Irene and Svante decided that Sven Andersson would have to decide if there would be a larger-scale Operation Knock-on-Doors at all three buildings in the apartment complex. Even if it had been rainy and dark yesterday afternoon, someone might have seen something suspicious.

IRENE AND SVANTE managed to wolf down a pizza at Torslanda Square before they drove to the farm in Björkil. Erik Johansson's sports car was already parked in the farm driveway. He was opening the barn door and waving to them as they got out of the car.

"Over here!" he called. His smile was wide and inviting.

"Are you sure he's a real estate agent and not an entertainer?" Svante muttered to Irene as they walked toward him.

Irene introduced Svante to Erik as they went into the

barn. It was a large building with a large space between the ground and the ceiling. The ceiling was lower over the horse stalls, with the hayloft above them. Erik led them right through the barn to a heavy wooden door, which looked rather new.

"This is the changing room," he said. He held the door open for them.

It was a long, narrow room with orange metal lockers along the walls. There were also massive hooks on which the students probably kept various pieces of horse equipment. There were a few small windows over the lockers.

"Why did the riding school leave the lockers behind?" asked Irene.

"All the interior fixtures belonged to the aunt," Erik said.

Next to the door was a small toilet.

The young agent walked over to a smooth oak door on the other side of the changing room. He unlocked it. He used a common ASSA key, but Irene saw that there was also a seven-lever tumbler lock.

"Here's the office," he said.

The room had no windows. It was hardly more than ten square meters and was completely empty of furnishings, except for one poster on the wall showing the anatomy of a horse. Erik Johansson strode across the floor and opened another door. "There's a toilet here, too."

"I'd prefer it if you wouldn't touch the door handles too much," Svante said and smiled. "Fingerprints and the like, you know."

"Oh, jeez! I hadn't thought of that!" Erik said with a guilt-stricken face. He let go of the door handle as if it were red hot. "But I do have to tell you," he added. "A number of people have come through here—potential buyers."

"Don't worry, but it would be nice if we didn't add any more traces," Svante said. He pulled out protective gloves and hats, and gave Irene a meaningful look. "Why don't you and our friend Erik here take a look at the stalls?"

Irene read his mind and told the young man, "Here's the deal. We'll just be in his way here. We'll be more useful looking around somewhere else."

Erik Johansson nodded, appearing relieved to turn the office room over to Svante. He looked curiously into Svante's toolbox. *He's observant and curious,* Irene thought. *He'd make a good police officer.*

The stalls still had a slight smell of horse and hay, although two years had passed since the animals were taken away. There was a rusty bridle hanging on one of the pegs, and some pitchforks and shovels were propped in a corner. Otherwise, the place was empty. It was neat and tidy, but nowhere near as sparkling clean as the office room had been. Erik was right. Someone had recently cleaned that area thoroughly.

"Not so much to see here," Erik said, gesturing as if to include the entire barn.

He went toward an old wooden door hanging crookedly on its hinges. He could walk through upright, but Irene had to bow her head.

"This was a large storage space or maybe even a garage. An old tractor and a few pieces of ancient machinery. Old stuff." Erik seemed to have little understanding of farm machinery.

The light was dim in the storage space. The tiny windows were covered with spider webs and layers of dust. In the dark, Irene could see the tractor and something that looked like a harvester.

"Are there any lights here?" Irene asked.

"Sure, just a moment," Erik said.

A few tired fluorescent light strips began to sputter. Even though the windows were as dim as ever, Irene was now able to see much more clearly what was in the storage area.

"Why don't you start over by the door and I'll start from this end," Irene said. "If you see anything interesting, don't touch it!"

"Aye-aye, Chief Inspector," Erik replied and gave a perfect military salute.

Irene couldn't help thinking that the influence of American television shows was getting much too strong.

Obviously, this area had been used to store all kinds of broken down machinery during the past decades. Irene felt a sting of nostalgia as she spied her father's old light blue moped. Well, of course, it wasn't her father's, but one exactly like it, just missing tires. He'd ridden his moped to work for years, no matter what the weather, until her parents bought their first car in 1962. Irene had been much too young to remember the time before her parents had the car. Still, she remembered the moped very well. Her father, Börje, had kept it and fixed it up to give to her on her fifteenth birthday. It ran like clockwork. Some of her friends had made fun of her old moped, but she didn't care. She loved her light blue Puch and rode around on it for many years.

She was pulled out of memory lane by Erik's voice on the other side of the storage area.

"Ahoy! A bed!"

Irene made her way over. He was pointing to an area where stairs went to the hayloft. Underneath it, between two slabs of Masonite, a wooden cot was folded up and stashed. Irene remembered sleeping in a bed like that when she spent her summer vacations at her paternal grandparent's place in Falkenberg. The edges of the bed were heavy wood, and there was a metal hinge in the middle. It had links on the bottom that rattled whenever the bed was unfolded or folded back up.

"It's not as filthy as the other stuff," Erik pointed out.

He couldn't hide his excitement. Police work often had

that effect on people, as long as they were not feeling threatened themselves.

"You're right. Let it be for now, and let's see if there's anything else, like clothes or sheets," Irene said.

Erik quickly rushed up the stairs and into the hayloft. He didn't seem to mind that his light blue pants and his mocha jacket were not suited to mucking around in a filthy old barn. Irene heard his footsteps above her head. *I hope he doesn't fall through the floor,* she thought. She hoped that his real estate insurance would cover any accidents in the course of a workday. *But is he actually doing real estate work now? They'd have to say he was if anything happened to him.*

Irene poked around the junk without finding anything else of interest. *Yet the bed is a good find,* she thought.

Erik came back down from the hayloft and reported that up there were just rotten hay and an impressive number of rats. Without thinking, he wiped his hands on his light blue pants, which was unfortunate. Palm prints now ran down both sides. He looked even worse when he rubbed his hand on his forehead. It looked like he was putting on camouflage.

"You'll have to go home and wash up before you meet your clients this afternoon," Irene said, laughing.

"Oh, it's not so bad. I'll have time to change. My next showing is at four thirty," he said happily.

SVANTE MALM THOUGHT the bed was an interesting item. Irene also put on protective gear, and together they managed to wrap the heavy bed in plastic.

"No bedclothes?" asked Svante.

"No, but she was on a mattress when she died in the fire. And fragments of the fabric used to set the fire indicated a cotton like the kind used in sheets. And there was a woolen blanket," Irene reminded him.

At her words, Erik turned a little pale. It had dawned on him that this was no game. They had gone on a scavenger hunt to find anything relevant to Sophie's murder, and she had not been much older than Erik.

Fredrik Stridh needed help investigating the pedophile sports trainer. As they went through the man's computers, both his home computer and the one he used at the office of the sports club, they found thousands of pictures of child pornography. Many of them were hardcore, showing rapes of boys not much older than three or four.

"He's been passing them around. We've found a whole new damned porn ring," Fredrik said with a sigh.

Simultaneous with this investigation was the need for a great deal of work on the gang killings. Irene decided to suspend her investigation over the weekend. Svante had promised to get back to her with some concrete results by Monday or Tuesday.

When Irene went home Friday evening, she felt drained. She needed to take it easy the entire weekend and rest up.

Sammie came rushing to greet her as soon as she stepped into the house, but no one else was around. The twins must have been home at some point, because they'd picked Sammie up from his dog-sitter. There was also a note on the kitchen table:

Hello Parental Units!
Jenny is making her record this weekend (the studio changed the day because they had something else come

up for next weekend). She's on the way to Skara with her band, and they won't be home until Sunday evening.

I'm going to capoeira, and Felipe and I will be going out afterward.

Love, Katarina

So only Irene and Krister would be home that evening. That would be nice and relaxing—just what she needed in her exhausted state. Still, she felt a twinge of missing her girls. Of course, the twins were much more independent at their age and had their own activities and friends. Irene missed her Friday night family time, tubs of hot popcorn and good movies on television. But most importantly she missed the sense of security as the four of them cuddled on the sofa. Other evenings they'd play games, although things could get hot when one of the girls lost her temper. Both girls hated to lose; for the sake of peace in the home, the girls often would play on the same team and were often allowed to win.

Irene went into the kitchen to prepare Sammie's food. Sammie was now lying in the hallway, watching to make sure the process was done correctly. He could hear the sound of dry food dropping into the bowl. Then there were leftover bits of Värmland sausage from Wednesday's dinner. Warm water was spread over all of it.

When Irene put the bowl on the floor, Sammie flung himself at it with enthusiasm. He began to chew loudly, content. At least one being on this planet appreciated Irene's food preparation abilities.

What were the humans going to eat this evening? Irene had no idea, but trusted that her husband was going to see to this part of the program. Krister always finished at 4 P.M. on Fridays when he had the weekend off. He'd often go to

Saluhallen, the food market, and shop before he headed home. For the past few months, the family had two cars. They still had their Saab, now thirteen years old, and they'd also taken over the Volvo that had once belonged to Krister's father. Both cars still ran well, though the Volvo was fairly old as well. According to Krister, they'd last for another few years. He'd given them names to boot: "Old Betty" and "Bosse." Their cars were the oldest ones in the townhouse parking lot. Irene felt it was a touch too luxurious to have two cars in the family, but it made things so much easier, especially since she and Krister had odd work schedules.

It was a quarter past six and Krister still hadn't come home. Irene tried to reach him on his cell phone, but only got the message that "this number cannot be reached now." She called Glady's Corner and asked for him, but found out that he'd left the restaurant at the normal time.

A dull apprehension churned in her stomach, but she told herself that there was nothing to worry about yet. Perhaps Krister had run into a friend and they had decided to have a cup of coffee together. Or perhaps he'd remembered an important errand. Or . . . or . . . what? Irene glanced at the clock and saw it was now six thirty. Why had Krister turned off his cell phone?

Sammie began to whine and circle in front of the door. What goes in must come out. The dog had to be walked.

Irene snapped on Sammie's leash and threw on her coat. They took a brisk walk through the wind and rain without running into any other humans or dogs. The other houses looked warm and inviting. Everyone was enjoying their Friday evening except her. She knew this was an illusion. As a police officer, she knew what was often hidden behind respectable house façades. For instance, the man suspected of child abuse lived in a brand new house in Askim with a wife and two young children. He'd been an elite athlete in the past and had a degree in sports psychology. When he was arrested, he'd just gone to pick up a brand new BMW 530i. He had certainly kept up appearances.

Every ten minutes, Irene called Krister's cell phone number. Still no answer. After an hour, Sammie wanted to go in. It was too wet and rainy even for him. When Irene opened the front door, she was hoping to be met with the aroma of wonderful food being prepared in the kitchen.

The house was just as empty as when she'd left. Krister had not come home.

At a quarter to eight, the phone rang, cutting through the silence of the house. Irene rushed to pick it up and she could hear her own lack of breath as she answered. "Irene here."

"Mrs. Huss?" The voice was that of a young woman. She sounded chilly and impersonal, but perhaps she was just being firm. "This is Ellen Brinkman. I'm a doctor at Sahlgren Hospital. We have admitted your husband through the emergency wing. He—"

"What happened?" Irene was practically screaming. She was surprised at how emotional her reaction was. She could hear her heart begin to pound wildly and she felt dizzy, as if she might faint.

"He's not in danger. He seems to have suffered temporary amnesia. He did not remember his name or where he lived. He's lost his cell phone and his wallet, so we weren't able to identify him right away. His memory's begun to come back, which is how I knew to reach you. Can you come here?"

"Of course, of course," Irene managed to croak out.

Her mouth felt dry and her hands were shaking as she replaced the receiver. She had to sit down on a kitchen chair to recover for a minute before she got ready to drive to Sahlgren Hospital.

• • •

BEFORE IRENE WAS allowed to see Krister, the nurse in charge of his case told her what had happened. Someone had called the police at 4:35 P.M., a butcher from Saluhall who said one of his customers was acting in an odd manner. He had purchased almost 2,000 Swedish kronor worth of meat and had not blinked as he paid in cash. When the butcher went for change, the customer had looked at him strangely. Then he'd turned on his heel and walked out, leaving both his money and his purchase.

The next call had come from NK half an hour later. They'd phoned to ask the police to come get a man who seemed sad and confused. He did not know his name or where he lived. His wallet was gone. The police officer who took down the call noted that the description matched the man the butcher at Saluhall had reported earlier.

When the police picked him up, they drove him straight to the emergency room.

The nurse laid a comforting hand on Irene's arm. She said, "The doctor who examined him says that he is not in danger of any acute mental harm. He is back to normal. On the other hand, we have no idea what made him suffer this temporary memory loss. Often when something like this happens, we find the patient is suffering from overwhelming stress and overexertion. Does this fit your husband?"

"Well . . . yes . . . he often works overtime. There's always so much to do, and they often don't have enough help," Irene replied.

KRISTER LOOKED PALE and exhausted. He tried to smile as Irene leaned over to give him a kiss on the mouth, but his smile seemed more like a grimace. At least he was making an effort, and he looked happy to see her.

"I want to go home," he said, tiredly.

"Tomorrow. Nurse Lena said you have to stay here overnight for observation."

"That's fine. I guess I *am* feeling a little weak."

The nurse who had brought Irene to his room shook his shoulder gently and said, "Krister, you can't fall asleep. Right now I need to check your pulse and blood pressure and look at the size of your pupils." She glanced up at Irene and smiled. "Just routine. We are going to do an ACT in about an hour. There is a small risk there is some intracranial bleeding, so we always check just to make sure."

The nurse performed the examination quickly and efficiently. Then she jotted the results on his chart on the nightstand next to a stethoscope and a blood pressure cuff.

She was middle-aged, slightly plump and rather short, but somehow she gave Irene a sense of comfort. She seemed competent and had a friendly, motherly way about her, which was just what Irene needed that moment.

Irene picked up her courage to ask: "What does intracranial bleeding mean?"

"We don't know why Krister lost his memory. We have to rule out a stroke or a blood clot. These things can be seen on an X-ray."

The nurse glanced at Krister, and Irene knew she didn't want to worry him. She felt worry gnaw at her own heart. *How sick is Krister really? What is going to happen to him? What will it mean if the doctors find something on the X-ray? What will it mean if they don't?*

Mostly to calm her own fearful thoughts, Irene asked, "Have the police been here yet? It seems someone took his cell phone and wallet."

"Since Krister had trouble with his memory, the police decided to wait until tomorrow morning to question him. Perhaps everything will be clearer then," Nurse Lena replied. She gave Krister an encouraging smile.

The police had probably made a good call, but Irene still felt frustrated. Her husband was likely the victim of a crime, and she wanted her colleagues to get right to work. At the same time, she knew it was Friday night in a big city. Parties were just getting started. There'd be many more thefts, fights and assaults before the night was through. Perhaps even a murder. The police department's resources were already stretched thin, so if they could put off questioning someone until the following morning, when things were calmer, they would do so.

Irene was suddenly overwhelmed by exhaustion. All her strength was gone, and all she wanted to do was cry. She couldn't upset Krister by giving in to that impulse. She'd have to keep her spirits up. She took his hand and gave it a squeeze.

"Do you remember anything at all about what happened?" she asked.

Krister turned his head to look at her. He wet his dry lips with his tongue before he replied. "I parked my car at the usual spot. It's on the top floor of the parking garage. I remember walking over Kungsportsplatsen and into the Saluhall. Then nothing. Everything went black. The next thing I remember is lying here in this hospital bed."

The nurse jokingly wagged her forefinger at Irene and Krister as she said, "No more interrogations today! Krister needs to rest."

As she was speaking, the door opened and a rolling bed was pushed into the room.

"Now you'll have some company," the nurse said to Krister. She turned to Irene and said, "Unfortunately, I'll have to ask you to leave now. This patient is in a bad state."

Irene nodded and got up from the chair beside Krister's bed. She gave Krister another kiss, and he did his best to respond. His eyes were already half-closed, and it looked like he was going back to sleep.

Irene glanced at the new patient. He was an old man lying completely still, his eyes closed. He was extremely thin and his yellow-tinged skin seemed to be glued to his cranium. *In a bad state*, the nurse had said. Irene thought the man looked dead, and she had certainly seen enough corpses in her line of work to know.

ON THE WAY home, Irene suddenly felt hungry; she hadn't eaten since lunch. For simplicity's sake, she drove to the pizzeria on Frölunda Square and bought a pizza to go. Then, as she held the warm pizza carton in her hands, she realized it had been a mistake. Now it was too late.

Sammie was overjoyed when she got home. He hated to be left home alone, and the feeling only intensified as the years passed, perhaps because his sight and hearing were starting to decline. Or perhaps he was fearful, as many old folks can be. He would be twelve in the spring, a considerable age for a dog.

Irene didn't bother to get out a plate; she'd eat the pizza right from the carton. Krister would have gotten angry if he saw her. Style and good manners at the dinner table were important to him. At least she'd gotten a glass for her beer. Even for her, drinking directly from the can was too much.

She put the pizza, the glass of beer, a small salad, tableware and the can containing the rest of the beer onto a tray and brought it upstairs to the television room. She surfed through the channels and finally found a Goldie Hawn film. Goldie was playing a confused, cute blonde as usual. She'd get herself into trouble and then get herself out again by the end of the film. Irene couldn't handle even that level of mindlessness. Her thoughts and concern for Krister overwhelmed her mind. She took a bite of pizza, and it tasted like styrofoam. The mouthful seemed to expand until, finally, she spat it out.

She'd ordered a Quattro Stagione with ham, cheese, tomatoes, shrimp, mussels and artichokes. How could she have been such an idiot and believed she'd be able to eat an entire pizza with all this happening? How had she . . .

The cold pizza in front of her unlocked a barrier in her mind. She understood the truth in a sentence, which had been repeated many times during the investigation into Sophie's murder. Sophie had her *idées fixes*, such as choosing the same pizza every single time. Sophie never lied. She could keep silent, in order not to tell the truth, but she never lied.

"How's Krister doing?" asked Tommy right away on Monday morning. Tommy and Irene usually met in their office a few minutes before they would have to gather for morning prayer.

"Under the circumstances, he's doing fine," Irene replied. "But I have to tell you that this has been the worst weekend of my life." She gave Tommy an exhausted look.

"Have they found his wallet and cell phone?"

"No. He seems to have just put them down somewhere and then walked away from them, just like he did with the bags of food. He also has no idea why he bought so much meat. It was enough to throw a party or something! He . . . he started to cry when he told me this. He's frightened about what he could have done during the time he had his memory loss. He's . . . deflated. Completely lacking energy." Irene sighed.

Tommy nodded and said in all seriousness, "That's probably exactly what's happened to him. He's used up all his energy and is burned out."

"Probably. The doctor says that there's nothing physically wrong with him. It's his mind, but he's not mentally ill. Just exhausted and depressed. The doctor says that this is a definite sign of burnout."

"Depression can be serious. It might even be easier if he had a physical illness. People are more sympathetic when it comes to physical illnesses and injuries. People can't see something invisible. They don't understand."

"I know. I remember when I was attacked out in Billdal. It's been more than six years, but just hearing the words 'Hell's Angels' makes me physically ill. Sometimes my heart starts to pound if I hear a loud motorcycle. Now and then, I still have nightmares. And now this damned Hoffa reappears in another murder investigation!"

"Yep. And we know why, now. Narcotics has informed us that Milan's gang is definitely linked to the Banditos. Just as we expected at the beginning—Roberto Oliviera was killed as part of a turf war. Hell's Angels was following Milan. When Milan knifed Roberto, it was a gift from heaven as far as Hoffa and his gang were concerned. Even those small players, the Pumas, suffered a blow when their leader was killed."

"Are all the guys in Roberto's gang from Latin America? The ones I've questioned were."

"Most of them are. The local police tell us that there are some Swedish guys, too, as well as two guys from Kosovo. They're not united by race or background; they are all part of the underclass."

"Any girls involved?"

"Nope. Their motto is No Girls Allowed." He smiled a teasing smile and got up from his desk chair. It was seven thirty. In other words, time for morning prayer.

SVANTE MALM LOOKED over the collection of police officers, who appeared half awake. Svante had forgotten to comb his hair after his bike ride into work. Since it was a cold morning, he had been wearing a small knit cap, so now his red hair, touched with grey, stuck out in all directions. The forensic technician never bothered about his appearance. His freckled face lit up when he smiled at Irene. He laid a few plastic bags on the table.

"Good news!" he exclaimed and gave her a meaningful wink.

In anticipation, she sat at the head of the table.

"We've made some breakthroughs in the Sophie murder investigation," Svante said. "But I'm going to start with the box of nougat candy from Ingrid Hagberg's apartment. We found no prints whatsoever on the box, which seems to have been wiped clean before it was given to her. On the other hand, we did find a great number of prints on the Pressbyrå plastic bag. They belong to Angelika Malmborg-Eriksson."

Although Irene had somewhat expected it, she was still rather surprised. It was just plain stupid to clean the box but not to use gloves when handling the plastic bag.

"We're going to look at the silver clasps found on Sophie's body. The maker's mark showed that they were made in Norway in nineteen fifty-nine. I've contacted some of our Norwegian colleagues, and they were able to fill me in. The clasps come from a Norwegian sweater. In the olden days, people used silver buttons and silver clasps to dress up their clothes. They were part of folk costume. The more wealthy people used more silver on their sweaters. Today, the use of real silver is rare. These days, they use tin. It's our good luck that these were made of silver, because tin would have melted at this temperature."

Svante held up the plastic bags with the beautiful silver clasps. Then he placed them back in the small red plastic box and reached for a new bag, which he also held up. It looked empty.

"Inside this bag we have two strands of hair. They were caught in the hinges from an old fold-up bed we found in the stable at Björkil, the farm owned by Ingrid Hagberg. The hair belongs to Sophie."

There was silence in the room as his words sank in.

Svante was pleased with their reaction. He continued. "There are no fingerprints on the bed frame. It had been wiped down—actually, thoroughly cleaned. We found traces of cleaning fluid on it."

"She must have been lying on top of the mattress," said Birgitta. "So how the heck did her hair get on the underside of the bed?"

Irene cleared her throat and said, "I can answer that. When I was young and visited my grandparents, I used to sleep in a bed like that. Whenever I wanted to retrieve something that had fallen under the bed, I would get my hair caught on those hinges underneath. It hurt because it was hard to get my hair loose again."

"Most likely that is how it happened. I also found Sophie's hair in the bathroom right next to the office, where we now believe Sophie was kept prisoner. Both the bathroom and the office had been thoroughly cleaned. Quite a bit of cleaning fluid was used, too," Svante said.

"How do we know that the hair belongs to Sophie?" protested Jonny. "The top half of her body was burned completely up!"

"We secured hair from her hairbrush. There's more than enough hair in her bedroom at the Änggården mansion."

Svante paused for dramatic effect. He looked out over the collection of police officers to make sure they were paying attention.

"The most valuable piece of concrete evidence is that we have found one of her palm prints on the wall above the toilet."

Irene looked at her boss, Superintendent Andersson, and said, "We have proof that Sophie was kept prisoner in Björkil. Our suspicions are now directed toward a specific suspect: Frej. Her half brother. He had access to the farm during his aunt's absence. Ingrid Hagberg was . . . oh my God! The Norwegian sweater!"

Her colleagues looked at her in surprise. Jonny Blom whispered theatrically to Hannu, "There she goes again."

Irene ignored Jonny and eagerly began to explain. "Those silver clasps came from a Norwegian sweater, and I know where I've seen it before!"

She glared at Jonny, who was circling his finger against his temple while rolling his eyes. When he stopped, she continued: "I talked to Ingrid Hagberg fifteen years ago, when I investigated the fire at Björkil—the one where Magnus Eriksson died. It was a cold winter day in February, and Ingrid was wearing a beautiful sweater in various shades of blue. I'm absolutely certain that this was the same sweater Sophie was wearing when she died. She was probably freezing cold in that stable, even with a heater."

"You spoke to Ingrid Hagberg back then?" Sven Andersson demanded, lifting an eyebrow.

"Just a short conversation," Irene said, trying for nonchalance and avoiding Andersson's gaze.

In order to direct her boss's thoughts elsewhere, she said, "Last Friday I was having a pizza, and I realized that Sophie had already told us what happened fifteen years ago. She never lied. She could be silent, but she never lied."

Irene took another twenty minutes to explain her train of thought to her colleagues. An additional five minutes went by while she tried to convince her boss that she was on the right track. Grudgingly, he agreed to let Irene and Tommy finish up Sophie's murder investigation. One justification for his decision was that their workload lightened when the narcotics division had been brought into the gang killings. If all went well, they'd soon be bringing in the entire bunch.

NURSE ULLA OPENED the door for them and smiled warmly at Tommy, so much so that Irene took note of it. The nurse had never given *her* a smile so filled with sunshine.

"I'll go with you," she twittered, with a new smile toward Tommy. "Ingrid is still weak from her latest episode."

Irene thought it was odd how many women thought Tommy was attractive. In her eyes, he was just average looking. His brown hair was always cut short. His brown eyes matched his hair. He was just a few inches taller than she was, and he wasn't in good shape since he didn't exercise. A slight beer belly was beginning to form, too, and Irene had teased him about it. He didn't let her get to him.

"Women like love handles. Can't lose!" Tommy would reply and smile mischievously.

Nurse Ulla seemed to conform to his assertion. She swung her hips as she walked in front of them toward the elevator. As they rode up, she said, "The truth is, Ingrid is a bit confused right now. More mixed-up than before. And she's often sad. The doctors are going to come take a look at her tomorrow."

The mechanical voice informed them they'd reached the fourth floor. The elevator came to a smooth stop. The nurse went to Ingrid's apartment door and unlocked it.

"Hello, Ingrid! It's me, Ulla. I have two people who want to talk to you," she called out into the apartment.

They could hear soft whimpering in the bedroom. Nurse Ulla led the way. The room had only room for the bed, a small nightstand and a small dresser. With three grown people, the room felt like a streetcar during rush hour. They stood rigidly upright, close to each other.

"I'll head back out," Tommy said, and walked out to the living room.

Ingrid looked ashen-faced and still very ill. It was clear she'd gone through an extreme medical crisis. The scars on her forehead shone bright red against her pale hairline.

"Ingrid, this is Irene Huss. Do you remember her?" asked the nurse.

Ingrid's thin eyelids fluttered. She opened them halfway and began to look around. When her gaze fastened on Irene, she said, "The policewoman." Her voice was thin and shaking, but her sour tone could not be mistaken. She closed her eyes again to shut out the unwelcome guest.

Irene cleared her throat and said, "I hope you will be able to answer a few questions for me."

"I know nothing about the girl. I never saw her after . . . after . . ." Ingrid began angrily, but she didn't have the energy to complete her sentence.

"I know. You never saw her again after the fire fifteen years ago. But that is the fire I want to talk to you about."

"Too long ago . . . I don't want to . . ." Ingrid grumbled.

She seems clear in her head right now at any rate, Irene thought. How confused was she really? She had to determine if the old lady was counterfeiting confusion so she wouldn't have to answer. Considering the secret she'd been carrying all those years, she must be a great actress.

"Before Sophie died, she wrote down exactly what happened the night the cottage at Björkil burned down. It took us a while to figure it out, because she wrote it in . . . ballet language. Now, however, we understand her description of the course of events."

Irene paused so that what she'd told the old woman had a chance to sink in. At the same time, Irene thought again about the ballet performance she'd seen. *The Fire Dance* contained the truth.

The party guests began to yawn, lie down, and fall asleep. The light diminished and the scene had a twilight feel. Only the Prince was still awake. He'd found a bottle and drunk what was left in it. On unsteady legs, he got up and began to stagger to the tower. Since the Guardian was not at her post, he had no trouble opening the door to the tower.

"You told me yourself that you picked up Frej at the bus

that afternoon. Your brother had told you he was going downtown and asked you to take care of the boy. Then you and Frej had dinner. Then he fell asleep and slept until eight thirty that night. Is this true?"

Not a single muscle twitched in Ingrid's haggard face, but Irene felt that she was listening intensely. Calmly, Irene continued: "Sophie's story is different. According to her version, she came home at the usual time in order to get ready and pick up her ballet things. Frej was already in the house. He was tipsy. He had found one of his father's bottles, and he'd drunk quite a bit. It doesn't take much to make an eight-year-old drunk. It wasn't Frej who'd fallen asleep after dinner. It was you. Sophie probably called you because she didn't know what to do. She didn't want to miss her ride, because then she would also miss ballet class, the most important thing in Sophie's life. So, she called you before she biked away to the convenience store. There was a time gap between when she left and when you arrived. Let's say, ten to fifteen minutes. During that time, Frej began to play with fire. When you arrived . . ."

"Go away!" Ingrid began to scream. "Go away! Get out of here!"

Her shriek was the most heartrending thing Irene had heard. Nurse Ulla came rushing through the bedroom door. Irene had not even noticed she'd left—presumably to spend more time with Tommy in the living room.

"What are you trying to do? Are you trying to be the death of poor Ingrid?"

Irene stretched to her full height and held up a warning finger toward the red, indignant face of the nurse.

"If 'poor Ingrid' had told the truth fifteen years ago, an innocent young girl would not have had to suffer so terribly. Perhaps she might not have been murdered!" Irene snapped at the nurse.

Right away, Irene regretted saying it, but it shut the nurse up.

Ingrid had also fallen silent and lay there with her eyes closed and her lips firmly pressed together. Irene would get nothing more from her.

Sophie had told the truth. The Guardian had existed in real life.

ANGELIKA HAD JUST finished her last class for the day when they reached her by phone at the House of Dance. Very unwillingly, she agreed to go directly to the police station to meet Tommy and Irene.

The first thing she did when she arrived was apologize for not having taken a shower and changed. She'd have to wait until she got home, she'd said while giving Tommy a coquettish look. She still wore her leotard underneath her coat. From her body came the scent of perfume, which was not at all unpleasant. The aroma gave her a strong, sensual attraction. She again ignored Irene completely. Apparently, Angelika never noticed any woman if there was a man in the room. She found her affirmation solely from men. Tommy appeared to give her all the attention she needed. In reciprocation, Angelika flirted with giggles and suggestive glances. Tommy's head was being turned.

Irene felt like a piece of furniture. An ugly, clunky piece badly placed. Certainly not something deserving attention.

Irene was tired of playing the role of third wheel. She decided to begin her questioning, with no help coming from Tommy.

"Perhaps you're wanting to know why we asked you here," Irene began.

Her statement seemed unnecessarily brusque, but it forced Angelika to look at her.

"Go ahead and sit down," Irene said.

Tommy pulled out a chair for Angelika to sit on. He looked at Irene quizzically and pointed to the other chair, but Irene shook her head. Tommy quickly took it instead.

Irene cleared her throat before the first question. "This morning we talked to your former sister-in-law, Ingrid Hagberg. As you know, she has just recovered from another diabetic coma. Someone gave her a box of the sweetest nougat imaginable."

Angelika crossed one leg over the other and began to jiggle her foot in its stylish boot. It was the only indication that she was actually listening.

"We have found your fingerprints on the bag the candy came in. How would you like to explain this?"

The tiny figure stiffened, and her foot stopped jiggling. She swallowed a few times. Finally, she was able to say, "That's impossible . . . I didn't . . ."

"They *are* your fingerprints," Irene insisted, without taking her gaze from the woman.

Angelika could not endure Irene's look, and she looked over to Tommy. Tommy was not able to offer support. He still had a smile, but his eyes held the same question that Irene had just asked. A question that needed a good answer.

"Maybe I left a bag there," she muttered.

"When would this have been?" Irene asked.

"Don't remember . . ."

"When I met you a week ago, you told me that Ingrid did not let you in. I watched you enter the building and then come out, so your statement seemed most likely true. You also told me that you and Ingrid hadn't been in touch for over fifteen years."

Irene let her words drop off and kept her eyes on Angelika, who kept her gaze fixed on a spot close to Irene's shoe.

"So when were you in her apartment?"

Silence.

Irene continued, "The truth is, you weren't in her apartment at all. You came through the front door and then stuffed the bag holding the box of candy through the mail slot. You knew that she wouldn't be able to resist it."

Angelika hadn't moved, but Irene knew that she was listening and that she was nervous, as she had every reason to be.

"Did Frej ask you to bring Ingrid the . . ."

"Frej didn't know anything!" Angelika yelled and jumped out of the chair. Her eyes were shimmering with rage, and it looked as if she wanted to punch Irene.

"So? Frej knew nothing. How was I supposed to know this? He will inherit everything from his aunt, and we know that the sale of her farm will bring in a fortune," Irene said, calmly.

Angelika swallowed hard a few times and then said, "I . . . I took his keys. That is, Ingrid's keys."

All her instinct to fight deserted her, and she sank back onto the chair.

"Where did you get them?" Irene asked.

"From the Änggården mansion. He wasn't home when I took them. He'd put them on the work table in his darkroom."

"Which keys were on the ring?"

"The keys for the farm and for the apartment."

"So you used Ingrid's keys to get into her building."

Angelika nodded, and it appeared she was about to start crying.

"When were you at Ingrid's place?"

"Wednesday. About six."

That was when Irene was talking to Frej in his darkroom. He'd been so stressed he'd probably forgotten that he'd put the key ring on his worktable. He probably hadn't missed them, either. At least, he hadn't said anything to Irene about them.

"Did you take the elevator?"

"No, the stairs," Angelika replied in a low voice.

"You met no one on the stairs."

Angelika shook her head and wiped away the tears that started running down her cheeks.

"When did you put the keys back?"

"The same evening. I knew Frej was taking capoeira and would be home late. He knew absolutely nothing about any of this! I did it on my own! I was the only one involved!"

Tommy leaned over and placed a hand on Angelika's arm. "Why did you, Angelika?"

She gave him a confused look and said, "I can't tell you!"

Her tears turned into heartbreaking sobs. Tommy took a box of paper tissues and handed it to her.

When she had calmed slightly, Irene said, "Angelika. I attended the premiere of *The Fire Dance*. I remember your face as you ran from the building. You looked scared to death, as if you'd seen a ghost. You certainly knew enough about dance to interpret the story Sophie had put in her creation."

Irene paused for effect. Angelika sat and stared at her with a paper tissue pressed to her nose. Her eyes were wide with fear.

The Guardian had found the peacefully sleeping Prince, who was holding the bottle so tenderly in his arms. She resolutely pulled him to his feet and hid him beneath the Queen's wide skirts. The Guardian took off her cape and flung it over the Queen's shoulders to help hide the Prince. The trick worked as none of the other guests saw how the two women took the Prince away from the scene.

"Sophie's *Fire Dance* is the true story of what happened at Björkil so long ago when the fire broke out. Ingrid was the

Guardian and you were the Queen. Together, the two of you have been protecting Prince Frej all these years. You were able to keep him out of the investigation. No one knew that he had been at the house that afternoon except three people: you, Ingrid and Sophie. Sophie protected her brother in the only way she knew: by keeping silent. And you kept silent, too."

"It was that old hag's fault! If she hadn't fallen asleep, nothing would have happened! She was responsible for him, but when she fell asleep, he sneaked out!"

"He went home."

"Yes," Angelika whispered.

"Did he know that his father was home?"

Angelika said nothing for a while, but then she shook her head. "No. Magnus was sleeping on the second floor. The house was dark. Frej didn't think anyone was at home, and I believe he was unhappy to come home with nobody there. Or he thought no one was there. The door must have been unlocked, so he could walk right in. I don't know where he found one of Magnus's bottles, but they were often lying around everywhere . . . I also don't know why he drank what he found . . . but kids are like that. They try things. He was so little!"

She was pleading as she said those words. Irene could understand her a bit. A mother is inclined to ignore and explain away anything to protect her child. In this case, however, it came at the price of her other child. This Irene found more difficult to comprehend.

"You told me earlier that Sophie was fascinated by fire at an early age. But it was really Frej you were talking about, right?"

Angelika opened her mouth to say something, but then realized that words weren't necessary. The fear in her eyes revealed everything.

INTERROGATING FREJ WENT well. In the beginning, he'd refused to answer the questions the police asked him, but in time he was ready to talk.

At first, he just answered in short syllables, but the urge to tell all about what happened soon made itself known, and then the words flowed so quickly it was hard to get him to stop. Irene played the recorded interrogation several times. She felt sad and sorrowful each time she listened to it.

Family secrets. The things that everyone knew but no one was supposed to talk about. As long as everyone kept quiet, the secret was invisible. The truth was still there like a wound ready to burst. The lies that were spun around it would keep growing like a cancer until the whole thing could no longer be contained and erupted all at once. The one frightful thing everyone was afraid of.

The truth.

Angelika, Ingrid and Sophie had all conspired to protect Frej. Had their silence actually helped him, or did it make his guilt grow along with their own?

Irene kept starting the tape where Frej revealed what happened on the night of September 24th, when Sophie disappeared from the Park Aveny Hotel:

Frej: *We had, like, a code. When we saw a fire truck. Or if we saw . . . something good. Something to set fire to . . . that is . . . Sophie wanted photographs, of course. So we texted FIRE and then we would meet at a predetermined place. That night I saw a really old shed, and I thought it was time . . . to set it on fire . . . out at Skrabro. Each time I'd drive over to Ingrid's place, I'd see it. It was just fifty meters from the road. I knew it was going to be torn down . . . they were going to build a shopping center. So I sent my text and she got it while she was going up the stairs at the hotel. They were supposed to have an after-party at that old man's suite . . . the one she's related to . . . that author. There's another staircase at the back of the hotel, and she just went right back down . . . I'd parked my car behind the hotel . . . there's a parking lot there. We drove out to Björlandavägen and out to Skrabro. The shed was there. It was already falling down, and they were going to get rid of it anyway . . . so, we, like, poured on some lighter fluid and lit it up. Then things went wrong because an old guy from a house down the road came running and started to yell at us. That son of a bitch had a rifle and started to shoot at us! Sophie was terrified and began to run to the car. She fell into a ditch. She didn't notice right away that she'd hurt her arm. We threw ourselves into the car and drove off as fast as we could. Sophie yelled, "We have to hide! He's going to call the police, and they're going to set up roadblocks!" I believed her—at least then. So we drove to Björkil because I had the keys to Ingrid's farm. We drove the car straight into the stable so that it wouldn't be seen. Sophie was out of her mind with hysteria. I've never seen her like that! She just lost it completely! She wanted to hide in the office in the stable, so that no one would think we were, like, burglars or something and start shooting at us. She went on and on about that guy. She was completely out of it! And . . . she'd been smoking pot—*

Irene: *Did Sophie often take drugs?*

Frej: *No, she didn't do drugs. Just some pot . . . not too often . . . but it made her weird. Still, she liked to use it . . .*

Irene: *Okay, go on.*

Frej: *I went into the house and got the spare bed and two*

mattresses. I took them to the office. Also sheets . . . everything we needed was in the house. Ingrid doesn't throw anything away. So, we just slept in the office. In the morning, I wanted to go home, but Sophie refused. She wanted to stay hidden. She thought that if she were gone, Marcelo would start to miss her. So I made some food for us, and then I went home and acted like nothing happened. On Saturday, my mom said Sophie was missing . . . and then things just kept going on from there. Sophie didn't want to come out. She thought it was exciting that people were out looking for her, and no one knew where she was. The police were involved . . . Mom was out of her mind with worry, and Sophie still thought that Marcelo would be missing her.

Irene remembered that Frej stopped at this point to give her a meaningful, crooked smile. They both knew that Marcelo would never miss any woman.

Frej: *But Sophie hurt her arm when she was running to the car. It really started to hurt, and a few days later it was swollen like you wouldn't believe. She asked me to get some pills that were in her father's bathroom cabinet back home. You know, he had these painkillers before he kicked the bucket. Really strong, because he had cancer. I took the whole carton so she could decide how many to take.*

Frej was silent for a moment. When he started to speak again, it was apparent that he was trying to keep from crying.

Frej: *I thought she took too much. She was really in pain, and I wanted to take her to the emergency room. I promise . . . I wanted to get her to come out of hiding, but she refused. She kept saying the police were after her. I began to think that she was starting to lose it . . . I wanted to talk with my mom about it . . . but when I came back to the stable that last night, she was lying dead on the bed.*

At this point, Frej began to cry. A few minutes later, he was able to calm down enough to continue his story.

Frej: *I tried to wake her up, but I couldn't. She was dead!*

I swear! I wanted to call my mom . . . or an ambulance . . . but then I started to think that the whole thing looked really sick. It didn't sound right that Sophie wanted to stay in hiding. No one would believe me! I mean . . . people would think I killed her!

His blue eyes looked pleadingly into Irene's.

Irene: *Why did you bring her to the shed at Högsbo and then set fire to it?*

A long silence with muffled weeping.

Frej: *I didn't know what I was supposed to do . . . I wrapped her in a blanket and brought her to the car. I threw a rug over her so no one could see her . . . I put the mattress into the trunk, and all the sheets and stuff . . . they were disgusting. She'd vomited and . . . before she died . . .*

Again, a long silence.

Frej: *Sophie and I talked about it a lot. When a person dies, he should be burned . . . because fire purifies . . . she repeated that all the time. I knew that she wanted to disappear in a fire . . . so I drove to that shed and put her on the mattress, and I put the rug over her . . . like a cover . . . and then I set her on fire. She would have wanted that.*

He was still crying.

Irene: *How did you know about the old shed?*

Frej: *We saw it last summer. There was another building that burned down in the area. I saw it then.*

Irene: *Were you and Sophie the people who set fire to the other building?*

Frej did not answer, and pressed his lips closed.

Irene: *There were many old buildings that were set on fire in that area. All of them were scheduled to be demolished. And there were some container fires, too. Were you and Sophie the people who started those fires?*

Frej said nothing for a while, but finally said something that sounded like a maybe.

Irene: *Could you speak louder so it can be heard on the recording?*

He shook his head and refused to answer.

Irene: *It is now fifteen thirty-two, and this interrogation is finished for the day.*

IRENE TOOK THE tape out of the recorder. She contemplated putting in the recording from the interrogation session regarding the Björkil fire, but then decided not to listen to it. It was not all that informative. Frej had insisted that he did not remember anything because he was so young. He had been shocked by the death of his father and probably repressed everything that had happened. Irene had the feeling that he remembered more than he let on. The only breakthrough was that he did not deny that he'd sneaked home when his aunt had fallen asleep after dinner.

The forensic psychologist was going to talk to Frej later that day. He would then make a determination if Frej was capable of standing trial.

They had checked into Frej's story about the arson at the old shed in Skrabro. The incident had been reported to the police. The old man backed up Frej's story, and even admitted to firing his rifle. He said that he didn't aim for the young people, but shot the rifle straight into the air. No, he hadn't put in the police report that he'd fired his rifle. He'd forgotten to mention it.

THE FORENSIC PSYCHOLOGIST, Torgny Wallén, peered at Sven Andersson and Irene from over his reading glasses. He was the same age as the superintendent, and the two of them knew each other well after the twenty years they'd both spent on the force. Torgny Wallén folded his sausage-like fingers over his round stomach and then sat back in his chair. It was right after lunch, and he needed to make room for his Thursday pea soup and pancakes. He began the conversation in his pleasant Scanian accent.

"I've ordered a more extensive psychological evaluation for Frej. It's going to take longer than a week. As far as I can determine so far, he seems to be telling the truth about his sister's last weeks of life. She appears to have been psychologically damaged, but that's another story. It could be that both of them were part of a *folie à deux*, where one psychologically damaged person has such a strong influence over the other that they both fall ill. As far as Sophie is concerned, her pot smoking could have contributed to a psychosis, especially when combined with the trauma around the unsuccessful arson attempt. She seems to have had a neuropsychological handicap as well."

"So, do you believe she became mentally ill shortly before her death?" asked Irene.

"Her actions just before her death indicate some kind of paranoia."

"Could Frej have become infected as well?"

"No, that's not how it works. It's a complicated process. Frej seems to have had a strong dependent relationship with his sister. Perhaps he has some kind of guilt complex because his sister had to bear the suspicion for the arson he'd started. He also had guilty feelings concerning his father's death. These are heavy things to deal with at such a young age. The boy should have had help fifteen years ago."

"Do you think he will be sent to a mental health institution instead of jail?" asked Andersson.

"I can't say right now. Perhaps he'll serve time in jail for arson or manslaughter or both. That will be judicial hairsplitting. His sister died from the fire. The autopsy showed she was still breathing when it started, even if she was unconscious from an extreme overdose of opiates, including both the pills and the suppositories."

"What's a suppository?" asked the superintendent.

"It's medicine that is inserted into the anal cavity. The medicine is absorbed more quickly that way. She'd taken the last of the pills and the suppository at the same time, and she took too much. A serious and often fatal side effect of an overdose is that breathing is suppressed. The part of the brain that regulates breathing is paralyzed. The person, quite simply, stops breathing. Before death arrives, the breathing is so shallow that even a doctor can have difficulty determining if the patient is still alive. Sophie had a high concentration of opiates in her body, and she would have probably died of the overdose before the fire took her life."

Andersson sat quietly for a long time. Finally, he gave a heavy sigh and said, "So, we've spent a great deal of time and resources investigating what we thought was premeditated murder, and it's really accidental manslaughter we're dealing with."

"So it seems," the psychiatrist agreed. After a moment, he

added, "Unfortunate circumstances. Unhappy people in an unhappy family."

Silence hovered over the room again. The forensic psychiatrist took off his reading glasses, and said, "Well, what do you say we go get a cup of coffee?"

Epilogue

"THE DOCTOR SAYS I shouldn't start working again until after Christmas," Krister sighed as he sank into the sofa.

"You should listen to the doctor's orders," Irene replied.

"How can I? Last weekend we had the first Christmas smorgasbord! It'll be fully packed between now and New Year's Eve! I have to be at my station!"

"You often tell me that no one is irreplaceable."

As she said that, she realized it was the wrong thing to say. Krister's face darkened as if he were angry enough to hit her.

"You're one to talk! You're never home!" He jumped up from the sofa and headed to the bedroom, slamming the door behind him.

Irene sat helplessly on the sofa. What had happened to her kind husband who was almost never angry? He'd rarely raised his voice and hardly complained at all—what happened to the man who loved his family and his job?

KRISTER DECIDED TO go ahead and take the medicine the doctor had prescribed. He didn't like it. He finally began to realize that he really did need to rest. He'd been working much too hard all through the fall. To tell the truth, he'd been working much too much for the past few years. He'd been under too much stress. He still did not remember what had happened during the hours he'd suffered amnesia.

On New Year's Day, he and Irene were sitting and drinking coffee. Krister was dipping the last saffron bun of the season into his coffee and eating it with great enjoyment. Irene had already been outside with Sammie and was warming her hands over her coffee cup. Both jumped when the phone rang, disturbing their holiday peace.

Krister said, "Don't get up. I'll get it."

He walked into the hallway. After a few minutes, Irene realized he was talking to his cousin Inga-Maja from Arvika. They talked for a long time. Irene could hear Krister say the words "burned out" over and over.

When Krister returned to the kitchen, he was chuckling to himself. "That was Inga-Maja. She was telling me about two of her colleagues from work, who had been hospitalized because they were burned out from working too much. Apparently, I'm not the only person who suffers from it. But you know what the people from Arvika call it? They don't say 'burned out.' Do you know what they say?"

He started to chortle again and looked teasingly at Irene. She shook her head.

"No, what do they say in Arvika?"

Krister spoke in a broad Värmland accent as he said, "There are many folks these days who have all burned up!"

Irene smiled, although she realized that she and her husband were thinking of different things. In her mind, she saw the heart-shaped face of a young girl, whose deep brown eyes were looking right into hers. Around the girl's serious mouth, a smile began to play, and her eyes began to shine. Then the picture began to fade. Irene understood that it would be the last time she saw it.

"All burned up," she said.

My thanks to:

FLORIAN MONTOYO, THE Head of Instruction at the Ballet Academy of Gothenburg, who guided me around the institution and informed me of the latest trends in the instruction of dance.

Tuula Dajén, my friend of many years. She is also a teacher as well as a trained dancer and choreographer. For the past few years, she has directed many cultural events and is now a cultural administrator. She founded the Ballet School of Sunne in 1980, which has graduated a number of professional dancers over the years. Her abilities and enthusiasm inspired my daughter's interest in dance. During the decade when my daughter studied it, I also learned a great deal about the world of dance.

Maina Sahlman, Detective Inspector in Göteborg, who has given me a great deal of valuable assistance, both with this book and with *The Glass Devil* (2002). I often say she is the template for Irene Huss, though we didn't actually meet until I was researching the fourth book in the series . . .

As usual, I have used a great deal of artistic license when describing the geography of Göteborg. I don't make my stories fit the real environment, but the environment must fit my story. None of the characters in this book are knowingly drawn from real life.

Helene Tursten